D1146791

The Card, A Story Of Adventure In The Five Towns

by

Arnold Bennett

The Echo Library 2005

Published by

The Echo Library

Paperbackshop Ltd
Cockrup Farm House
Coln St Aldwyns
Cirencester GL7 5AZ

www.echo-library.com

ISBN 1-84637-671-8

CONTENTS

THE CARD

CHAPTER I

THE DANCE

I

Edward Henry Machin first saw the smoke on the 27th May 1867, in Brougham Street, Bursley, the most ancient of the Five Towns. Brougham Street runs down from St Luke's Square straight into the Shropshire Union Canal, land consists partly of buildings known as "potbanks" (until they come to be sold by auction, when auctioneers describe them as "extensive earthenware manufactories") and partly of cottages whose highest rent is four-and-six a week. In such surroundings was an extraordinary man born. He was the only anxiety of a widowed mother, who gained her livelihood and his by making up "ladies' own materials" in ladies' own houses. Mrs Machin, however, had a speciality apart from her vocation: she could wash flannel with less shrinking than any other woman in the district, and she could wash fine lace without ruining it; thus often she came to sew and remained to wash. A somewhat gloomy woman; thin, with a tongue! But I liked her. She saved a certain amount of time every day by addressing her son as Denry, instead of Edward Henry.

Not intellectual, not industrious, Denry would have maintained the average dignity of labour on a potbank had he not at the age of twelve won a scholarship from the Board School to the Endowed School. He owed his triumph to audacity rather than learning, and to chance rather than design. On the second day of the examination he happened to arrive in the examination-room ten minutes too soon for the afternoon sitting. He wandered about the place exercising his curiosity, and reached the master's desk. On the desk was a tabulated form with names of candidates and the number of marks achieved by each in each subject of the previous day. He had done badly in geography, and saw seven marks against his name, in the geographical column, out of a possible thirty. The figures had been written in pencil. The pencil lay on the desk. He picked it up, glanced at the door and at the rows of empty desks, and a neat "2" in front of the 7; then he strolled innocently forth and came back late. His trick ought to have been found out—the odds were against him—but it was not found out. Of course it was dishonest. Yes, but I will not agree that Denry was uncommonly vicious. Every schoolboy is dishonest, by the adult standard. If I knew an honest schoolboy I would begin to count my silver spoons as he grew up. All is fair between schoolboys and schoolmasters.

This dazzling feat seemed to influence not only Denry's career but also his character. He gradually came to believe that he had won the scholarship by genuine merit, and that he was a remarkable boy and destined to great ends. His new companions, whose mothers employed Denry's mother, also believed that he was a remarkable boy; but they did not forget, in their gentlemanly way, to call him "washer-woman." Happily Denry did not mind.

He had a thick skin, and fair hair and bright eyes and broad shoulders, and the jolly gaiety of his disposition developed daily. He did not shine at the school; he failed to fulfil the rosy promise of the scholarship; but he was not stupider than the majority; and his opinion of himself, having once risen, remained at "set fair." It was inconceivable that he should work in clay with his hands.

II

When he was sixteen his mother, by operations [**words missing in original] a yard and a half of Brussels point lace, put [**words missing in original] Emery under an obligation. Mrs Emery [**words missing in original] the sister of Mr Duncalf. Mr Duncalf was town Clerk of Bursley, and a solicitor. It is well known that all bureaucracies are honey-combed with intrigue. Denry Machin left school to be clerk to Mr Duncalf, on the condition that within a year he should be able to write shorthand at the rate of a hundred and fifty words a minute. In those days mediocre and incorrect shorthand was not a drug on the market. He complied (more or less, and decidedly less than more) with the condition. And for several years he really thought that he had nothing further to hope for. Then he met the Countess.

The Countess of Chell was born of poor but picturesque parents, and she could put her finger on her great-grandfather's grandfather. Her mother gained her livelihood and her daughter's by allowing herself to be seen a great deal with humbler but richer people's daughters. The Countess was brought up to matrimony. She was aimed and timed to hit a given mark at a given moment. She succeeded. She married the Earl of Chell. She also married about twenty thousand acres in England, about a fifth of Scotland, a house in Piccadilly, seven country seats (including Sneyd), a steam yacht, and five hundred thousand pounds' worth of shares in the Midland Railway. She was young and pretty. She had travelled in China and written a book about China. She sang at charity concerts and acted in private theatricals. She sketched from nature. She was one of the great hostesses of London. And she had not the slightest tendency to stoutness. All this did not satisfy her. She was ambitious! She wanted to be taken seriously. She wanted to enter into the life of the people. She saw in the quarter of a million souls that constitute the Five Towns a unique means to her end, an unrivalled toy. And she determined to be identified with all that was most serious in the social progress of the Five Towns. Hence some fifteen thousand pounds were spent in refurbishing Sneyd Hall, which lies on the edge of the Five Towns, and the Earl and Countess passed four months of the year there. Hence the Earl, a mild, retiring man, when invited by the Town Council to be the ornamental Mayor of Bursley, accepted the invitation. Hence the Mayor and Mayoress gave an immense afternoon reception to practically the entire roll of burgesses. And hence, a little later, the Mayoress let it be known that she meant to give a municipal ball. The news of the ball thrilled Bursley more than anything had thrilled Bursley since the signing of Magna

Charta. Nevertheless, balls had been offered by previous mayoresses. One can only suppose that in Bursley there remains a peculiar respect for land, railway stock, steam yachts, and great-grandfathers' grandfathers.

Now, everybody of account had been asked to the reception. But everybody could not be asked to the ball, because not more than two hundred people could dance in the Town Hall. There were nearly thirty-five thousand inhabitants in Bursley, of whom quite two thousand "counted," even though they did not dance.

III

Three weeks and three days before the ball Denry Machin was seated one Monday alone in Mr Duncalf's private offices in Duck Square (where he carried on his practice as a solicitor), when in stepped a tall and pretty young woman, dressed very smartly but soberly in dark green. On the desk in front of Denry were several wide sheets of "abstract" paper, concealed by a copy of that morning's *Athletic News*. Before Denry could even think of reversing the positions of the abstract paper and the *Athletic News* the young woman said "Good-morning!" in a very friendly style. She had a shrill voice and an efficient smile.

"Good-morning, madam," said Denry.

"Mr Duncalf in?" asked the young woman brightly.

(Why should Denry have slipped off his stool? It is utterly against etiquette for solicitors' clerks to slip off their stools while answering inquiries.)

"No, madam; he's across at the Town Hall," said Denry.

The young lady shook her head playfully, with a faint smile.

"I've just been there," she said. "They said he was here."

"I daresay I could find him, madam—if you would——"

She now smiled broadly. "Conservative Club, I suppose?" she said, with an air deliciously confidential.

He, too, smiled.

"Oh, no," she said, after a little pause; "just tell him I've called."

"Certainly, madam. Nothing I can do?"

She was already turning away, but she turned back and scrutinised his face, as Denry thought, roguishly.

"You might just give him this list," she said, taking a paper from her satchel and spreading it. She had come to the desk; their elbows touched. "He isn't to take any notice of the crossings-out in red ink— you understand? Of course, I'm relying on him for the other lists, and I expect all the invitations to be out on Wednesday. Good-morning."

She was gone. He sprang to the grimy window. Outside, in the snow, were a brougham, twin horses, twin men in yellow, and a little crowd of youngsters and oldsters. She flashed across the footpath, and vanished; the door of the carriage banged, one of the twins in yellow leaped up to his brother, and the whole affair dashed dangerously away. The face of the leaping twin was familiar to Denry. The man had, indeed, once inhabited Brougham Street, being known to the street as Jock, and his mother had for long years been a friend of Mrs Machin's.

It was the first time Denry had seen the Countess, save at a distance. Assuredly she was finer even than her photographs. Entirely different from what one would have expected! So easy to talk to! (Yet what had he said to her? Nothing—and everything.)

He nodded his head and murmured, "No mistake about that lot!" Meaning, presumably, that all that one had read about the brilliance of the aristocracy was true, and more than true.

"She's the finest woman that ever came into this town," he murmured.

The truth was that she surpassed his dreams of womanhood. At two o'clock she had been a name to him. At five minutes past two he was in love with her. He felt profoundly thankful that, for a church tea-meeting that evening, he happened to be wearing his best clothes.

It was while looking at her list of invitations to the ball that he first conceived the fantastic scheme of attending the ball himself. Mr Duncalf was, fussily and deferentially, managing the machinery of the ball for the Countess. He had prepared a little list of his own of people who ought to be invited. Several aldermen had been requested to do the same. There were thus about half-a-dozen lists to be combined into one. Denry did the combining. Nothing was easier than to insert the name of E.H. Machin inconspicuously towards the centre of the list! Nothing was easier than to lose the original lists, inadvertently, so that if a question arose as to any particular name, the responsibility for it could not be ascertained without inquiries too delicate to be made. On Wednesday Denry received a lovely Bristol board, stating in copper-plate that the Countess desired the pleasure of his company at the ball; and on Thursday his name was ticked off as one who had accepted.

IV

He had never been to a dance. He had no dress-suit, and no notion of dancing.

He was a strange, inconsequent mixture of courage and timidity. You and I are consistent in character; we are either one thing or the other but Denry Machin had no consistency.

For three days he hesitated, and then, secretly trembling, he slipped into Shillitoe's, the young tailor who had recently set up, and who was gathering together the *jeunesse dorée* of the town.

"I want a dress-suit," he said.

Shillitoe, who knew that Denry only earned eighteen shillings a week, replied with only superficial politeness that a dress-suit was out of the question; he had already taken more orders than he could execute without killing himself. The whole town had uprisen as one man and demanded a dress-suit.

"So you're going to the ball, are you?" said Shillitoe, trying to condescend, but, in fact, slightly impressed.

"Yes," said Denry; "are you?"

Shillitoe started and then shook his head. "No time for balls," said he.

"I can get you an invitation, if you like," said Denry, glancing at the door precisely as he had glanced at the door before adding 2 to 7.

"Oh!" Shillitoe cocked his ears. He was not a native of the town, and had no alderman to protect his legitimate interests.

To cut a shameful story short, in a week Denry was being tried on. Shillitoe allowed him two years' credit.

The prospect of the ball gave an immense impetus to the study of the art of dancing in Bursley, and so put quite a nice sum of money info the pocket of Miss Earp, a young mistress in that art. She was the daughter of a furniture dealer with a passion for the Bankruptcy Court. Miss Earp's evening classes were attended by Denry, but none of his money went into her pocket. She was compensated by an expression of the Countess's desire for the pleasure of her company at the ball.

The Countess had aroused Denry's interest in women as a sex; Ruth Earp quickened the interest. She was plain, but she was only twenty-four, and very graceful on her feet. Denry had one or two strictly private lessons from her in reversing. She said to him one evening, when he was practising reversing and they were entwined in the attitude prescribed by the latest fashion: "Never mind me! Think about yourself. It's the same in dancing as it is in life—the woman's duty is to adapt herself to the man." He did think about himself. He was thinking about himself in the middle of the night, and about her too. There had been something in her tone... her eye... At the final lesson he inquired if she would give him the first waltz at the ball. She paused, then said yes.

V

On the evening of the ball, Denry spent at least two hours in the operation which was necessary before he could give the Countess the pleasure of his company. This operation took place in his minute bedroom at the back of the cottage in Brougham Street, and it was of a complex nature. Three weeks ago he had innocently thought that you had only to order a dress-suit and there you were! He now knew that a dress-suit is merely the beginning of anxiety. Shirt! Collar! Tie! Studs! Cuff-links! Gloves! Handkerchief! (He was very glad to learn authoritatively from Shillitoe that handkerchiefs were no longer worn in the waistcoat opening, and that men who so wore them were barbarians and the truth was not in them. Thus, an everyday handkerchief would do.) Boots!... Boots were the rock on which he had struck. Shillitoe, in addition to being a tailor was a hosier, but by some flaw in the scheme of the universe hosiers do not sell boots. Except boots, Denry could get all he needed on credit; boots he could not get on credit, and he could not pay cash for them. Eventually he decided that his church boots must be dazzled up to the level of this great secular occasion. The pity was that he forgot—not that he was of a forgetful disposition in great matters; he was simply over-excited—he forgot to dazzle them up until after he had fairly put his collar on and his necktie in a bow. It is imprudent to touch blacking in a dress-shirt, so Denry had to undo the past and begin again. This hurried him. He was not afraid of being late for the first waltz with Miss Ruth Earp, but he was afraid of not being out of the house before his mother returned. Mrs Machin had been making up a lady's own materials all day, naturally—the day being what it was! If she had had twelve hands instead of two, she might have made up the own materials of half-a-dozen ladies instead of one, and earned twenty-four shillings instead of four. Denry did not want his mother to see him ere he departed. He had lavished an enormous amount of brains and energy to the end of displaying himself in this refined and novel attire to the gaze of two hundred persons, and yet his secret wish was to deprive his mother of the beautiful spectacle.

However, she slipped in, with her bag and her seamy fingers and her rather sardonic expression, at the very moment when Denry was putting on his overcoat in the kitchen (there being insufficient room in the passage). He did what he could to hide his shirt-front (though she knew all about it), and failed.

"Bless us!" she exclaimed briefly, going to the fire to warm her hands.

A harmless remark. But her tone seemed to strip bare the vanity of human greatness.

"I'm in a hurry," said Denry, importantly, as if he was going forth to sign a treaty involving the welfare of the nations.

"Well," said she, "happen ye are, Denry. But th' kitchen table's no place for boot-brushes."

He had one piece of luck. It froze. Therefore no anxiety about the condition of boots.

VI

The Countess was late; some trouble with a horse. Happily the Earl had been in Bursley all day, and had dressed at the Conservative Club; and his lordship had ordered that the programme of dances should be begun. Denry learned this as soon as he emerged, effulgent, from the gentlemen's cloak-room into the broad red-carpeted corridor which runs from end to end of the ground-floor of the Town Hall. Many important townspeople were chatting in the corridor—the innumerable Swetnam family, the Stanways, the great Etches, the Fearnses, Mrs Clayton Vernon, the Suttons, including Beatrice Sutton. Of course everybody knew him for Duncalf's shorthand clerk and the son of the flannel-washer; but universal white kid gloves constitute a democracy, and Shillitoe could put more style into a suit than any other tailor in the Five Towns.

"How do?" the eldest of the Swetnam boys nodded carelessly.

"How do, Swetnam?" said Denry, with equal carelessness.

The thing was accomplished! That greeting was like a Masonic initiation, and henceforward he was the peer of no matter whom. At first he had thought that four hundred eyes would be fastened on him, their glance saying, "This youth is wearing a dress-suit for the first time, and it is not paid for, either!" But it was not so. And the reason was that the entire population of the Town Hall was heartily engaged in pretending that never in its life had it been seen after seven o'clock of a night apart from a dress-suit. Denry observed with joy that, while numerous middle-aged and awkward men wore red or white silk handkerchiefs in their waistcoats, such people as Charles Fearns, the Swetnams, and Harold Etches did not. He was, then, in the shyness of his handkerchief, on the side of the angels.

He passed up the double staircase (decorated with white or pale frocks of unparalleled richness), and so into the grand hall. A scarlet orchestra was on the platform, and many people strolled about the floor in attitudes of expectation. The walls were festooned with flowers. The thrill of being magnificent seized him, and he was drenched in a vast desire to be truly magnificent himself. He dreamt of magnificence and boot-brushes kept sticking out of this dream like black mud out of snow. In his reverie he looked about for Ruth Earp, but she was invisible. Then he went downstairs again, idly; gorgeously feigning that he spent six evenings a week in ascending and descending monumental staircases, appropriately clad. He was determined to be as sublime as any one.

There was a stir in the corridor, and the sublimest consented to be excited.

The Countess was announced to be imminent. Everybody was grouped round the main portal, careless of temperatures. Six times was the Countess announced to be imminent before she actually appeared, expanding from the narrow gloom of her black carriage like a magic vision. Aldermen received her—and they did not do it with any excess of gracefulness. They seemed afraid of her, as though she was recovering from influenza and they feared to catch it. She had precisely the same high voice, and precisely the same efficient smile, as she had employed to Denry, and these instruments worked marvels on aldermen; they were as melting as salt on snow. The Countess disappeared upstairs in a cloud of shrill apologies and trailing aldermen. She seemed to have greeted everybody except Denry. Somehow he was relieved that she had not drawn attention to him. He lingered, hesitating, and then he saw a being in a long yellow overcoat, with a bit of peacock's feather at the summit of a shiny high hat. This being held a lady's fur mantle. Their eyes met. Denry had to decide instantly. He decided.

"Hello, Jock!" he said.

"Hello, Denry!" said the other, pleased.

"What's been happening?" Denry inquired, friendly.

Then Jock told him about the antics of one of the Countess's horses.

He went upstairs again, and met Ruth Earp coming down. She was glorious in white. Except that nothing glittered in her hair, she looked the very equal of the Countess, at a little distance, plain though her features were.

"What about that waltz?" Denry began informally.

"That waltz is nearly over," said Ruth Earp, with chilliness. "I suppose you've been staring at her ladyship with all the other men."

"I'm awfully sorry," he said. "I didn't know the waltz was——"

"Well, why didn't you look at your programme?"

"Haven't got one," he said naïvely.

He had omitted to take a programme. Ninny! Barbarian!

"Better get one," she said cuttingly, somewhat in her *rôle* of dancing mistress.

"Can't we finish the waltz?" he suggested, crestfallen.

"No!" she said, and continued her solitary way downwards.

She was hurt. He tried to think of something to say that was equal to the situation, and equal to the style of his suit. But he could not. In a moment he heard her, below him, greeting some male acquaintance in the most effusive way.

Yet, if Denry had not committed a wicked crime for her, she could never have come to the dance at all!

He got a programme, and with terror gripping his heart he asked sundry young and middle-aged women whom he knew by sight and by name for a dance. (Ruth had taught him how to ask.) Not one of them had a dance left. Several looked at him as much as to say: "You must be a goose to suppose that my programme is not filled up in the twinkling of my eye!"

Then he joined a group of despisers of dancing near the main door. Harold Etches was there, the wealthiest manufacturer of his years (barely twenty-four) in the Five Towns. Also Shillitoe, cause of another of Denry's wicked crimes. The group was taciturn, critical, and very doggish.

The group observed that the Countess was not dancing. The Earl was dancing (need it be said with Mrs Jos Curtenty, second wife of the Deputy Mayor?), but the Countess stood resolutely smiling, surrounded by aldermen. Possibly she was getting her breath; possibly nobody had had the pluck to ask her. Anyhow, she seemed to be stranded there, on a beach of aldermen. Very wisely she had brought with her no members of a house-party from Sneyd Hall. Members of a house-party, at a municipal ball, invariably operate as a bar between greatness and democracy; and the Countess desired to participate in the life of the people.

"Why don't some of those johnnies ask her?" Denry burst out. He had hitherto said nothing in the group, and he felt that he must be a man with the rest of them.

"Well, *you* go and do it. It's a free country," said Shillitoe.

"So I would, for two pins!" said Denry.

Harold Etches glanced at him, apparently resentful of his presence there. Harold Etches was determined to put the extinguisher on *him*.

"I'll bet you a fiver you don't," said Etches scornfully.

"I'll take you," said Denry, very quickly, and very quickly walked off.

VII

"She can't eat me. She can't eat me!"

This was what he said to himself as he crossed the floor. People seemed to make a lane for him, divining his incredible intention. If he had not started at once, if his legs had not started of themselves, he would never have started; and, not being in command of a fiver, he would afterwards have cut a preposterous figure in the group. But started he was, like a piece of clockwork that could not be stopped! In the grand crises of his life something not himself, something more powerful than himself, jumped up in him and forced him to do things. Now for the first time he seemed to understand what had occurred within him in previous crises.

In a second—so it appeared—he had reached the Countess. Just behind her was his employer, Mr Duncalf, whom Denry had not previously noticed there. Denry regretted this, for he had never mentioned to Mr Duncalf that he was coming to the ball, and he feared Mr Duncalf.

"Could I have this dance with you?" he demanded bluntly, but smiling and showing his teeth.

No ceremonial title! No mention of "pleasure" or "honour." Not a trace of the formula in which Ruth Earp had instructed him! He forgot all such trivialities.

"I've won that fiver, Mr Harold Etches," he said to himself.

The mouths of aldermen inadvertently opened. Mr Duncalf blenched.

"It's nearly over, isn't it?" said the Countess, still efficiently smiling. She did not recognise Denry. In that suit he might have been a Foreign Office attaché.

"Oh! that doesn't matter, I'm sure," said Denry.

She yielded, and he took the paradisaical creature in his arms. It was her business that evening to be universally and inclusively polite. She could not have begun with a refusal. A refusal might have dried up all other invitations whatsoever. Besides, she saw that the aldermen wanted a lead. Besides, she was young, though a countess, and adored dancing.

Thus they waltzed together, while the flower of Bursley's chivalry gazed in enchantment. The Countess's fan, depending from her arm, dangled against Denry's suit in a rather confusing fashion, which withdrew his attention from his feet. He laid hold of it gingerly between two unemployed fingers. After that he managed fairly well. Once they came perilously near the Earl and his partner; nothing else. And then the dance ended, exactly when Denry had begun to savour the astounding spectacle of himself enclasping the Countess.

The Countess had soon perceived that he was the merest boy.

"You waltz quite nicely!" she said, like an aunt, but with more than an aunt's smile.

"Do I?" he beamed. Then something compelled him to say: "Do you know, it's the first time I've ever waltzed in my life, except in a lesson, you know?"

"Really!" she murmured. "You pick things up easily, I suppose?"

"Yes," he said. "Do you?"

Either the question or the tone sent the Countess off into carillons of amusement. Everybody could see that Denry had made the Countess laugh tremendously. It was on this note that the waltz finished. She was still laughing when he bowed to her (as taught by Ruth Earp). He could not comprehend why she had so laughed, save on the supposition that he was more humorous than he had suspected. Anyhow, he laughed too, and they parted laughing. He remembered that he had made a marked effect (though not one of laughter) on the tailor by quickly returning the question, "Are you?" And his unpremeditated stroke with the Countess was similar. When he had got ten yards on his way towards Harold Etches and a fiver he felt something in his hand. The Countess's fan was sticking between his fingers. It had unhooked itself from her chain. He furtively pocketed it.

VIII

"Just the same as dancing with any other woman!" He told this untruth in reply to a question from Shillitoe. It was the least he could do. And any other young man in his place would have said as much or as little.

"What was she laughing at?" somebody asked.

"Ah!" said Denry, judiciously, "wouldn't you like to know?"

"Here you are!" said Etches, with an inattentive, plutocratic gesture handing over a five-pound note. He was one of those men who never venture out of sight of a bank without a banknote in their pockets— "Because you never know what may turn up."

Denry accepted the note with a silent nod. In some directions he was gifted with astounding insight, and he could read in the faces of the haughty males surrounding him that in the space of a few minutes he had risen from nonentity into renown. He had become a great man. He did not at once realise how great, how renowned. But he saw enough in those eyes to cause his heart to glow, and to rouse in his brain those ambitious dreams which stirred him upon occasion. He left the group; he had need of motion, and also of that mental privacy which one may enjoy while strolling about on a crowded floor in the midst of a considerable noise. He noticed that the Countess was now dancing with an alderman, and that the alderman, by an oversight inexcusable in an alderman, was not wearing gloves. It was he, Denry, who had broken the ice, so that the alderman might plunge into the water. He first had danced with the Countess, and had rendered her up to the alderman with delicious gaiety upon her countenance. By instinct he knew Bursley, and he knew that he would be talked of. He knew that, for a time at any rate, he would displace even Jos Curtenty, that almost professional "card" and amuser of burgesses, in the popular imagination. It would not be: "Have ye heard Jos's latest?" It would be: "Have ye heard about young Machin, Duncalf's clerk?"

Then he met Ruth Earp, strolling in the opposite direction with a young girl, one of her pupils, of whom all he knew was that her name was Nellie, and that this was her first ball: a childish little thing with a wistful face. He could not decide whether to look at Ruth or to avoid her glance. She settled the point by smiling at him in a manner that could not be ignored.

"Are you going to make it up to me for that waltz you missed?" said Ruth Earp. She pretended to be vexed and stern, but he knew that she was not. "Or is your programme full?" she added.

"I should like to," he said simply.

"But perhaps you don't care to dance with us poor, ordinary people, now you've danced with the *Countess*!" she said, with a certain lofty and bitter pride.

He perceived that his tone had lacked eagerness.

"Don't talk like that," he said, as if hurt.

"Well," she said, "you can have the supper dance."

He took her programme to write on it.

"Why," he said, "there's a name down here for the supper dance. 'Herbert,' it looks like."

"Oh!" she replied carelessly, "that's nothing. Cross it out."

So he crossed Herbert out.

"Why don't you ask Nellie here for a dance?" said Ruth Earp.

And Nellie blushed. He gathered that the possible honour of dancing with the supremely great man had surpassed Nellie's modest expectations.

"Can I have the next one?" he said.

"Oh, yes!" Nellie timidly whispered.

"It's a polka, and you aren't very good at polking, you know," Ruth warned him. "Still, Nellie will pull you through."

Nellie laughed, in silver. The naïve child thought that Ruth was trying to joke at Denry's expense. Her very manifest joy and pride in being seen with the unique Mr Machin, in being the next after the Countess to dance with him, made another mirror in which Denry could discern the reflection of his vast importance.

At the supper, which was worthy of the hospitable traditions of the Chell family (though served standing-up in the police-court), he learnt all the gossip of the dance from Ruth Earp; amongst other things that more than one young man had asked the Countess for a dance, and had been refused, though Ruth Earp for her part declined to believe that aldermen and councillors had utterly absorbed the Countess's programme. Ruth hinted that the Countess was keeping a second dance open for him, Denry. When she asked him squarely if he meant to request another from the Countess, he said no, positively. He knew when to let well alone, a knowledge which is more precious than a knowledge of geography. The supper was the summit of Denry's triumph. The best people spoke to him without being introduced. And lovely creatures mysteriously and intoxicatingly discovered that programmes which had been crammed two hours before were not, after all, quite full.

"Do tell us what the Countess was laughing at?" This question was shot at him at least thirty times. He always said he would not tell. And one girl who had danced with Mr Stanway, who had danced with the Countess, said that Mr Stanway had said that the Countess would not tell either. Proof, here, that he was being extensively talked about!

Towards the end of the festivity the rumour floated abroad that the Countess had lost her fan. The rumour reached Denry, who maintained a culpable silence. But when all was over, and the Countess was departing, he rushed down after her, and, in a dramatic fashion which demonstrated his genius for the effective, he caught her exactly as she was getting into her carriage.

"I've just picked it up," he said, pushing through the crowd of worshippers.

"On! thank you so much!" she said. And the Earl also thanked Denry. And then the Countess, leaning from the carriage, said, with archness in her efficient smile: "You do pick things up easily, don't you?"

And both Demo and the Countess laughed without restraint, and the pillars of Bursley society were mystified.

Denry winked at Jock as the horses pawed away. And Jock winked back.

The envied of all, Denry walked home, thinking violently. At a stroke he had become possessed of more than he could earn from Duncalf in a month. The faces of the Countess, of Ruth Earp, and of the timid Nellie mingled in exquisite hallucinations before his tired eyes. He was inexpressibly happy. Trouble, however, awaited him.

CHAPTER II

THE WIDOW HULLINS'S HOUSE

I

The simple fact that he first, of all the citizens of Bursley, had asked a countess for a dance (and not been refused) made a new man of Denry Machin. He was not only regarded by the whole town as a fellow wonderful and dazzling, but he so regarded himself. He could not get over it. He had always been cheerful, even to optimism. He was now in a permanent state of calm, assured jollity. He would get up in the morning with song and dance. Bursley and the general world were no longer Bursley and the general world; they had been mysteriously transformed into an oyster; and Denry felt strangely that the oyster-knife was lying about somewhere handy, but just out of sight, and that presently he should spy it and seize it. He waited for something to happen. And not in vain.

A few days after the historic revelry, Mrs Codleyn called to see Denry's employer. Mr Duncalf was her solicitor. A stout, breathless, and yet muscular woman of near sixty, the widow of a chemist and druggist who had made money before limited companies had taken the liberty of being pharmaceutical. The money had been largely invested in mortgage on cottage property; the interest on it had not been paid, and latterly Mrs Codleyn had been obliged to foreclose, thus becoming the owner of some seventy cottages. Mrs Codleyn, though they brought her in about twelve pounds a week gross, esteemed these cottages an infliction, a bugbear, an affront, and a positive source of loss. Invariably she talked as though she would willingly present them to anybody who cared to accept— "and glad to be rid of 'em!" Most owners of property talk thus. She particularly hated paying the rates on them.

Now there had recently occurred, under the direction of the Borough Surveyor, a revaluation of the whole town. This may not sound exciting; yet a revaluation is the most exciting event (save a municipal ball given by a titled mayor) that can happen in any town. If your house is rated at forty pounds a year, and rates are seven shillings in the pound, and the revaluation lifts you up to forty-five pounds, it means thirty-five shillings a year right out of your pocket, which is the interest on thirty-five pounds. And if the revaluation drops you to thirty-five pounds, it means thirty-five shillings *in* your pocket, which is a box of Havanas or a fancy waistcoat. Is not this exciting? And there are seven thousand houses in Bursley. Mrs Codleyn hoped that her rateable value would be reduced. She based the hope chiefly on the fact that she was a client of Mr Duncalf, the Town Clerk. The Town Clerk was not the Borough Surveyor and had nothing to do with the revaluation. Moreover, Mrs Codleyn presumably [Transcriber's note: sic] entrusted him with her affairs because she considered him an honest man, and an honest man could not honestly have sought to tickle the Borough Surveyor out of the narrow path of rectitude in order to oblige a client.

Nevertheless, Mrs Codleyn thought that because she patronised the Town Clerk her rates ought to be reduced! Such is human nature in the provinces! So different from human nature in London, where nobody ever dreams of offering even a match to a municipal official, lest the act might be construed into an insult.

It was on a Saturday morning that Mrs Codleyn called to impart to Mr Duncalf the dissatisfaction with which she had learned the news (printed on a bit of bluish paper) that her rateable value, far from being reduced, had been slightly augmented.

The interview, as judged by the clerks through a lath-and-plaster wall and by means of a speaking tube, atoned by its vivacity for its lack of ceremony. When the stairs had finished creaking under the descent of Mrs Codleyn's righteous fury, Mr Duncalf whistled sharply twice. Two whistles meant Denry. Denry picked up his shorthand note-book and obeyed the summons.

"Take this down!" said his master, rudely and angrily.

Just as though Denry had abetted Mrs Codleyn! Just as though Denry was not a personage of high importance in the town, the friend of countesses, and a shorthand clerk only on the surface.

"Do you hear?"

"Yes, sir."

"MADAM"—hitherto it had always been "Dear Madam," or "Dear Mrs Codleyn"—"MADAM,—Of course I need hardly say that if, after our interview this morning, and your extraordinary remarks, you wish to place your interests in other hands, I shall be most happy to hand over all the papers, on payment of my costs. Yours truly ... To Mrs Codleyn."

Denry reflected: "Ass! Why doesn't he let her cool down?" Also: "He's got 'hands' and 'hand' in the same sentence. Very ugly. Shows what a temper he's in!" Shorthand clerks are always like that—hypercritical. Also: "Well, I jolly well hope she does chuck him! Then I shan't have those rents to collect." Every Monday, and often on Tuesday, too, Denry collected the rents of Mrs Codleyn's cottages—an odious task for Denry. Mr Duncalf, though not affected by its odiousness, deducted 7-1/2 per cent. for the job from the rents.

"That'll do," said Mr Duncalf.

But as Denry was leaving the room Mr Duncalf called with formidable brusqueness—

"Machin!"

"Yes, sir?"

In a flash Denry knew what was coming. He felt sickly that a crisis had supervened with the suddenness of a tidal wave. And for one little second it seemed to him that to have danced with a countess while the flower of Bursley's chivalry watched in envious wonder was not, after all, the key to the door of success throughout life.

Undoubtedly he had practised fraud in sending to himself an invitation to the ball. Undoubtedly he had practised fraud in sending invitations to his tailor and his dancing-mistress. On the day after the ball, beneath his great glory, he had trembled to meet Mr Duncalf's eye, lest Mr Duncalf should ask him: "Machin, what were *you* doing at the Town Hall last night, behaving as if you were the Shah of Persia, the Prince of Wales, and Henry Irving?" But Mr Duncalf had said nothing, and Mr Duncalf's eye had said nothing, and Denry thought that the danger was past.

Now it surged up. "Who invited you to the Mayor's ball?" demanded Mr Duncalf like thunder.

Yes, there it was! And a very difficult question.

"I did, sir," he blundered out. Transparent veracity. He simply could not think of a lie.

"Why?"

"I thought you'd perhaps forgotten to put my name down on the list of invitations, sir."

"Oh!" This grimly. "And I suppose you thought I'd also forgotten to put down that tailor chap, Shillitoe?"

So it was all out! Shillitoe must have been chattering. Denry remembered that the classic established tailor of the town, Hatterton, whose trade Shillitoe was getting, was a particular friend of Mr Duncalf's. He saw the whole thing.

"Well?" persisted Mr Duncalf, after a judicious silence from Denry.

Denry, sheltered in the castle of his silence, was not to be tempted out.

"I suppose you rather fancy yourself dancing with your betters?" growled Mr Duncalf, menacingly.

"Yes," said Denry. "Do *you*?"

He had not meant to say it. The question slipped out of his mouth. He had recently formed the habit of retorting swiftly upon people who put queries to him: "Yes, are *you*?" or "No, do *you*?" The trick of speech had been enormously effective with Shillitoe, for instance, and with the Countess. He was in process of acquiring renown for it. Certainly it was effective now. Mr Duncalf's dance with the Countess had come to an ignominious conclusion in the middle, Mr Duncalf preferring to dance on skirts rather than on the floor, and the fact was notorious.

"You can take a week's notice," said Mr Duncalf, pompously.

It was no argument. But employers are so unscrupulous in an altercation.

"Oh, very well," said Denry; and to himself he said: "Something *must* turn up, now."

He felt dizzy at being thus thrown upon the world—he who had been meditating the propriety of getting himself elected to the stylish and newly-established Sports Club at Hillport! He felt enraged, for Mr Duncalf had only been venting on Denry the annoyance induced in him by Mrs Codleyn. But it is remarkable that he was not depressed at all. No! he went about with songs and whistling, though he had no prospects except starvation or living on his mother. He traversed the streets in his grand, new manner, and his thoughts ran: "What on earth can I do to live up to my reputation?" However, he possessed intact the five-pound note won from Harold Etches in the matter of the dance.

II

Every life is a series of coincidences. Nothing happens that is not rooted in coincidence. All great changes find their cause in coincidence. Therefore I shall not mince the fact that the next change in Denry's career was due to an enormous and complicated coincidence. On the following morning both Mrs Codleyn and Denry were late for service at St Luke's Church—Mrs Codleyn by accident and obesity, Denry by design. Denry was later than Mrs Codleyn, whom he discovered waiting in the porch. That Mrs Codleyn was waiting is an essential part of the coincidence. Now Mrs Codleyn would not have been waiting if her pew had not been right at the front of the church, near the choir. Nor would she have been waiting if she had been a thin woman and not given to breathing loudly after a hurried walk. She waited partly to get her breath, and partly so that she might take advantage of a hymn or a psalm to gain her seat without attracting attention. If she had not been late, if she had not been stout, if she had not had a seat under the pulpit, if she had not had an objection to making herself conspicuous, she would have been already in the church and Denry would not have had a private colloquy with her.

"Well, you're nice people, I must say!" she observed, as he raised his hat.

She meant Duncalf and all Duncalf's myrmidons. She was still full of her grievance. The letter which she had received that morning had startled her. And even the shadow of the sacred edifice did not prevent her from referring to an affair that was more suited to Monday than to Sunday morning. A little more, and she would have snorted.

"Nothing to do with me, you know!" Denry defended himself.

"Oh!" she said, "you're all alike, and I'll tell you this, Mr Machin, I'd take him at his word if it wasn't that I don't know who else I could trust to collect my rents. I've heard such tales about rent-collectors.... I reckon I shall have to make my peace with him."

"Why," said Denry, "I'll keep on collecting your rents for you if you like."

"You?"

"I've given him notice to leave," said Denry. "The fact is, Mr Duncalf and I don't hit it off together."

Another procrastinator arrived in the porch, and, by a singular simultaneous impulse, Mrs Codleyn and Denry fell into the silence of the overheard and wandered forth together among the graves.

There, among the graves, she eyed him. He was a clerk at eighteen shillings a week, and he looked it. His mother was a sempstress, and he looked it. The idea of neat but shabby Denry and the mighty Duncalf not hitting it off together seemed excessively comic. If only Denry could have worn his dress-suit at church! It vexed him exceedingly that he had only worn that expensive dress-suit once, and saw no faintest hope of ever being able to wear it again.

"And what's more," Denry pursued, "I'll collect 'em for five per cent, instead of seven-and-a-half. Give me a free hand, and see if I don't get better results than *he* did. And I'll settle accounts every month, or week if you like, instead of once a quarter, like *he* does."

The bright and beautiful idea had smitten Denry like some heavenly arrow. It went through him and pierced Mrs Codleyn with equal success. It was an idea that appealed to the reason, to the pocket, and to the instinct of revenge. Having revengefully settled the hash of Mr Duncalf, they went into church.

No need to continue this part of the narrative. Even the text of the rector's sermon has no bearing on the issue.

In a week there was a painted board affixed to the door of Denry's mother:

E.H. MACHIN, *Rent Collector and Estate Agent*.

There was also an advertisement in the *Signal*, announcing that Denry managed estates large or small.

III

The next crucial event in Denry's career happened one Monday morning, in a cottage that was very much smaller even than his mother's. This cottage, part of Mrs Codleyn's multitudinous property, stood by itself in Chapel Alley, behind the Wesleyan chapel; the majority of the tenements were in Carpenter's Square, near to. The neighbourhood was not distinguished for its social splendour, but existence in it was picturesque, varied, exciting, full of accidents, as existence is apt to be in residences that cost their occupiers an average of three shillings a week. Some persons referred to the quarter as a slum, and ironically insisted on its adjacency to the Wesleyan chapel, as though that was the Wesleyan chapel's fault. Such people did not understand life and the joy thereof.

The solitary cottage had a front yard, about as large as a blanket, surrounded by an insecure brick wall and paved with mud. You went up two steps, pushed at a door, and instantly found yourself in the principal reception-room, which no earthly blanket could possibly have covered. Behind this chamber could be seen obscurely an apartment so tiny that an auctioneer would have been justified in terming it "bijou," Furnished simply but practically with a slopstone; also the beginnings of a stairway. The furniture of the reception-room comprised two chairs and a table, one or two saucepans, and some antique crockery. What lay at the upper end of the stairway no living person knew, save the old woman who slept there. The old woman sat at the fireplace, "all bunched up," as they say in the Five Towns. The only fire in the room, however, was in the short clay pipe which she smoked; Mrs Hullins was one of the last old women in Bursley to smoke a cutty; and even then the pipe was considered coarse, and cigarettes were coming into fashion—though not in Chapel Alley. Mrs Hullins smoked her pipe, and thought about nothing in particular. Occasionally some vision of the past floated through her drowsy brain. She had lived in that residence for over forty years. She had brought up eleven children and two husbands there. She had coddled thirty-five grand-children there, and given instruction to some half-dozen daughters-in-law. She had known midnights when she could scarcely move in that residence without disturbing somebody asleep. Now she was alone in it. She never left it, except to fetch water from the pump in the square. She had seen a lot of life, and she was tired.

Denry came unceremoniously in, smiling gaily and benevolently, with his bright, optimistic face under his fair brown hair. He had large and good teeth. He was getting—not stout, but plump.

"Well, mother!" he greeted Mrs Hullins, and sat down on the other chair.

A young fellow obviously at peace with the world, a young fellow content with himself for the moment. No longer a clerk; one of the employed; saying "sir" to persons with no more fingers and toes than he had himself; bound by servile agreement to be in a fixed place at fixed hours! An independent unit, master of his own time and his own movements! In brief, a man! The truth was that he earned now in two days a week slightly more than Mr Duncalf paid him for the labour of five and a half days. His income, as collector of rents and manager of estates large or small, totalled about a pound a week. But, he walked forth in the town, smiled, joked, spoke vaguely, and said, "Do *you*?" to such a tune that his income might have been guessed to be anything from ten pounds a week to ten thousand a year. And he had four days a week in which to excogitate new methods of creating a fortune.

"I've nowt for ye," said the old woman, not moving.

"Come, come, now! That won't do," said Denry. "Have a pinch of my tobacco."

She accepted a pinch of his tobacco, and refilled her pipe, and he gave her a match.

"I'm not going out of this house without half-a-crown at any rate!" said Denry, blithely.

And he rolled himself a cigarette, possibly to keep warm. It was very chilly in the stuffy residence, but the old woman never shivered. She was one of those old women who seem to wear all the skirts of all their lives, one over the other.

"Ye're here for th' better part o' some time, then," observed Mrs Hullins, looking facts in the face. "I've told you about my son Jack. He's been playing [out of work] six weeks. He starts to-day, and he'll gi'me summat Saturday."

"That won't do," said Denry, curtly and kindly.

He then, with his bluff benevolence, explained to Mother Hullins that Mrs Codleyn would stand no further increase of arrears from anybody, that she could not afford to stand any further increase of arrears, that her tenants were ruining her, and that he himself, with all his cheery good-will for the rent-paying classes, would be involved in her fall.

"Six-and-forty years have I been i' this 'ere house!" said Mrs Hullins.

"Yes, I know," said Denry. "And look at what you owe, mother!"

It was with immense good-humoured kindliness that he invited her attention to what she owed. She tacitly declined to look at it.

"Your children ought to keep you," said Denry, upon her silence.

"Them as is dead, can't," said Mrs Hullins, "and them as is alive has their own to keep, except Jack."

"Well, then, it's bailiffs," said Denry, but still cheerfully.

"Nay, nay! Ye'll none turn me out."

Denry threw up his hands, as if to exclaim: "I've done all I can, and I've given you a pinch of tobacco. Besides, you oughtn't to be here alone. You ought to be with one of your children."

There was more conversation, which ended in Denry's repeating, with sympathetic resignation:

"No, you'll have to get out. It's bailiffs."

Immediately afterwards he left the residence with a bright filial smile. And then, in two minutes, he popped his cheerful head in at the door again.

"Look here, mother," he said, "I'll lend you half-a-crown if you like."

Charity beamed on his face, and genuinely warmed his heart.

"But you must pay me something for the accommodation," he added. "I can't do it for nothing. You must pay me back next week and give me threepence. That's fair. I couldn't bear to see you turned out of your house. Now get your rent-book."

And he marked half-a-crown as paid in her greasy, dirty rent-book, and the same in his large book.

"Eh, you're a queer 'un, Mester Machin!" murmured the old woman as he left. He never knew precisely what she meant. Fifteen—twenty—years later in his career her intonation of that phrase would recur to him and puzzle him.

On the following Monday everybody in Chapel Alley and Carpenter's Square seemed to know that the inconvenience of bailiffs and eviction could be avoided by arrangement with Denry the philanthropist. He did quite a business. And having regard to the fantastic nature of the security, he could not well charge less than threepence a week for half-a-crown. That was about 40 per cent. a month and 500 per cent. per annum. The security was merely fantastic, but nevertheless he had his remedy against evil-doers. He would take what they paid him for rent and refuse to mark it as rent, appropriating it to his loans, so that the fear of bailiffs was upon them again. Thus, as the good genius of Chapel Alley and Carpenter's Square, saving the distressed from the rigours of the open street, rescuing the needy from their tightest corners, keeping many a home together when but for him it would have fallen to pieces—always smiling, jolly, sympathetic, and picturesque—Denry at length employed the five-pound note won from Harold Etches. A five-pound note— especially a new and crisp one, as this was—is a miraculous fragment of matter, wonderful in the pleasure which the sight of it gives, even to millionaires; but perhaps no five-pound note was ever so miraculous as Denry's. Ten per cent. per week, compound interest, mounts up; it ascends, and it lifts. Denry never talked precisely. But the town soon began to comprehend that he was a rising man, a man to watch. The town admitted that, so far, he had lived up to his reputation as a dancer with countesses. The town felt that there was something indefinable about Denry.

Denry himself felt this. He did not consider himself clever or brilliant. But he considered himself peculiarly gifted. He considered himself different from other men. His thoughts would run:

"Anybody but me would have knuckled down to Duncalf and remained a shorthand clerk for ever."

"Who but me would have had the idea of going to the ball and asking the Countess to dance?... And then that business with the fan!"

"Who but me would have had the idea of taking his rent-collecting off Duncalf?"

"Who but me would have had the idea of combining these loans with the rent-collecting? It's simple enough! It's just what they want! And yet nobody ever thought of it till I thought of it!"

And he knew of a surety that he was that most admired type in the bustling, industrial provinces—a card.

IV

The desire to become a member of the Sports Club revived in his breast. And yet, celebrity though he was, rising though he was, he secretly regarded the Sports Club at Hillport as being really a bit above him. The Sports Club was the latest and greatest phenomenon of social life in Bursley, and it was emphatically the club to which it behoved the golden youth of the town to belong. To Denry's generation the Conservative Club and the Liberal Club did not seem like real clubs; they were machinery for politics, and membership carried nearly no distinction with it. But the Sports Club had been founded by the most dashing young men of Hillport, which is the most aristocratic suburb of Bursley and set on a lofty eminence. The sons of the wealthiest earthenware manufacturers made a point of belonging to it, and, after a period of disdain, their fathers also made a point of belonging to it. It was housed in an old mansion, with extensive grounds and a pond and tennis courts; it had a working agreement with the Golf Club and with the Hillport Cricket Club. But chiefly it was a social affair. The correctest thing was to be seen there at nights, rather late than early; and an exact knowledge of card games and billiards was worth more in it than prowess on the field.

It was a club in the Pall Mall sense of the word.

And Denry still lived in insignificant Brougham Street, and his mother was still a sempstress! These were apparently insurmountable truths. All the men whom he knew to be members were somehow more dashing than Denry —and it was a question of dash; few things are more mysterious than dash. Denry was unique, knew himself to be unique; he had danced with a countess, and yet... these other fellows!... Yes, there are puzzles, baffling puzzles, in the social career.

In going over on Tuesdays to Hanbridge, where he had a few trifling rents to collect, Denry often encountered Harold Etches in the tramcar. At that time Etches lived at Hillport, and the principal Etches manufactory was at Hanbridge. Etches partook of the riches of his family, and, though a bachelor, was reputed to have the spending of at least a thousand a year. He was famous, on summer Sundays, on the pier at Llandudno, in white flannels. He had been one of the originators of the Sports Club. He spent far more on clothes alone than Denry spent in the entire enterprise of keeping his soul in his body. At their first meeting little was said. They were not equals, and nothing but dress-suits could make them equals. However, even a king could not refuse speech with a scullion whom he had allowed to win money from him.

And Etches and Denry chatted feebly. Bit by bit they chatted less feebly. And once, when they were almost alone on the car, they chatted with vehemence during the complete journey of twenty minutes.

"He isn't so bad," said Denry to himself, of the dashing Harold Etches.

And he took a private oath that at his very next encounter with Etches he would mention the Sports Club—"just to see." This oath disturbed his sleep for several night. But with Denry an oath was sacred. Having sworn that he would mention the club to Etches, he was bound to mention it. When Tuesday came, he hoped that Etches would not be on the tram, and the coward in him would have walked to Hanbridge instead of taking the tram. But he was brave. And he boarded the tram, and Etches was already in it. Now that he looked at it close, the enterprise of suggesting to Harold Etches that he, Denry, would be a suitable member of the Sports Club at Hillport, seemed in the highest degree preposterous. Why! He could not play any games at all! He was a figure only in the streets! Nevertheless—the oath!

He sat awkwardly silent for a few moments, wondering how to begin. And then Harold Etches leaned across the tram to him and said:

"I say, Machin, I've several times meant to ask you. Why don't you put up for the Sports Club? It's really very good, you know."

Denry blushed, quite probably for the last time in his life. And he saw with fresh clearness how great he was, and how large he must loom in the life of the town. He perceived that he had been too modest.

V

You could not be elected to the Sports Club all in a minute. There were formalities; and that these formalities were complicated and took time is simply a proof that the club was correctly exclusive and worth belonging to. When at length Denry received notice from the "Secretary and Steward" that he was elected to the most sparkling fellowship in the Five Towns, he was positively afraid to go and visit the club. He wanted some old and experienced member to lead him gently into the club and explain its usages and introduce him to the chief habitués. Or else he wanted to slip in unobserved while the heads of clubmen were turned. And then he had a distressing shock. Mrs Codleyn took it into her head that she must sell her cottage property. Now, Mrs Codleyn's cottage property was the back-bone of Denry's livelihood, and he could by no means be sure that a new owner would employ him as rent-collector. A new owner might have the absurd notion of collecting rents in person. Vainly did Denry exhibit to Mrs Codleyn rows of figures, showing that her income from the property had increased under his control. Vainly did he assert that from no other form of investment would she derive such a handsome interest. She went so far as to consult an auctioneer. The auctioneer's idea of what could constitute a fair reserve price shook, but did not quite overthrow her. At this crisis it was that Denry happened to say to her, in his new large manner: "Why! If I could afford, I'd buy the property off you myself, just to show you...!" (He did not explain, and he did not perhaps know himself, what had to be shown.) She answered that she wished to goodness he would! Then he said wildly that he *would*, in instalments! And he actually did buy the Widow Hullins's half-a-crown-a-week cottage for forty-five pounds, of which he paid thirty pounds in cash and arranged that the balance should be deducted gradually from his weekly commission. He chose the Widow Hullins's because it stood by itself—an odd piece, as it were, chipped off from the block of Mrs Codleyn's realty. The transaction quietened Mrs Codleyn. And Denry felt secure because she could not now dispense with his services without losing her security for fifteen pounds. (He still thought in these small sums instead of thinking in thousands.)

He was now a property owner.

Encouraged by this great and solemn fact, he went up one afternoon to the club at Hillport. His entry was magnificent, superficially. No one suspected that he was nervous under the ordeal. The truth is that no one suspected because the place was empty. The emptiness of the hall gave him pause. He saw a large framed copy of the "Rules" hanging under a deer's head, and he read them as carefully as though he had not got a copy in his pocket. Then he read the notices, as though they had been latest telegrams from some dire seat of war. Then, perceiving a massive open door of oak (the club-house had once been a pretty stately mansion), he passed through it, and saw a bar (with bottles) and a number of small tables and wicker chairs, and on one of the tables an example of the *Staffordshire Signal* displaying in vast letters the fearful question:—"Is your skin troublesome?" Denry's skin was troublesome; it crept. He crossed the hall and went into another room which was placarded "Silence." And silence was. And on a table with copies of *The Potter's World*, *The British Australasian*, *The Iron Trades Review*, and the *Golfers' Annual*, was a second copy of the *Signal*, again demanding of Denry in vast letters whether his skin was troublesome. Evidently the reading-room.

He ascended the stairs and discovered a deserted billiard-room with two tables. Though he had never played at billiards, he seized a cue, but when he touched them the balls gave such a resounding click in the hush of the chamber that he put the cue away instantly. He noticed another door, curiously opened it, and started back at the sight of a small room, and eight middle-aged men, mostly hatted, playing cards in two groups. They had the air of conspirators, but they were merely some of the finest solo-whist players in Bursley. (This was before bridge had quitted Pall Mall.) Among them was Mr Duncalf. Denry shut the door quickly. He felt like a wanderer in an enchanted castle who had suddenly come across something that ought not to be come across. He returned to earth, and in the hall met a man in shirt-sleeves—the Secretary and Steward, a nice, homely man, who said, in the accents of ancient friendship, though he had never spoken to Denry before: "Is it Mr Machin? Glad to see you, Mr Machin! Come and have a drink with me, will you? Give it a name." Saying which, the Secretary and

Steward went behind the bar, and Denry imbibed a little whisky and much information.

"Anyhow, I've *been!*" he said to himself, going home.

VI

The next night he made another visit to the club, about ten o'clock. The reading-room, that haunt of learning, was as empty as ever; but the bar was full of men, smoke, and glasses. It was so full that Denry's arrival was scarcely observed. However, the Secretary and Steward observed him, and soon he was chatting with a group at the bar, presided over by the Secretary and Steward's shirt-sleeves. He glanced around, and was satisfied. It was a scene of dashing gaiety and worldliness that did not belie the club's reputation. Some of the most important men in Bursley were there. Charles Fearns, the solicitor, who practised at Hanbridge, was arguing vivaciously in a corner. Fearns lived at Bleakridge and belonged to the Bleakridge Club, and his presence at Hillport (two miles from Bleakridge) was a dramatic tribute to the prestige of Hillport's Club.

Fearns was apparently in one of his anarchistic moods. Though a successful business man who voted right, he was pleased occasionally to uproot the fabric of society and rebuild it on a new plan of his own. To-night he was inveighing against landlords—he who by "conveyancing" kept a wife and family, and a French governess for the family, in rather more than comfort. The Fearns's French governess was one of the seven wonders of the Five Towns. Men enjoyed him in these moods; and as he raised his voice, so he enlarged the circle of his audience.

"If the by-laws of this town were worth a bilberry," he was saying, "about a thousand so-called houses would have to come down to-morrow. Now there's that old woman I was talking about just now—Hullins. She's a Catholic—and my governess is always slumming about among Catholics— that's how I know. She's paid half-a-crown a week for pretty near half a century for a hovel that isn't worth eighteen-pence, and now she's going to be pitched into the street because she can't pay any more. And she's seventy if she's a day! And that's the basis of society. Nice refined society, eh?"

"Who's the grasping owner?" some one asked.

"Old Mrs Codleyn," said Fearns.

"Here, Mr Machin, they're talking about you," said the Secretary and Steward, genially. He knew that Denry collected Mrs Codleyn's rents.

"Mrs Codleyn isn't the owner," Denry called out across the room, almost before he was aware what he was doing. There was a smile on his face and a glass in his hand.

"Oh!" said Fearns. "I thought she was. Who is?"

Everybody looked inquisitively at the renowned Machin, the new member.

"I am," said Denry.

He had concealed the change of ownership from the Widow Hullins. In his quality of owner he could not have lent her money in order that she might pay it instantly back to himself.

"I beg your pardon," said Fearns, with polite sincerity. "I'd no idea...!" He saw that unwittingly he had come near to committing a gross outrage on club etiquette.

"Not at all!" said Denry. "But supposing the cottage was *yours*, what would *you* do, Mr Fearns? Before I bought the property I used to lend her money myself to pay her rent."

"I know," Fearns answered, with a certain dryness of tone.

It occurred to Denry that the lawyer knew too much.

"Well, what should you do?" he repeated obstinately.

"She's an old woman," said Fearns. "And honest enough, you must admit. She came up to see my governess, and I happened to see her."

"But what should you do in my place?" Denry insisted.

"Since you ask, I should lower the rent and let her off the arrears," said Fearns.

"And supposing she didn't pay then? Let her have it rent-free because she's seventy? Or pitch her into the street?"

"Oh—Well—"

"Fearns would make her a present of the blooming house and give her a conveyance free!" a voice said humorously, and everybody laughed.

"Well, that's what I'll do," said Denry. "If Mr Fearns will do the conveyance free, I'll make her a present of the blooming house. That's the sort of grasping owner I am."

There was a startled pause. "I mean it," said Denry firmly, even fiercely, and raised his glass. "Here's to the Widow Hullins!"

There was a sensation, because, incredible though the thing was, it had to be believed. Denry himself was not the least astounded person in the crowded, smoky room. To him, it had been like somebody else talking, not himself. But, as always when he did something crucial, spectacular, and effective, the deed had seemed to be done by a mysterious power within him, over which he had no control.

This particular deed was quixotic, enormously unusual; a deed assuredly without precedent in the annals of the Five Towns. And he, Denry, had done it. The cost was prodigious, ridiculously and dangerously beyond his means. He could find no rational excuse for the deed. But he had done it. And men again wondered. Men had wondered when he led the Countess out to waltz. That was nothing to this. What! A smooth-chinned youth giving houses away—out of mere, mad, impulsive generosity.

And men said, on reflection, "Of course, that's just the sort of thing Machin *would* do!" They appeared to find a logical connection between dancing with a Countess and tossing a house or so to a poor widow. And the next morning every man who had been in the Sports Club that night was remarking eagerly to his friends: "I say, have you heard young Machin's latest?"

And Denry, inwardly aghast at his own rashness, was saying to himself: "Well, no one but me would ever have done that!"

He was now not simply a card; he was *the* card.

CHAPTER III

THE PANTECHNICON

I

"How do you do, Miss Earp?" said Denry, in a worldly manner, which he had acquired for himself by taking the most effective features of the manners of several prominent citizens, and piecing them together so that, as a whole, they formed Denry's manner.

"Oh! How do you do, Mr Machin?" said Ruth Earp, who had opened her door to him at the corner of Tudor Passage and St Luke's Square.

It was an afternoon in July. Denry wore a new summer suit, whose pattern indicated not only present prosperity but the firm belief that prosperity would continue. As for Ruth, that plain but piquant girl was in one of her simpler costumes; blue linen; no jewellery. Her hair was in its usual calculated disorder; its outer fleeces held the light. She was now at least twenty-five, and her gaze disconcertingly combined extreme maturity with extreme candour. At one moment a man would be saying to himself: "This woman knows more of the secrets of human nature than I can ever know." And the next he would be saying to himself: "What a simple little thing she is!" The career of nearly every man is marked at the sharp corners with such women. Speaking generally, Ruth Earp's demeanour was hard and challenging. It was evident that she could not be subject to the common weaknesses of her sex. Denry was glad.

A youth of quick intelligence, he had perceived all the dangers of the mission upon which he was engaged, and had planned his precautions.

"May I come in a minute?" he asked in a purely business tone. There was no hint in that tone of the fact that once she had accorded him a supper-dance.

"Please do," said Ruth.

An agreeable flouncing swish of linen skirts as she turned to precede him down the passage! But he ignored it. That is to say, he easily steeled himself against it.

She led him to the large room which served as her dancing academy—the bare-boarded place in which, a year and a half before, she had taught his clumsy limbs the principles of grace and rhythm. She occupied the back part of a building of which the front part was an empty shop. The shop had been tenanted by her father, one of whose frequent bankruptcies had happened there; after which his stock of the latest novelties in inexpensive furniture had been seized by rapacious creditors, and Mr Earp had migrated to Birmingham, where he was courting the Official Receiver anew. Ruth had remained solitary and unprotected, with a considerable amount of household goods which had been her mother's. (Like all professional bankrupts, Mr Earp had invariably had belongings which, as he could prove to his creditors, did not belong to him.) Public opinion had justified Ruth in her enterprise of staying in Bursley on her own responsibility and renting part of the building, in order not to lose her "connection" as a dancing-mistress. Public opinion said that "there would have been no sense in her going dangling after her wastrel of a father."

"Quite a long time since we saw anything of each other," observed Ruth in rather a pleasant style, as she sat down and as he sat down.

It was. The intimate ecstasy of the supper-dance had never been repeated. Denry's exceeding industry in carving out his career, and his desire to graduate as an accomplished clubman, had prevented him from giving to his heart that attention which it deserved, having regard to his tender years.

"Yes, it is, isn't it?" said Denry.

Then there was a pause, and they both glanced vaguely about the inhospitable and very wooden room. Now was the moment for Denry to carry out his pre-arranged plan in all its savage simplicity. He did so. "I've called about the rent, Miss Earp," he said, and by an effort looked her in the eyes.

"The rent?" exclaimed Ruth, as though she had never in all her life heard of such a thing as rent; as though June 24 (recently past) was an ordinary day like any other day.

"Yes," said Denry.

"What rent?" asked Ruth, as though for aught she guessed it might have been the rent of Buckingham Palace that he had called about.

"Yours," said Denry.

"Mine!" she murmured. "But what has my rent got to do with you?" she demanded. And it was just as if she had said, "But what has my rent got to do with you, little boy?"

"Well," he said, "I suppose you know I'm a rent-collector?"

"No, I didn't," she said.

He thought she was fibbing out of sheer naughtiness. But she was not. She did not know that he collected rents. She knew that he was a card, a figure, a celebrity; and that was all. It is strange how the knowledge of even the cleverest woman will confine itself to certain fields.

"Yes," he said, always in a cold, commercial tone, "I collect rents."

"I should have thought you'd have preferred postage-stamps," she said, gazing out of the window at a kiln that was blackening all the sky.

If he could have invented something clever and cutting in response to this sally he might have made the mistake of quitting his *rôle* of hard, unsentimental man of business. But he could think of nothing. So he proceeded sternly:

"Mr Herbert Calvert has put all his property into my hands, and he has given me strict instructions that no rent is to be allowed to remain in arrear."

No answer from Ruth. Mr Calvert was a little fellow of fifty who had made money in the mysterious calling of a "commission agent." By reputation he was really very much harder than Denry could even pretend to be, and indeed Denry had been considerably startled by the advent of such a client. Surely if any man in Bursley were capable of unmercifully collecting rents on his own account, Herbert Calvert must be that man!

"Let me see," said Denry further, pulling a book from his pocket and peering into it, "you owe five quarters' rent—thirty pounds."

He knew without the book precisely what Ruth owed, but the book kept him in countenance, supplied him with needed moral support.

Ruth Earp, without the least warning, exploded into a long peal of gay laughter. Her laugh was far prettier than her face. She laughed well. She might, with advantage to Bursley, have given lessons in laughing as well as in dancing, for Bursley laughs without grace. Her laughter was a proof that she had not a care in the world, and that the world for her was naught but a source of light amusement.

Denry smiled guardedly.

"Of course, with me it's purely a matter of business," said he.

"So that's what Mr Herbert Calvert has done!" she exclaimed, amid the embers of her mirth. "I wondered what he would do! I presume you know all about Mr Herbert Calvert," she added.

"No," said Denry, "I don't know anything about him, except that he owns some property and I'm in charge of it. Stay," he corrected himself, "I think I do remember crossing his name off your programme once."

And he said to himself: "That's one for her. If she likes to be so desperately funny about postage-stamps, I don't see why I shouldn't have my turn." The recollection that it was precisely Herbert Calvert whom he had supplanted in the supper-dance at the Countess of Chell's historic ball somehow increased his confidence in his ability to manage the interview with brilliance.

Ruth's voice grew severe and chilly. It seemed incredible that she had just been laughing.

"I will tell you about Mr Herbert Calvert," she enunciated her words with slow, stern clearness. "Mr Herbert Calvert took advantage of his visits here for his rent to pay his attentions to me. At one time he was so far—well—gone, that he would scarcely take his rent."

"Really!" murmured Denry, genuinely staggered by this symptom of the distance to which Mr Herbert Calvert was once "gone."

"Yes," said Ruth, still sternly and inimically. "Naturally a woman can't make up her mind about these things all of a sudden," she continued. "Naturally!" she repeated.

"Of course," Denry agreed, perceiving that his experience of life, and deep knowledge of human nature were being appealed to.

"And when I did decide definitely, Mr Herbert Calvert did not behave like a gentleman. He forgot what was due to himself and to me. I won't describe to you the scene he made. I'm simply telling you this, so that you may know. To cut a long story short, he behaved in a very vulgar way. And a woman doesn't forget these things, Mr Machin." Her eyes threatened him. "I decided to punish Mr Herbert Calvert. I thought if he wouldn't take his rent before—well, let him wait for it now! I might have given him notice to leave. But I didn't. I didn't see why I should let myself be upset because Mr Herbert Calvert had forgotten that he was a gentleman. I said, 'Let him wait for his rent,' and I promised myself I would just see what he would dare to do."

"I don't quite follow your argument," Denry put in.

"Perhaps you don't," she silenced him. "I didn't expect you would. You and Mr Herbert Calvert...! So he didn't dare to do anything himself, and he's paying you to do his dirty work for him! Very well! Very well!..." She lifted her head defiantly. "What will happen if I don't pay the rent?"

"I shall have to let things take their course," said Denry with a genial smile.

"All right, then," Ruth Earp responded. "If you choose to mix yourself up with people like Mr Herbert Calvert, you must take the consequences! It's all the same to me, after all."

"Then it isn't convenient for you to pay anything on account?" said Denry, more and more affable.

"Convenient!" she cried. "It's perfectly convenient, only I don't care to. I won't pay a penny until I'm forced. Let Mr Herbert Calvert do his worst, and then I'll pay. And not before! And the whole town shall hear all about Mr Herbert Calvert!"

"I see," he laughed easily.

"Convenient!" she reiterated, contemptuously. "I think everybody in Bursley knows how my *clientèle* gets larger and larger every year!... Convenient!"

"So that's final, Miss Earp?"

"Perfectly!" said Miss Earp.

He rose. "Then the simplest thing will be for me to send round a bailiff to-morrow morning, early." He might have been saying: "The simplest thing will be for me to send round a bunch of orchids."

Another man would have felt emotion, and probably expressed it. But not Denry, the rent-collector and manager of estates large and small. There were several different men in Denry, but he had the great gift of not mixing up two different Denrys when he found himself in a complicated situation.

Ruth Earp rose also. She dropped her eyelids and looked at him from under them. And then she gradually smiled.

"I thought I'd just see what you'd do," she said, in a low, confidential voice from which all trace of hostility had suddenly departed. "You're a strange creature," she went on curiously, as though fascinated by the problems presented by his individuality. "Of course, I shan't let it go as far as that. I only thought I'd see what you'd say. I'll write you to-night."

"With a cheque?" Denry demanded, with suave, jolly courtesy. "I don't collect postage-stamps."

(And to himself: "She's got her stamps back.")

She hesitated. "Stay!" she said. "I'll tell you what will be better. Can you call to-morrow afternoon? The bank will be closed now."

"Yes," he said, "I can call. What time?"

"Oh!" she answered, "any time. If you come in about four, I'll give you a cup of tea into the bargain. Though you don't deserve it!" After an instant, she added reassuringly: "Of course I know business is business with you. But I'm glad I've told you the real truth about your precious Mr Herbert Calvert, all the same."

And as he walked slowly home Denry pondered upon the singular, erratic, incalculable strangeness of woman, and of the possibly magic effect of his own personality on women.

II

It was the next afternoon, in July. Denry wore his new summer suit, but with a necktie of higher rank than the previous day's. As for Ruth, that plain but piquant girl was in one of her more elaborate and foamier costumes. The wonder was that such a costume could survive even for an hour the smuts that lend continual interest and excitement to the atmosphere of Bursley. It was a white muslin, spotted with spots of opaque white, and founded on something pink. Denry imagined that he had seen parts of it before—at the ball; and he had; but it was now a tea-gown, with long, languishing sleeves; the waves of it broke at her shoulders, sending lacy surf high up the precipices of Ruth's neck. Denry did not know it was a tea-gown. But he knew that it had a most peculiar and agreeable effect on himself, and that she had promised him tea. He was glad that he had paid her the homage of his best necktie.

Although the month was July, Ruth wore a kind of shawl over the tea-gown. It was not a shawl, Denry noted; it was merely about two yards of very thin muslin. He puzzled himself as to its purpose. It could not be for warmth, for it would not have helped to melt an icicle. Could it be meant to fulfil the same function as muslin in a confectioner's shop? She was pale. Her voice was weak and had an imploring quality.

She led him, not into the inhospitable wooden academy, but into a very small room which, like herself, was dressed in muslin and bows of ribbon. Photographs of amiable men and women decorated the pinkish-green walls. The mantelpiece was concealed in drapery as though it had been a sin. A writing-desk as green as a leaf stood carelessly in one corner; on the desk a vase containing some Cape gooseberries. In the middle of the room a small table, on the table a spirit-lamp in full blast, and on the lamp a kettle practising scales; a tray occupied the remainder of the table. There were two easy chairs; Ruth sank delicately into one, and Denry took the other with precautions.

He was nervous. Nothing equals muslin for imparting nervousness to the naïve. But he felt pleased.

"Not much of the Widow Hullins touch about this!" he reflected privately.

And he wished that all rent-collecting might be done with such ease, and amid such surroundings, as this particular piece of rent-collecting. He saw what a fine thing it was to be a free man, under orders from nobody; not many men in Bursley were in a position to accept invitations to four o'clock tea at a day's notice. Further 5 per cent. on thirty pounds was thirty shillings, so that if he stayed an hour—and he meant to stay an hour—he would, while enjoying himself, be earning money steadily at the rate of sixpence a minute.

It was the ideal of a business career.

When the kettle, having finished its scales, burst into song with an accompaniment of castanets and vapour, and Ruth's sleeves rose and fell as she made the tea, Denry acknowledged frankly to himself that it was this sort of thing, and not the Brougham Street sort of thing, that he was really born for. He acknowledged to himself humbly that this sort of thing was "life," and that hitherto he had had no adequate idea of what "life" was. For, with all his ability as a card and a rising man, with all his assiduous frequenting of the Sports Club, he had not penetrated into the upper domestic strata of Bursley society. He had never been invited to any house where, as he put it, he would have had to mind his p's and q's. He still remained the kind of man whom you familiarly chat with in the street and club, and no more. His mother's fame as a flannel-washer was against him; Brougham Street was against him; and, chiefly, his poverty was against him. True, he had gorgeously given a house away to an aged widow! True, he succeeded in transmitting to his acquaintances a vague idea that he was doing well and waxing financially from strength to strength! But the idea was too vague, too much in the air. And save by a suit of clothes, he never gave ocular proof that he had money to waste. He could not. It was impossible for him to compete with even the more modest of the bloods and the blades. To keep a satisfactory straight crease down the middle of each leg of his trousers was all he could accomplish with the money regularly at his disposal. The town was wafting for him to do something decisive in the matter of what it called "the stuff."

Thus Ruth Earp was the first to introduce him to the higher intimate civilisations, the refinements lurking behind the foul walls of Bursley.

"Sugar?" she questioned, her head on one side, her arm uplifted, her sleeve drooping, and a bit of sugar caught like a white mouse between the claws of the tongs.

Nobody before had ever said "Sugar?" to him like that. His mother never said "Sugar?" to him. His mother was aware that he liked three pieces, but she would not give him more than two. "Sugar?" in that slightly weak, imploring voice seemed to be charged with a significance at once tremendous and elusive.

"Yes, please."

"Another?"

And the "Another?" was even more delicious.

He said to himself: "I suppose this is what they call flirting."

When a chronicler tells the exact truth, there is always a danger that he will not be believed. Yet, in spite of the risk, it must be said plainly that at this point Denry actually thought of marriage. An absurd and childish thought, preposterously rash; but it came into his mind, and—what is more—it stuck there! He pictured marriage as a perpetual afternoon tea alone with an elegant woman, amid an environment of ribboned muslin. And the picture appealed to him very strongly. And Ruth appeared to him in a new light. It was perhaps the change in her voice that did it. She appeared to him at once as a creature very feminine and enchanting, and as a creature who could earn her own living in a manner that was both original and ladylike. A woman such as Ruth would be a delight without being a drag. And, truly, was she not a remarkable woman, as remarkable as he was a man? Here she was living amid the refinements of luxury. Not an expensive luxury (he had an excellent notion of the monetary value of things), but still luxury. And the whole affair was so stylish. His heart went out to the stylish.

The slices of bread-and-butter were rolled up. There, now, was a pleasing device! It cost nothing to roll up a slice of bread-and-butter —her fingers had doubtless done the rolling—and yet it gave quite a different taste to the food.

"What made you give that house to Mrs Hullins?" she asked him suddenly, with a candour that seemed to demand candour.

"Oh," he said, "just a lark! I thought I would. It came to me all in a second, and I did."

She shook her head. "Strange boy!" she observed.

There was a pause.

"It was something Charlie Fearns said, wasn't it?" she inquired.

She uttered the name "Charlie Fearns" with a certain faint hint of disdain, as if indicating to Denry that of course she and Denry were quite able to put Fearns into his proper place in the scheme of things.

"Oh!" he said. "So you know all about it?"

"Well," said she, "naturally it was all over the town. Mrs Fearns's girl, Annunciata—what a name, eh?—is one of my pupils—the youngest, in fact."

"Well," said he, after another pause, "I wasn't going to have Fearns coming the duke over me!" She smiled sympathetically. He felt that they understood each other deeply.

"You'll find some cigarettes in that box," she said, when he had been there thirty minutes, and pointed to the mantelpiece.

"Sure you don't mind?" he murmured.

She raised her eyebrows.

There was also a silver match-box in the larger box. No detail lacked. It seemed to him that he stood on a mountain and had only to walk down a winding path in order to enter the promised land. He was decidedly pleased with the worldly way in which he had said: "Sure you don't mind?"

He puffed out smoke delicately. And, the cigarette between his lips, as with his left hand he waved the match into extinction, he demanded:

"You smoke?"

"Yes," she said, "but not in public. I know what you men are."

This was in the early, timid days of feminine smoking.

"I assure you!" he protested, and pushed the box towards her. But she would not smoke.

"It isn't that I mind *you*," she said, "not at all. But I'm not well. I've got a frightful headache."

He put on a concerned expression.

"I *thought* you looked rather pale," he said awkwardly.

"Pale!" she repeated the word. "You should have seen me this morning: I have fits of dizziness, you know, too. The doctor says it's nothing but dyspepsia.

However, don't let's talk about poor little me and my silly complaints. Perhaps the tea will do me good."

He protested again, but his experience of intimate civilisation was too brief to allow him to protest with effectiveness. The truth was, he could not say these things naturally. He had to compose them, and then pronounce them, and the result failed in the necessary air of spontaneity. He could not help thinking what marvellous self-control women had. Now, when he had a headache—which happily was seldom—he could think of nothing else and talk of nothing else; the entire universe consisted solely of his headache. And here she was overcome with a headache, and during more than half-an-hour had not even mentioned it!

She began talking gossip about the Fearnses and the Swetnams, and she mentioned rumours concerning Henry Mynors (who had scruples against dancing) and Anna Tellwright, the daughter of that rich old skinflint Ephraim Tellwright. No mistake; she was on the inside of things in Bursley society! It was just as if she had removed the front walls of every house and examined every room at her leisure, with minute particularity. But of course a teacher of dancing had opportunities.... Denry had to pretend to be nearly as omniscient as she was.

Then she broke off, without warning, and lay back in her chair.

"I wonder if you'd mind going into the barn for me?" she murmured.

She generally referred to her academy as the barn. It had once been a warehouse.

He jumped up. "Certainly," he said, very eager.

"I think you'll see a small bottle of eau-de-Cologne on the top of the piano," she said, and shut her eyes.

He hastened away, full of his mission, and feeling himself to be a terrific cavalier and guardian of weak women. He felt keenly that he must be equal to the situation. Yes, the small bottle of eau-de-Cologne was on the top of the piano. He seized it and bore it to her on the wings of chivalry. He had not been aware that eau-de-Cologne was a remedy for, or a palliative of, headaches.

She opened her eyes, and with a great effort tried to be bright and better. But it was a failure. She took the stopper out of the bottle and sniffed first at the stopper and then at the bottle; then she spilled a few drops of the liquid on her handkerchief and applied the handkerchief to her temples.

"It's easier," she said.

"Sure?" he asked. He did not know what to do with himself—whether to sit down and feign that she was well, or to remain standing in an attitude of respectful and grave anxiety. He thought he ought to depart; yet would it not be ungallant to desert her under the circumstances? She was alone. She had no servant, only an occasional charwoman.

She nodded with brave, false gaiety. And then she had a relapse.

"Don't you think you'd better lie down?" he suggested in more masterful accents. And added; "And I'll go....? You ought to lie down. It's the only thing." He was now speaking to her like a wise uncle.

"Oh no!" she said, without conviction. "Besides, you can't go till I've paid you."

It was on the tip of his tongue to say, "Oh! don't bother about that now!" But he restrained himself. There was a notable core of common-sense in Denry. He had been puzzling how he might neatly mention the rent while departing in a hurry so that she might lie down. And now she had solved the difficulty for him.

She stretched out her arm, and picked up a bunch of keys from a basket on a little table.

"You might just unlock that desk for me, will you?" she said. And, further, as she went through the keys one by one to select the right key: "Each quarter I've put your precious Mr Herbert Calvert's rent in a drawer in that desk. ... Here's the key." She held up the whole ring by the chosen key, and he accepted it. And she lay back once more in her chair, exhausted by her exertions.

"You must turn the key sharply in the lock," she said weakly, as he fumbled at the locked part of the desk.

So he turned the key sharply.

"You'll see a bag in the little drawer on the right," she murmured.

The key turned round and round. It had begun by resisting, but now it yielded too easily.

"It doesn't seem to open," he said, feeling clumsy.

The key clicked and slid, and the other keys rattled together.

"Oh yes," she replied. "I opened it quite easily this morning. It *is* a bit catchy."

The key kept going round and round.

"Here! I'll do it," she said wearily.

"Oh no!" he urged.

But she rose courageously, and tottered to the desk, and took the bunch from him.

"I'm afraid you've broken something in the lock," she announced, with gentle resignation, after she had tried to open the desk and failed.

"Have I?" he mumbled. He knew that he was not shining.

"Would you mind calling in at Allman's," she said, resuming her chair, "and tell them to send a man down at once to pick the lock? There's nothing else for it. Or perhaps you'd better say first thing to-morrow morning. And then as soon as he's done it I'll call and pay you the money myself. And you might tell your precious Mr Herbert Calvert that next quarter I shall give notice to leave."

"Don't you trouble to call, please," said he. "I can easily pop in here."

She sped him away in an enigmatic tone. He could not be sure whether he had succeeded or failed, in her estimation, as a man of the world and a partaker of delicate teas.

"Don't *forget* Allman's!" she enjoined him as he left the room. He was to let himself out.

III

He was coming home late that night from the Sports Club, from a delectable evening which had lasted till one o'clock in the morning, when just as he put the large door-key into his mother's cottage he grew aware of peculiar phenomena at the top end of Brougham Street, where it runs into St Luke's Square. And then in the gas-lit gloom of the warm summer night he perceived a vast and vague rectangular form in the slow movement towards the slope of Brougham Street.

It was a pantechnicon van.

But the extraordinary thing was, not that it should be a pantechnicon van, but that if should be moving of its own accord and power. For there were no horses in front of it, and Denry saw that the double shafts had been pushed up perpendicularly, after the manner of carmen when they outspan. The pantechnicon was running away. It had perceived the wrath to come and was fleeing. Its guardians had evidently left it imperfectly scotched or braked, and it had got loose.

It proceeded down the first bit of Brougham Street with a dignity worthy of its dimensions, and at the same time with apparently a certain sense of the humour of the situation. Then it seemed to be saying to itself: "Pantechnicons will be pantechnicons." Then it took on the absurd gravity of a man who is perfectly sure that he is not drunk. Nevertheless it kept fairly well to the middle of the road, but as though the road were a tight-rope.

The rumble of it increased as it approached Denry. He withdrew the key from his mother's cottage and put it in his pocket. He was always at his finest in a crisis. And the onrush of the pantechnicon constituted a clear crisis. Lower down the gradient of Brougham Street was more dangerous, and it was within the possibilities that people inhabiting the depths of the street might find themselves pitched out of bed by the sharp corner of a pantechnicon that was determined to be a pantechnicon. A pantechnicon whose ardour is fairly aroused may be capable of surpassing deeds. Whole thoroughfares might crumble before it.

As the pantechnicon passed Denry, at the rate of about three and a half miles an hour, he leaped, or rather he scrambled, on to it, losing nothing in the process except his straw hat, which remained a witness at his mother's door that her boy had been that way and departed under unusual circumstances. Denry had the bright idea of dropping the shafts down to act as a brake. But, unaccustomed to the manipulation of shafts, he was rather slow in accomplishing the deed, and ere the first pair of shafts had fallen the pantechnicon was doing quite eight miles an hour and the steepest declivity was yet to come. Further, the dropping of the left-hand shafts jerked the van to the left, and Denry dropped the other pair only just in time to avoid the sudden uprooting of a lamp-post. The four points of the shafts digging and prodding into the surface of the road gave the pantechnicon something to think about for a few seconds. But unfortunately the precipitousness of the street encouraged its head-strong caprices, and a few seconds later all four shafts were broken, and the pantechnicon seemed to scent the open prairie. (What it really did scent was the canal.) Then Denry discovered the brake, and furiously struggled with the iron handle. He turned it and turned it, some forty revolutions. It seemed to have no effect. The miracle was that the pantechnicon maintained its course in the middle of the street. Presently Denry could vaguely distinguish the wall and double wooden gates of the canal wharf. He could not jump off; the pantechnicon was now an express, and I doubt whether he would have jumped off, even if jumping off had not been madness. His was the kind of perseverance that, for the fun of it, will perish in an attempt. The final fifty or sixty yards of Brougham Street were level, and the pantechnicon slightly abated its haste. Denry could now plainly see, in the radiance of a gas-lamp, the gates of the wharf, and on them the painted letters:—

SHROPSHIRE UNION CANAL COY., LTD..

GENERAL CARRIERS.

No Admittance except on Business

He was heading straight for those gates, and the pantechnicon evidently had business within. It jolted over the iron guard of the weighing-machine, and this jolt deflected it, so that instead of aiming at the gates it aimed for part of a gate and part of a brick pillar. Denry ground his teeth together and clung to his seat. The gate might have been paper, and the brick pillar a cardboard pillar. The pantechnicon went through them as a sword will go through a ghost, and Denry was still alive. The remainder of the journey was brief and violent, owing partly to a number of bags of cement, and partly to the propinquity of the canal basin. The pantechnicon jumped into the canal like a mastodon, and drank.

Denry, clinging to the woodwork, was submerged for a moment, but, by standing on the narrow platform from which sprouted the splintered ends of the shafts, he could get his waist clear of the water. He was not a swimmer.

All was still and dark, save for the faint stream of starlight on the broad bosom of the canal basin. The pantechnicon had encountered nobody whatever *en route*. Of its strange escapade Denry had been the sole witness.

"Well, I'm dashed!" he murmured aloud.

And a voice replied from the belly of the pantechnicon:

"Who is there?"

All Denry's body shook.

"It's me!" said he.

"Not Mr Machin?" said the voice.

"Yes," said he. "I jumped on as it came down the street—and here we are!"

"Oh!" cried the voice. "I do wish you could get round to me."

Ruth Earp's voice.

He saw the truth in a moment of piercing insight. Ruth had been playing with him! She had performed a comedy for him in two acts. She had meant to do what is called in the Five Towns "a moonlight flit." The pantechnicon (doubtless from Birmingham, where her father was) had been brought to her door late in the evening, and was to have been filled and taken away during the night. The horses had been stabled, probably in Ruth's own yard, and while the carmen were reposing the pantechnicon had got off, Ruth in it. She had no money locked in her unlockable desk. Her reason for not having paid the precious Mr Herbert Calvert was not the reason which she had advanced.

His first staggered thought was:

"She's got a nerve! No mistake!"

Her duplicity, her wickedness, did not shock him. He admired her tremendous and audacious enterprise; it appealed strongly to every cell in his brain. He felt that she and he were kindred spirits.

He tried to clamber round the side of the van so as to get to the doors at the back, but a pantechnicon has a wheel-base which forbids leaping from wheel to wheel, especially, when the wheels are under water. Hence he was obliged to climb on to the roof, and so slide down on to the top of one of the doors, which was swinging loose. The feat was not simple. At last he felt the floor of the van under half a yard of water.

"Where are you?"

"I'm here," said Ruth, very plaintively. "I'm on a table. It was the only thing they had put into the van before they went off to have their supper or something. Furniture removers are always like that. Haven't you got a match?"

"I've got scores of matches," said Denry. "But what good do you suppose they'll be now, all soaked through?"

A short silence. He noticed that she had offered no explanation of her conduct towards himself. She seemed to take it for granted that he would understand.

"I'm frightfully bumped, and I believe my nose is bleeding," said Ruth, still more plaintively. "It's a good thing there was a lot of straw and sacks here."

Then, after much groping, his hand touched her wet dress.

"You know you're a very naughty girl," he said.

He heard a sob, a wild sob. The proud, independent creature had broken down under the stress of events. He climbed out of the water on to the part of the table which she was not occupying. And the van was as black as Erebus.

Gradually, out of the welter of sobs, came faint articulations, and little by little he learnt the entire story of her difficulties, her misfortunes, her struggles, and her defeats. He listened to a frank confession of guilt. But what could she do? She had meant well. But what could she do? She had been driven into a corner. And she had her father to think of! Honestly, on the previous day, she had intended to pay the rent, or part of it. But there had been a disappointment! And she had been so unwell. In short...

The van gave a lurch. She clutched at him and he at her. The van was settling down for a comfortable night in the mud.

(Queer that it had not occurred to him before, but at the first visit she had postponed paying him on the plea that the bank was closed, while at the second visit she had stated that the actual cash had been slowly accumulating in her desk! And the discrepancy had not struck him. Such is the influence of a teagown. However, he forgave her, in consideration of her immense audacity.)

"What can we do?" she almost whispered.

Her confidence in him affected him.

"Wait till it gets light," said he.

So they waited, amid the waste of waters. In a hot July it is not unpleasant to dangle one's feet in water during the sultry dark hours. She told him more and more.

When the inspiring grey preliminaries of the dawn began, Denry saw that at the back of the pantechnicon the waste of waters extended for at most a yard, and that it was easy, by climbing on to the roof, to jump therefrom to the wharf. He did so, and then fixed a plank so that Ruth could get ashore. Relieved of their weight the table floated out after them. Denry seized it, and set about smashing it to pieces with his feet.

"What *are* you doing?" she asked faintly. She was too enfeebled to protest more vigorously.

"Leave it to me," said Denry. "This table is the only thing that can give your show away. We can't carry it back. We might meet some one."

He tied the fragments of the table together with rope that was afloat in the van, and attached the heavy iron bar whose function was to keep the doors closed. Then he sank the faggot of wood and iron in a distant corner of the basin.

"There!" he said. "Now you understand. Nothing's happened except that a furniture van's run off and fallen into the canal owing to the men's carelessness. We can settle the rest later—I mean about the rent and so on."

They looked at each other.

Her skirts were nearly dry. Her nose showed no trace of bleeding, but there was a bluish lump over her left eye. Save that he was hatless, and that his trousers clung, he was not utterly unpresentable.

They were alone in the silent dawn.

"You'd better go home by Acre Lane, not up Brougham Street," he said. "I'll come in during the morning."

It was a parting in which more was felt than said.

They went one after the other through the devastated gateway, baptising the path as they walked. The Town Hall clock struck three as Denry crept up his mother's stairs. He had seen not a soul.

IV

The exact truth in its details was never known to more than two inhabitants of Bursley. The one thing clear certainly appeared to be that Denry, in endeavouring to prevent a runaway pantechnicon from destroying the town, had travelled with it into the canal. The romantic trip was accepted as perfectly characteristic of Denry. Around this island of fact washed a fabulous sea of uninformed gossip, in which assertion conflicted with assertion, and the names of Denry and Ruth were continually bumping against each other.

Mr Herbert Calvert glanced queerly and perhaps sardonically at Denry when Denry called and handed over ten pounds (less commission) which he said Miss Earp had paid on account.

"Look here," said the little Calvert, his mean little eyes gleaming. "You must get in the balance at once."

"That's all right," said Denry. "I shall."

"Was she trying to hook it on the q.t.?" Calvert demanded.

"Oh, no!" said Denry. "That was a very funny misunderstanding. The only explanation I can think of is that that van must have come to the wrong house."

"Are you engaged to her?" Calvert asked, with amazing effrontery.

Denry paused. "Yes," he said. "Are you?"

Mr Calvert wondered what he meant.

He admitted to himself that the courtship had begun in a manner surpassingly strange.

CHAPTER IV

WRECKING OF A LIFE

I

In the Five Towns, and perhaps elsewhere, there exists a custom in virtue of which a couple who have become engaged in the early summer find themselves by a most curious coincidence at the same seaside resort, and often in the same street thereof, during August. Thus it happened to Denry and to Ruth Earp. There had been difficulties—there always are. A business man who lives by collecting weekly rents obviously cannot go away for an indefinite period. And a young woman who lives alone in the world is bound to respect public opinion. However, Ruth arranged that her girlish friend, Nellie Cotterill, who had generous parents, should accompany her. And the North Staffordshire Railway's philanthropic scheme of issuing four-shilling tourist return tickets to the seaside enabled Denry to persuade himself that he was not absolutely mad in contemplating a fortnight on the shores of England.

Ruth chose Llandudno, Llandudno being more stylish than either Rhyl or Blackpool, and not dearer. Ruth and Nellie had a double room in a boarding-house, No. 26 St Asaph's Road (off the Marine Parade), and Denry had a small single room in another boarding-house, No. 28 St Asaph's Road. The ideal could scarcely have been approached more nearly.

Denry had never seen the sea before. As, in his gayest clothes, he strolled along the esplanade or on the pier between those two girls in their gayest clothes, and mingled with the immense crowd of pleasure-seekers and money-spenders, he was undoubtedly much impressed by the beauty and grandeur of the sea. But what impressed him far more than the beauty and grandeur of the sea was the field for profitable commercial enterprise which a place like Llandudno presented. He had not only his first vision of the sea, but his first genuine vision of the possibilities of amassing wealth by honest ingenuity. On the morning after his arrival he went out for a walk and lost himself near the Great Orme, and had to return hurriedly along the whole length of the Parade about nine o'clock. And through every ground-floor window of every house he saw a long table full of people eating and drinking the same kinds of food. In Llandudno fifty thousand souls desired always to perform the same act at the same time; they wanted to be distracted and they would do anything for the sake of distraction, and would pay for the privilege. And they would all pay at once.

This great thought was more majestic to him than the sea, or the Great Orme, or the Little Orme.

It stuck in his head because he had suddenly grown into a very serious person. He had now something to live for, something on which to lavish his energy. He was happy in being affianced, and more proud than happy, and more startled than proud. The manner and method of his courtship had sharply differed from his previous conception of what such an affair would be. He had not passed through the sensations which he would have expected to pass through. And then this question was continually presenting itself: *What could she see in him?* She must have got a notion that he was far more wonderful than he really was. Could it be true that she, his superior in experience and in splendour of person, had kissed him? *Him!* He felt that it would be his duty to live up to this exaggerated notion which she had of him. But how?

II

They had not yet discussed finance at all, though Denry would have liked to discuss it. Evidently she regarded him as a man of means. This became clear during the progress of the journey to Llandudno. Denry was flattered, but the next day he had slight misgivings, and on the following day he was alarmed; and on the day after that his state resembled terror. It is truer to say that she regarded him less as a man of means than as a magic and inexhaustible siphon of money.

He simply could not stir out of the house without spending money, and often in ways quite unforeseen. Pier, minstrels, Punch and Judy, bathing, buns, ices, canes, fruit, chairs, row-boats, concerts, toffee, photographs, char-à-bancs: any of these expenditures was likely to happen whenever they went forth for a simple stroll. One might think that strolls were gratis, that the air was free! Error! If he had had the courage he would have left his purse in the house as Ruth invariably did. But men are moral cowards.

He had calculated thus:—Return fare, four shillings a week. Agreed terms at boarding-house, twenty-five shillings a week. Total expenses per week, twenty-nine shillings,—say thirty!

On the first day he spent fourteen shillings on nothing whatever—which was at the rate of five pounds a week of supplementary estimates! On the second day he spent nineteen shillings on nothing whatever, and Ruth insisted on his having tea with herself and Nellie at their boarding-house; for which of course he had to pay, while his own tea was wasting next door. So the figures ran on, jumping up each day. Mercifully, when Sunday dawned the open wound in his pocket was temporarily stanched. Ruth wished him to come in for tea again. He refused—at any rate he did not come—and the exquisite placidity of the stream of their love was slightly disturbed.

Nobody could have guessed that she was in monetary difficulties on her own account. Denry, as a chivalrous lover, had assisted her out of the fearful quagmire of her rent; but she owed much beyond rent. Yet, when some of her quarterly fees had come in, her thoughts had instantly run to Llandudno, joy, and frocks. She did not know what money was, and she never would. This was, perhaps, part of her superior splendour. The gentle, timid, silent Nellie occasionally let Denry see that she, too, was scandalised by her bosom friend's recklessness. Often Nellie would modestly beg for permission to pay her share of the cost of an amusement. And it seemed just to Denry that she should pay her share, and he violently wished to accept her money, but he could not. He would even get quite curt with her when she insisted. From this it will be seen how absurdly and irrationally different he was from the rest of us.

Nellie was continually with them, except just before they separated for the night. So that Denry paid consistently for three. But he liked Nellie Cotterill. She blushed so easily, and she so obviously worshipped Ruth and admired himself, and there was a marked vein of common-sense in her ingenuous composition.

On the Monday morning he was up early and off to Bursley to collect rents and manage estates. He had spent nearly five pounds beyond his expectation. Indeed, if by chance he had not gone to Llandudno with a portion of the previous week's rents in his pockets, he would have been in what the Five Towns call a fix.

While in Bursley he thought a good deal. Bursley in August encourages nothing but thought. His mother was working as usual. His recitals to her of the existence led by betrothed lovers at Llandudno were vague.

On the Tuesday evening he returned to Llandudno, and, despite the general trend of his thoughts, it once more occurred that his pockets were loaded with a portion of the week's rents. He did not know precisely what was going to happen, but he knew that something was going to happen; for the sufficient reason that his career could not continue unless something did happen. Without either a quarrel, an understanding, or a miracle, three months of affianced bliss with Ruth Earp would exhaust his resources and ruin his reputation as one who was ever equal to a crisis.

III

What immediately happened was a storm at sea. He heard it mentioned at Rhyl, and he saw, in the deep night, the foam of breakers at Prestatyn. And when the train reached Llandudno, those two girls in ulsters and caps greeted him with wondrous tales of the storm at sea, and of wrecks, and of lifeboats. And they were so jolly, and so welcoming, so plainly glad to see their cavalier again, that Denry instantly discovered himself to be in the highest spirits. He put away the dark and brooding thoughts which had disfigured his journey, and became the gay Denry of his own dreams. The very wind intoxicated him. There was no rain.

It was half-past nine, and half Llandudno was afoot on the Parade and discussing the storm—a storm unparalleled, it seemed, in the month of August. At any rate, people who had visited Llandudno yearly for twenty-five years declared that never had they witnessed such a storm. The new lifeboat had gone forth, amid cheers, about six o'clock to a schooner in distress near Rhos, and at eight o'clock a second lifeboat (an old one which the new one had replaced and which had been bought for a floating warehouse by an aged fisherman) had departed to the rescue of a Norwegian barque, the *Hjalmar*, round the bend of the Little Orme.

"Let's go on the pier," said Denry. "It will be splendid."

He was not an hour in the town, and yet was already hanging expense!

"They've closed the pier," the girls told him.

But when in the course of their meanderings among the excited crowd under the gas-lamps they arrived at the pier-gates, Denry perceived figures on the pier.

"They're sailors and things, and the Mayor," the girls explained.

"Pooh!" said Denry, fired.

He approached the turnstile and handed a card to the official. It was the card of an advertisement agent of the *Staffordshire Signal*, who had called at Brougham Street in Denry's absence about the renewal of Denry's advertisement.

"Press," said Denry to the guardian at the turnstile, and went through with the ease of a bird on the wing.

"Come along," he cried to the girls.

The guardian seemed to hesitate.

"These ladies are with me," he said.

The guardian yielded.

It was a triumph for Denry. He could read his triumph in the eyes of his companions. When she looked at him like that, Ruth was assuredly marvellous among women, and any ideas derogatory to her marvellousness which he might have had at Bursley and in the train were false ideas.

At the head of the pier beyond the pavilion, there were gathered together some fifty people, and the tale ran that the second lifeboat had successfully accomplished its mission and was approaching the pier.

"I shall write an account of this for the *Signal*," said Denry, whose thoughts were excusably on the Press.

"Oh, do!" exclaimed Nellie.

"They have the *Signal* at all the newspaper shops here," said Ruth.

Then they seemed to be merged in the storm. The pier shook and trembled under the shock of the waves, and occasionally, though the tide was very low, a sprinkle of water flew up and caught their faces. The eyes could see nothing save the passing glitter of the foam on the crest of a breaker. It was the most thrilling situation that any of them had ever been in.

And at last came word from the mouths of men who could apparently see as well in the dark as in daylight, that the second lifeboat was close to the pier. And then everybody momentarily saw it—a ghostly thing that heaved up pale out of the murk for an instant, and was lost again. And the little crowd cheered.

The next moment a Bengal light illuminated the pier, and the lifeboat was silhouetted with strange effectiveness against the storm. And some one flung a rope, and then another rope arrived out of the sea, and fell on Denry's shoulder.

"Haul on there!" yelled a hoarse voice. The Bengal light expired.

Denry hauled with a will. The occasion was unique. And those few seconds were worth to him the whole of Denry's precious life—yes, not excluding the seconds in which he had kissed Ruth and the minutes in which he had danced with the Countess of Chell. Then two men with beards took the rope from his hands. The air was now alive with shoutings. Finally there was a rush of men down the iron stairway to the lower part of the pier, ten feet nearer the water.

"You stay here, you two!" Denry ordered.

"But, Denry—"

"Stay here, I tell you!" All the male in him was aroused. He was off, after the rush of men. "Half a jiffy," he said, coming back. "Just take charge of this, will you?" And he poured into their hands about twelve shillings' worth of copper, small change of rents, from his hip-pocket. "If anything happened, that might sink me," he said, and vanished.

It was very characteristic of him, that effusion of calm sagacity in a supreme emergency.

IV

Beyond getting his feet wet Denry accomplished but little in the dark basement of the pier. In spite of his success in hauling in the thrown rope, he seemed to be classed at once down there by the experts assembled as an eager and useless person who had no right to the space which he occupied. However, he witnessed the heaving arrival of the lifeboat and the disembarking of the rescued crew of the Norwegian barque, and he was more than ever decided to compose a descriptive article for the *Staffordshire Signal.* The rescued and the rescuing crews disappeared in single file to the upper floor of the pier, with the exception of the coxswain, a man with a spreading red beard, who stayed behind to inspect the lifeboat, of which indeed he was the absolute owner. As a journalist Denry did the correct thing and engaged him in conversation. Meanwhile, cheering could be heard above. The coxswain, who stated that his name was Cregeen, and that he was a Manxman, seemed to regret the entire expedition. He seemed to be unaware that it was his duty now to play the part of the modest hero to Denry's interviewing. At every loose end of the chat he would say gloomily:

"And look at her now, I'm telling ye!" Meaning the battered craft, which rose and fell on the black waves.

Denry ran upstairs again, in search of more amenable material. Some twenty men in various sou'-westers and other headgear were eating thick slices of bread and butter and drinking hot coffee, which with foresight had been prepared for them in the pier buffet. A few had preferred whisky. The whole crowd was now under the lee of the pavilion, and it constituted a spectacle which Denry said to himself he should refer to in his article as "Rembrandtesque." For a few moments he could not descry Ruth and Nellie in the gloom. Then he saw the indubitable form of his betrothed at a penny-in-the-slot machine, and the indubitable form of Nellie at another penny-in-the-slot machine. And then he could hear the click-click-click of the machines, working rapidly. And his thoughts took a new direction.

Presently Ruth ran with blithe gracefulness from her machine and commenced a generous distribution of packets to the members of the crews. There was neither calculation nor exact justice in her generosity. She dropped packets on to heroic knees with a splendid gesture of largesse. Some packets even fell on the floor. But she did not mind.

Denry could hear her saying:

"You must eat it. Chocolate is so sustaining. There's nothing like it."

She ran back to the machines, and snatched more packets from Nellie, who under her orders had been industrious; and then began a second distribution.

A calm and disinterested observer would probably have been touched by this spectacle of impulsive womanly charity. He might even have decided that it was one of the most beautifully human things that he had ever seen. And the fact that the hardy heroes and Norsemen appeared scarcely to know what to do with the silver-wrapped bonbons would not have impaired his admiration for these two girlish figures of benevolence. Denry, too, was touched by the spectacle, but in another way. It was the rents of his clients that were being thus dissipated in a very luxury of needless benevolence. He muttered:

"Well, that's a bit thick, that is!" But of course he could do nothing.

As the process continued, the clicking of the machine exacerbated his ears.

"Idiotic!" he muttered.

The final annoyance to him was that everybody except himself seemed to consider that Ruth was displaying singular ingenuity, originality, enterprise, and goodness of heart.

In that moment he saw clearly for the first time that the marriage between himself and Ruth had not been arranged in Heaven. He admitted privately then that the saving of a young woman from violent death in a pantechnicon need not inevitably involve espousing her. She was without doubt a marvellous creature, but it was as wise to dream of keeping a carriage and pair as to dream of keeping Ruth. He grew suddenly cynical. His age leaped to fifty or so, and the curve of his lips changed.

Ruth, spying around, saw him and ran to him with a glad cry.

"Here!" she said, "take these. They're no good." She held out her hands.

"What are they?" he asked.

"They're the halfpennies."

"So sorry!" he said, with an accent whose significance escaped her, and took the useless coins.

"We've exhausted all the chocolate," said she. "But there's butterscotch left— it's nearly as good—and gold-tipped cigarettes. I daresay some of them would enjoy a smoke. Have you got any more pennies?"

"No!" he replied. "But I've got ten or a dozen half-crowns. They'll work the machine just as well, won't they?"

This time she did notice a certain unusualness in the flavour of his accent. And she hesitated.

"Don't be silly!" she said.

"I'll try not to be," said Denry. So far as he could remember, he had never used such a tone before. Ruth swerved away to rejoin Nellie.

Denry surreptitiously counted the halfpennies. There were eighteen. She had fed those machines, then, with over a hundred and thirty pence.

He murmured, "Thick, thick!"

Considering that he had returned to Llandudno in the full intention of putting his foot down, of clearly conveying to Ruth that his conception of finance differed from hers, the second sojourn had commenced badly. Still, he had promised to marry her, and he must marry her. Better a lifetime of misery and insolvency than a failure to behave as a gentleman should. Of course, if she chose to break it off.... But he must be minutely careful to do nothing which might lead to a breach. Such was Denry's code. The walk home at midnight, amid the reverberations of the falling tempest, was marked by a slight pettishness on the part of Ruth, and by Denry's polite taciturnity.

V

Yet the next morning, as the three companions sat together under the striped awning of the buffet on the pier, nobody could have divined, by looking at them, that one of them at any rate was the most uncomfortable young man in all Llandudno. The sun was hotly shining on their bright attire and on the still turbulent waves. Ruth, thirsty after a breakfast of herrings and bacon, was sucking iced lemonade up a straw. Nellie was eating chocolate, undistributed remains of the night's benevolence. Demo was yawning, not in the least because the proceedings failed to excite his keen interest, but because he had been a journalist till three a.m. and had risen at six in order to despatch a communication to the editor of the *Staffordshire Signal* by train. The girls were very playful. Nellie dropped a piece of chocolate into Ruth's glass, and Ruth fished it out, and bit at it.

"What a jolly taste!" she exclaimed.

And then Nellie bit at it.

"Oh, it's just lovely!" said Nellie, softly.

"Here, dear!" said Ruth, "try it."

And Denry had to try it, and to pronounce it a delicious novelty (which indeed it was) and generally to brighten himself up. And all the time he was murmuring in his heart, "This can't go on."

Nevertheless, he was obliged to admit that it was he who had invited Ruth to pass the rest of her earthly life with him, and not *vice versa*.

"Well, shall we go on somewhere else?" Ruth suggested.

And he paid yet again. He paid and smiled, he who had meant to be the masterful male, he who deemed himself always equal to a crisis. But in this crisis he was helpless.

They set off down the pier, brilliant in the brilliant crowd. Everybody was talking of wrecks and lifeboats. The new lifeboat had done nothing, having been forestalled by the Prestatyn boat; but Llandudno was apparently very proud of its brave old worn-out lifeboat which had brought ashore the entire crew of the *Hjalmar*, without casualty, in a terrific hurricane.

"Run along, child," said Ruth to Nellie, "while uncle and auntie talk to each other for a minute."

Nellie stared, blushed, and walked forward in confusion. She was startled. And Denry was equally startled. Never before had Ruth so brazenly hinted that lovers must be left alone at intervals. In justice to her, it must be said that she was a mirror for all the proprieties. Denry had even reproached her, in his heart, for not sufficiently showing her desire for his exclusive society. He wondered, now, what was to be the next revelation of her surprising character.

"I had our bill this morning," said Ruth.

She leaned gracefully on the handle of her sunshade, and they both stared at the sea. She was very elegant, with an aristocratic air. The bill, as she mentioned it, seemed a very negligible trifle. Nevertheless, Denry's heart quaked.

"Oh!" he said. "Did you pay it?"

"Yes," said she. "The landlady wanted the money, she told me. So Nellie gave me her share, and I paid it at once."

"Oh!" said Denry.

There was a silence. Denry felt as though he were defending a castle, or as though he were in a dark room and somebody was calling him, calling him, and he was pretending not to be there and holding his breath.

"But I've hardly enough money left," said Ruth. "The fact is, Nellie and I spent such a lot yesterday and the day before.... You've no idea how money goes!"

"Haven't I?" said Denry. But not to her—only to his own heart.

To her he said nothing.

"I suppose we shall have to go back home," she ventured lightly. "One can't run into debt here. They'd claim your luggage."

"What a pity!" said Denry, sadly.

Just those few words—and the interesting part of the interview was over! All that followed counted not in the least. She had meant to induce him to offer to defray the whole of her expenses in Llandudno—no doubt in the form of a loan; and she had failed. She had intended him to repair the disaster caused by her chronic extravagance. And he had only said: "What a pity!"

"Yes, it is!" she agreed bravely, and with a finer disdain than ever of petty financial troubles. "Still, it can't be helped."

"No, I suppose not," said Denry.

There was undoubtedly something fine about Ruth. In that moment she had it in her to kill Denry with a bodkin. But she merely smiled. The situation was terribly strained, past all Denry's previous conceptions of a strained situation; but she deviated with superlative *sang-froid* into frothy small talk. A proud and an unconquerable woman! After all, what were men for, if not to pay?

"I think I shall go home to-night," she said, after the excursion into prattle.

"I'm sorry," said Denry.

He was not coming out of his castle.

At that moment a hand touched his shoulder. It was the hand of Cregeen, the owner of the old lifeboat.

"Mister," said Cregeen, too absorbed in his own welfare to notice Ruth. "It's now or never! Five-and-twenty'll buy the *Fleetwing*, if ten's paid down this mornun."

And Denry replied boldly:

"You shall have it in an hour. Where shall you be?"

"I'll be in John's cabin, under the pier," said Cregeen, "where ye found me this mornun."

"Right," said Denry.

If Ruth had not been caracoling on her absurdly high horse, she would have had the truth out of Denry in a moment concerning these early morning interviews and mysterious transactions in shipping. But from that height she could not deign to be curious. And so she said naught. Denry had passed the whole morning since breakfast and had uttered no word of pre-prandial encounters with mariners, though he had talked a lot about his article for the *Signal* and of how he had risen betimes in order to despatch it by the first train.

And as Ruth showed no curiosity Denry behaved on the assumption that she felt none. And the situation grew even more strained.

As they walked down the pier towards the beach, at the dinner-hour, Ruth bowed to a dandiacal man who obsequiously saluted her.

"Who's that?" asked Denry, instinctively.

"It's a gentleman that I was once engaged to," answered Ruth, with cold, brief politeness.

Denry did not like this.

The situation almost creaked under the complicated stresses to which it was subject. The wonder was that it did not fly to pieces long before evening.

VI

The pride of the principal actors being now engaged, each person was compelled to carry out the intentions which he had expressed either in words or tacitly. Denry's silence had announced more efficiently than any words that he would under no inducement emerge from his castle. Ruth had stated plainly that there was nothing for it but to go home at once, that very night. Hence she arranged to go home, and hence Denry refrained from interfering with her arrangements. Ruth was lugubrious under a mask of gaiety; Nellie was lugubrious under no mask whatever. Nellie was merely the puppet of these betrothed players, her elders. She admired Ruth and she admired Denry, and between them they were spoiling the little thing's holiday for their own adult purposes. Nellie knew that dreadful occurrences were in the air—occurrences compared to which the storm at sea was a storm in a tea-cup. She knew partly because Ruth had been so queenly polite, and partly because they had come separately to St Asaph's Road and had not spent the entire afternoon together.

So quickly do great events loom up and happen that at six o'clock they had had tea and were on their way afoot to the station. The odd man of No. 26 St Asaph's Road had preceded them with the luggage. All the rest of Llandudno was joyously strolling home to its half-past six high tea— grand people to whom weekly bills were as dust and who were in a position to stop in Llandudno for ever and ever, if they chose! And Ruth and Nellie were conscious of the shame which always afflicts those whom necessity forces to the railway station of a pleasure resort in the middle of the season. They saw omnibuses loaded with luggage and jolly souls were actually *coming*, whose holiday had not yet properly commenced. And this spectacle added to their humiliation and their disgust. They genuinely felt that they belonged to the lower orders.

Ruth, for the sake of effect, joked on the most solemn subjects. She even referred with giggling laughter to the fact that she had borrowed from Nellie in order to discharge her liabilities for the final twenty-four hours at the boarding-house. Giggling laughter being contagious, as they were walking side by side close together, they all laughed. And each one secretly thought how ridiculous was such behaviour, and how it failed to reach the standard of true worldliness.

Then, nearer the station, some sprightly caprice prompted Denry to raise his hat to two young women who were crossing the road in front of them. Neither of the two young women responded to the homage.

"Who are they?" asked Ruth, and the words were out of her mouth before she could remind herself that curiosity was beneath her.

"It's a young lady I was once engaged to," said Denry.

"Which one?" asked the ninny, Nellie, astounded.

"I forget," said Denry.

He considered this to be one of his greatest retorts—not to Nellie, but to Ruth. Nellie naturally did not appreciate its loveliness. But Ruth did. There was no facet of that retort that escaped Ruth's critical notice.

At length they arrived at the station, quite a quarter of an hour before the train was due, and half-an-hour before it came in.

Denry tipped the odd man for the transport of the luggage.

"Sure it's all there?" he asked the girls, embracing both of them in his gaze.

"Yes," said Ruth, "but where's yours?"

"Oh!" he said. "I'm not going to-night. I've got some business to attend to here. I thought you understood. I expect you'll be all right, you two together."

After a moment, Ruth said brightly: "Oh yes! I was quite forgetting about your business." Which was completely untrue, since she knew nothing of his business, and he had assuredly not informed her that he would not return with them.

But Ruth was being very brave, haughty, and queenlike, and for this the precise truth must sometimes be abandoned. The most precious thing in the world to Ruth was her dignity—and who can blame her? She meant to keep it at no matter what costs.

In a few minutes the bookstall on the platform attracted them as inevitably as a prone horse attracts a crowd. Other people were near the bookstall, and as these people were obviously leaving Llandudno, Ruth and Nellie felt a certain solace. The social outlook seemed brighter for them. Denry bought one or two penny papers, and then the newsboy began to paste up the contents poster of the *Staffordshire Signal*, which had just arrived. And on this poster, very prominent, were the words:—"The Great Storm in North Wales. Special Descriptive Report." Denry snatched up one of the green papers and opened it, and on the first column of the news-page saw his wondrous description, including the word "Rembrandtesque." "Graphic Account by a Bursley Gentleman of the Scene at

Llandudno," said the sub-title. And the article was introduced by the phrase: "We are indebted to Mr E.H. Machin, a prominent figure in Bursley," etc.

It was like a miracle. Do what he would, Denry could not stop his face from glowing.

With false calm he gave the paper, to Ruth. Her calmness in receiving it upset him.

"We'll read it in the train," she said primly, and started to talk about something else. And she became most agreeable and companionable.

Mixed up with papers and sixpenny novels on the bookstall were a number of souvenirs of Llandudno—paper-knives, pens, paper-weights, watch-cases, pen-cases, all in light wood or glass, and ornamented with coloured views of Llandudno, and also the word "Llandudno" in large German capitals, so that mistakes might not arise. Ruth remembered that she had even intended to buy a crystal paper-weight with a view of the Great Orme at the bottom. The bookstall clerk had several crystal paper-weights with views of the pier, the Hotel Majestic, the Esplanade, the Happy Valley, but none with a view of the Great Orme. He had also paper-knives and watch-cases with a view of the Great Orme. But Ruth wanted a combination of paper-weight and Great Orme, and nothing else would satisfy her. She was like that. The clerk admitted that such a combination existed, but he was sold "out of it."

"Couldn't you get one and send it to me?" said Ruth.

And Denry saw anew that she was incurable.

"Oh yes, miss," said the clerk. "Certainly, miss. To-morrow at latest." And he pulled out a book. "What name?"

Ruth looked at Denry, as women do look on such occasions.

"Rothschild," said Denry.

It may seem perhaps strange that that single word ended their engagement. But it did. She could not tolerate a rebuke. She walked away, flushing. The bookstall clerk received no order. Several persons in the vicinity dimly perceived that a domestic scene had occurred, in a flash, under their noses, on a platform of a railway station. Nellie was speedily aware that something very serious had happened, for the train took them off without Ruth speaking a syllable to Denry, though Denry raised his hat and was almost effusive.

The next afternoon Denry received by post a ring in a box. "I will not submit to insult," ran the brief letter.

"I only said 'Rothschild'!" Denry murmured to himself. "Can't a fellow say 'Rothschild'?"

But secretly he was proud of himself.

CHAPTER V

THE MERCANTILE MARINE

I

The decisive scene, henceforward historic, occurred in the shanty known as "John's cabin"—John being the unacknowledged leader of the long-shore population under the tail of Llandudno pier. The cabin, festooned with cordage, was lighted by an oil-lamp of a primitive model, and round the orange case on which the lamp was balanced sat Denry, Cregeen, the owner of the lifeboat, and John himself (to give, as it were, a semi-official character to whatever was afoot).

"Well, here you are," said Denry, and handed to Cregeen a piece of paper.

"What's this, I'm asking ye?" said Cregeen, taking the paper in his large fingers and peering at it as though it had been a papyrus.

But he knew quite well what it was. It was a cheque for twenty-five pounds. What he did not know was that, with the ten pounds paid in cash earlier in the day, it represented a very large part indeed of such of Denry's savings as had survived his engagement to Ruth Earp. Cregeen took a pen as though it had been a match-end and wrote a receipt. Then, after finding a stamp in a pocket of his waistcoat under his jersey, he put it in his mouth and lost it there for a long time. Finally Denry got the receipt, certifying that he was the owner of the lifeboat formerly known as *Llandudno*, but momentarily without a name, together with all her gear and sails.

"Are ye going to live in her?" the rather curt John inquired.

"Not in her. On her," said Denry.

And he went out on to the sand and shingle, leaving John and Cregeen to complete the sale to Cregeen of the *Fleetwing*, a small cutter specially designed to take twelve persons forth for "a pleasant sail in the bay." If Cregeen had not had a fancy for the *Fleetwing* and a perfect lack of the money to buy her, Denry might never have been able to induce him to sell the lifeboat.

Under another portion of the pier Denry met a sailor with a long white beard, the aged Simeon, who had been one of the crew that rescued the *Hjalmar*, but whom his colleagues appeared to regard rather as an ornament than as a motive force.

"It's all right," said Demo.

And Simeon, in silence, nodded his head slowly several times.

"I shall give you thirty shilling for the week," said Denry.

And that venerable head oscillated again in the moon-lit gloom and rocked gradually to a stand-still.

Presently the head said, in shrill, slow tones:

"I've seen three o' them Norwegian chaps. Two of 'em can no more speak English than a babe unborn; no, nor understand what ye say to 'em, though I fair bawled in their ear-holes."

"So much the better," said Denry.

"I showed 'em that sovereign," said the bearded head, wagging again.

"Well," said Denry, "you won't forget. Six o'clock to-morrow morning."

"Ye'd better say five," the head suggested. "Quieter like."

"Five, then," Denry agreed.

And he departed to St Asaph's Road burdened with a tremendous thought. The thought was:

"I've gone and done it this time!"

Now that the transaction was accomplished and could not be undone, he admitted to himself that he had never been more mad. He could scarcely comprehend what had led him to do that which he had done. But he obscurely imagined that his caprice for the possession of sea-going craft must somehow be the result of his singular adventure with the pantechnicon in the canal at Bursley. He was so preoccupied with material interests as to be capable of forgetting, for a quarter of an hour at a stretch, that in all essential respects his life was wrecked, and that he had nothing to hope for save hollow worldly success. He knew that Ruth would return the ring. He could almost see the postman holding the little cardboard cube which would contain the rendered ring. He had loved, and loved tragically. (That was how he put it—in his unspoken thoughts; but the truth was merely that he had loved something too expensive.) Now the dream was done. And a man of disillusion walked along the Parade towards St Asaph's Road among revellers, a man with a past, a man who had probed women, a man who had nothing to learn about the sex. And amid all the tragedy of his heart, and all his apprehensions concerning hollow, worldly success, little thoughts of absurd unimportance kept running about like clockwork mice in his head. Such as that it would be a bit of a bore to have to tell people at Bursley that his engagement, which truly had thrilled the town, was broken off. Humiliating, that! And, after all, Ruth was a glittering gem among women. Was there another girl in Bursley so smart, so effective, so truly ornate?

Then he comforted himself with the reflection: "I'm certainly the only man that ever ended an engagement by just saying 'Rothschild!'" This was probably true. But it did not help him to sleep.

II

The next morning at 5.20 the youthful sun was shining on the choppy water of the Irish Sea, just off the Little Orme, to the west of Llandudno Bay. Oscillating on the uneasy waves was Denry's lifeboat, manned by the nodding bearded head, three ordinary British longshoremen, a Norwegian who could speak English of two syllables, and two other Norwegians who by a strange neglect of education could speak nothing but Norwegian.

Close under the headland, near a morsel of beach lay the remains of the *Hjalmar* in an attitude of repose. It was as if the *Hjalmar*, after a long struggle, had lain down like a cab-horse and said to the tempest: "Do what you like now!"

"Yes," the venerable head was piping. "Us can come out comfortable in twenty minutes, unless the tide be setting east strong. And, as for getting back, it'll be the same, other way round, if ye understand me."

There could be no question that Simeon had come out comfortable. But he was the coxswain. The rowers seemed to be perspiringly aware that the boat was vast and beamy.

"Shall we row up to it?" Simeon inquired, pointing to the wreck.

Then a pale face appeared above the gunwale, and an expiring, imploring voice said: "No. We'll go back." Whereupon the pale face vanished again.

Denry had never before been outside the bay. In the navigation of pantechnicons on the squall-swept basins of canals he might have been a great master, but he was unfitted for the open sea. At that moment he would have been almost ready to give the lifeboat and all that he owned for the privilege of returning to land by train. The inward journey was so long that Denry lost hope of ever touching his native island again. And then there was a bump. And he disembarked, with hope burning up again cheerfully in his bosom. And it was a quarter to six.

By the first post, which arrived at half-past seven, there came a brown package. "The ring!" he thought, starting horribly. But the package was a cube of three inches, and would have held a hundred rings. He undid the cover, and saw on half a sheet of notepaper the words:—

"Thank you so much for the lovely time you gave me. I hope you will like this, NELLIE."

He was touched. If Ruth was hard, mercenary, costly, her young and ingenuous companion could at any rate be grateful and sympathetic. Yes, he was touched. He had imagined himself to be dead to all human affections, but it was not so. The package contained chocolate, and his nose at once perceived that it was chocolate impregnated with lemon—the surprising but agreeable compound accidentally invented by Nellie on the previous day at the pier buffet. The little thing must have spent a part of the previous afternoon in preparing it, and she must have put the package in the post at Crewe. Secretive and delightful little thing! After his recent experience beyond the bay he had imagined himself to be incapable of ever eating again, but it was not so. The lemon gave a peculiar astringent, appetising, *settling* quality to the chocolate. And he ate even with gusto. The result was that, instead of waiting for the nine o'clock boarding-house breakfast, he hurried energetically into the streets and called on a jobbing printer whom he had seen on the previous evening. As Ruth had said, "There is nothing like chocolate for sustaining you."

III

At ten o'clock two Norwegian sailors, who could only smile in answer to the questions which assailed them, were distributing the following handbill on the Parade:—

WRECK OF THE *HJALMAR*

HEROISM AT LLANDUDNO

Every hour, at 11, 12, 2, 3, 4, 5, and 6 o'oclock,[sic] THE IDENTICAL
(guaranteed) LIFEBOAT which rescued the crew of the *JALMAR*
**will leave the beach for the scene of the wreck.   Manned
by Simeon Edwards, the oldest boatman in LLANDUDNO, and by
members of the rescued crew, genuine Norwegians (guaranteed)**

SIMEON EDWARDS, *Coxswain.*
Return Fare, with use of Cork Belt and Life-lines if desired, 2s. 6d.

A UNIQUE OPPORTUNITY

A UNIQUE EXPERIENCE

P.S.—The bravery of the lifeboatmen has been the theme of the Press
throughout the Principality and neighbouring counties.
E.D. MACHIN

At eleven o'clock there was an eager crowd down on the beach where, with
some planks and a piece of rock, Simeon had arranged an embarkation pier for
the lifeboat. One man, in overalls, stood up to his knees in the water and escorted
passengers up the planks, while Simeon's confidence-generating beard received
them into the broad waist of the boat. The rowers wore sou'westers and were
secured to the craft by life-lines, and these conveniences were also offered, with
life-belts, to the intrepid excursionists. A paper was pinned in the stern: "Licensed
to carry Fourteen." (Denry had just paid the fee.) But quite forty people were
anxious to make the first voyage.

"No more," shrilled Simeon, solemnly. And the wader scrambled in and the
boat slid away.

"Fares, please!" shrilled Simeon.

He collected one pound fifteen, and slowly buttoned it up in the right-hand
pocket of his blue trousers.

"Now, my lads, with a will," he gave the order. And then, with deliberate
method, he lighted his pipe. And the lifeboat shot away.

Close by the planks stood a young man in a negligent attitude, and with a look
on his face as if to say: "Please do not imagine that I have the slightest interest in
this affair." He stared consistently out to sea until the boat had disappeared round
the Little Orme, and then he took a few turns on the sands, in and out amid the
castles. His heart was beating in a most disconcerting manner. After a time he
resumed his perusal of the sea. And the lifeboat reappeared and grew larger and

larger, and finally arrived at the spot from which it had departed, only higher up the beach because the tide was rising. And Simeon debarked first, and there was a small blue and red model of a lifeboat in his hand, which he shook to a sound of coins.

"*For* the Lifeboat Fund! *For* the Lifeboat Fund!" he gravely intoned.

Every debarking passenger dropped a coin into the slit.

In five minutes the boat was refilled, and Simeon had put the value of fourteen more half-crowns into his pocket.

The lips of the young man on the beach moved, and he murmured:

"That makes over three pounds! Well, I'm dashed!"

At the hour appointed for dinner he went to St Asaph's Road, but could eat nothing. He could only keep repeating very softly to himself, "Well, I'm dashed!"

Throughout the afternoon the competition for places in the lifeboat grew keener and more dangerous. Denry's craft was by no means the sole craft engaged in carrying people to see the wreck. There were dozens of boats in the business, which had suddenly sprung up that morning, the sea being then fairly inoffensive for the first time since the height of the storm. But the other boats simply took what the lifeboat left. The guaranteed identity of the lifeboat, and of the Norsemen (who replied to questions in gibberish), and of Simeon himself; the sou'westers, the life-belts and the lines; even the collection for the Lifeboat Fund at the close of the voyage: all these matters resolved themselves into a fascination which Llandudno could not resist.

And in regard to the collection, a remarkable crisis arose. The model of a lifeboat became full, gorged to the slot. And the Local Secretary of the Fund had the key. The model was despatched to him by special messenger to open and to empty, and in the meantime Simeon used his sou'-wester as a collecting-box. This contretemps was impressive. At night Denry received twelve pounds odd at the hands of Simeon Edwards. He showered the odd in largesse on his heroic crew, who had also received many tips. By the evening post the fatal ring arrived from Ruth, as he anticipated. He was just about to throw it into the sea, when he thought better of the idea, and stuck it in his pocket. He tried still to feel that his life had been blighted by Ruth. But he could not. The twelve pounds, largely in silver, weighed so heavy in his pocket. He said to himself: "Of course this can't last!"

IV

Then came the day when he first heard some one saying discreetly behind him:

"That's the lifeboat chap!"

Or more briefly:

"That's him!"

Implying that in all Llandudno "him" could mean only one person.

And for a time he went about the streets self-consciously. However, that self-consciousness soon passed off, and he wore his fame as easily as he wore his collar.

The lifeboat trips to the *Hjalmar* became a feature of daily life in Llandudno. The pronunciation of the ship's name went through a troublous period. Some said the "j" ought to be pronounced to the exclusion of the "h," and others maintained the contrary. In the end the first two letters were both abandoned utterly, also the last—but nobody had ever paid any attention to the last. The facetious had a trick of calling the wreck *Inkerman*. This definite settlement of the pronunciation of the name was a sign that the pleasure-seekers of Llandudno had definitely fallen in love with the lifeboat-trip habit. Denry's timid fear that the phenomenon which put money into his pocket could not continue, was quite falsified. It continued violently. And Denry wished that the *Hjalmar* had been wrecked a month earlier. He calculated that the tardiness of the *Hjalmar* in wrecking itself had involved him in a loss of some four hundred pounds. If only the catastrophe had happened early in July, instead of early in August, and he had been there. Why, if forty *Hjalmars* had been wrecked, and their forty crews saved by forty different lifeboats, and Denry had bought all the lifeboats, he could have filled them all!

Still, the regularity of his receipts was extremely satisfactory and comforting. The thing had somehow the air of being a miracle; at any rate of being connected with magic. It seemed to him that nothing could have stopped the visitors to Llandudno from fighting for places in his lifeboat and paying handsomely for the privilege. They had begun the practice, and they looked as if they meant to go on with the practice eternally. He thought that the monotony of it would strike them unfavourably. But no! He thought that they would revolt against doing what every one had done. But no! Hundreds of persons arrived fresh from the railway station every day, and they all appeared to be drawn to that lifeboat as to a magnet. They all seemed to know instantly and instinctively that to be correct in Llandudno they must make at least one trip in Denry's lifeboat.

He was pocketing an income which far exceeded his most golden visions. And therefore naturally his first idea was to make that income larger and larger still. He commenced by putting up the price of the afternoon trips. There was a vast deal too much competition for seats in the afternoon. This competition led to quarrels, unseemly language, and deplorable loss of temper. It also led to loss of time. Denry was therefore benefiting humanity by charging three shillings after two o'clock. This simple and benign device equalised the competition throughout the day, and made Denry richer by seven or eight pounds a week.

But his fertility of invention did not stop there. One morning the earliest excursionists saw a sort of Robinson Crusoe marooned on the strip of beach near the wreck. All that heartless fate had left him appeared to be a machine on a tripod and a few black bags. And there was no shelter for him save a shallow cave. The poor fellow was quite respectably dressed. Simeon steered the boat round by the beach, which shelved down sharply, and as he did so the Robinson Crusoe hid his head in a cloth, as though ashamed, or as though he had gone mad and believed himself to be an ostrich. Then apparently he thought the better of it, and gazed boldly forth again. And the boat passed on its starboard side within a dozen feet of him and his machine. Then it put about and passed on the port side. And the same thing occurred on every trip. And the last trippers of the day left Robinson Crusoe on the strip of beach in his solitude.

The next morning a photographer's shop on the Parade pulled down its shutters and displayed posters all over the upper part of its windows. And the lower part of the windows held sixteen different large photographs of the lifeboat broad-side on. The likenesses of over a hundred visitors, many of them with sou'-westers, cork belts, and life-lines, could be clearly distinguished in these picturesque groups. A notice said:—

"Copies of any of these magnificent permanent holographs can be supplied, handsomely mounted, at a charge of two shillings each. Orders executed in rotation, and delivered by post if necessary. It is respectfully requested that cash be paid with order. Otherwise orders cannot be accepted."

Very few of those who had made the trip could resist the fascination of a photograph of themselves in a real lifeboat, manned by real heroes and real Norwegians on real waves, especially if they had worn the gear appropriate to lifeboats. The windows of the shop were beset throughout the day with crowds anxious to see who was in the lifeboat, and who had come out well, and who was a perfect fright. The orders on the first day amounted to over fifteen pounds, for not everybody was content with one photograph. The novelty was acute and enchanting, and it renewed itself each day. "Let's go down and look at the lifeboat photographs," people would say, when they were wondering what to do next. Some persons who had not "taken nicely" would perform a special trip in the lifeboat and would wear special clothes and compose special faces for the ordeal. The Mayor of Ashby-de-la-Zouch for that year ordered two hundred copies of a photograph which showed himself in the centre, for presentation as New Year's cards. On the mornings after very dull days or wet days, when photography had been impossible or unsatisfactory, Llandudno felt that something lacked. Here it may be mentioned that inclement weather (of which, for the rest, there was little) scarcely interfered with Denry's receipts. Imagine a lifeboat being deterred by rain or by a breath of wind! There were tarpaulins. When the tide was strong and adverse, male passengers were allowed to pull, without extra charge, though naturally they would give a trifle to this or that member of the professional crew.

Denry's arrangement with the photographer was so simple that a child could have grasped it. The photographer paid him sixpence on every photograph sold. This was Denry's only connection with the photographer. The sixpences totalled over a dozen pounds a week. Regardless of cost, Denry reprinted his article from the *Staffordshire Signal* descriptive of the night of the wreck, with a photograph of the lifeboat and its crew, and presented a copy to every client of his photographic department.

V

Llandudno was next titillated by the mysterious "Chocolate Remedy," which made its first appearance in a small boat that plied off Robinson Crusoe's strip of beach. Not infrequently passengers in the lifeboat were inconvenienced by displeasing and even distressing sensations, as Denry had once been inconvenienced. He felt deeply for them. The Chocolate Remedy was designed to alleviate the symptoms while captivating the palate. It was one of the most agreeable remedies that the wit of man ever invented. It tasted like chocolate and yet there was an astringent flavour of lemon in it—a flavour that flattered the stomach into a good opinion of itself, and seemed to say, "All's right with the world." The stuff was retailed in sixpenny packets, and you were advised to eat only a very little of it at a time, and not to masticate, but merely to permit melting. Then the Chocolate Remedy came to be sold on the lifeboat itself, and you were informed that if you "took" it before starting on the wave, no wave could disarrange you. And, indeed, many persons who followed this advice suffered no distress, and were proud accordingly, and duly informed the world. Then the Chocolate Remedy began to be sold everywhere. Young people bought it because they enjoyed it, and perfectly ignored the advice against over-indulgence and against mastication. The Chocolate Remedy penetrated like the refrain of a popular song to other seaside places. It was on sale from Morecambe to Barmouth, and at all the landing-stages of the steamers for the Isle of Man and Anglesey. Nothing surprised Denry so much as the vogue of the Chocolate Remedy. It was a serious anxiety to him, and he muddled both the manufacture and distribution of the remedy, from simple ignorance and inexperience. His chief difficulty at first had been to obtain small cakes of chocolate that were not stamped with the maker's name or mark. Chocolate manufacturers seemed to have a passion for imprinting their Quakerly names on every bit of stuff they sold. Having at length obtained a supply, he was silly enough to spend time in preparing the remedy himself in his bedroom! He might as well have tried to feed the British Army from his mother's kitchen. At length he went to a confectioner in Rhyl and a greengrocer in Llandudno, and by giving away half the secret to each, he contrived to keep the whole secret to himself. But even then he was manifestly unequal to the situation created by the demand for the Chocolate Remedy. It was a situation that needed the close attention of half a dozen men of business. It was quite different from the affair of the lifeboat.

One night a man who had been staying a day or two in the boarding-house in St Asaph's Road said to Denry:

"Look here, mister. I go straight to the point. What'll you take?"

And he explained what he meant. What would Denry take for the entire secret and rights of the Chocolate Remedy and the use of the name "Machin" ("without which none was genuine").

"What do you offer?" Denry asked.

"Well, I'll give you a hundred pounds down, and that's my last word."

Denry was staggered. A hundred pounds for simply nothing at all—for dipping bits of chocolate in lemon-juice!

He shook his head.

"I'll take two hundred," he replied.

And he got two hundred. It was probably the worst bargain that he ever made in his life. For the Chocolate Remedy continued obstinately in demand for ten years afterwards. But he was glad to be rid of the thing; it was spoiling his sleep and wearing him out.

He had other worries. The boatmen of Llandudno regarded him as an enemy of the human race. If they had not been nature's gentlemen they would have burned him alive at a stake. Cregeen, in particular, consistently referred to him in terms which could not have been more severe had Denry been the assassin of Cregeen's wife and seven children. In daring to make over a hundred pounds a week out of a ramshackle old lifeboat that Cregeen had sold to him for thirty-five pounds, Denry was outraging Cregeen's moral code. Cregeen had paid thirty-five pounds for the *Fleetwing*, a craft immeasurably superior to Denry's nameless tub. And was Cregeen making a hundred pounds a week out of it? Not a hundred shillings! Cregeen genuinely thought that he had a right to half Denry's profits. Old Simeon, too, seemed to think that *he* had a right to a large percentage of the same profits. And the Corporation, though it was notorious that excursionists visited the town purposely to voyage in the lifeboat, the Corporation made difficulties—about the embarking and disembarking, about the photographic strip of beach, about the crowds on the pavement outside the photograph shop. Denry learnt that he had committed the sin of not being a native of Llandudno. He was a stranger, and he was taking money out of the town. At times he wished he could have been born again. His friend and saviour was the Local Secretary of the Lifeboat Institution, who happened to be a Town Councillor. This worthy man, to whom Denry paid over a pound a day, was invaluable to him. Further, Denry was invited—nay commanded—to contribute to nearly every church, chapel, mission, and charity in Carnarvonshire, Flintshire, and other counties. His youthfulness was not accepted as an excuse. And as his gross profits could be calculated by any dunce who chose to stand on the beach for half a day, it was not easy for him to pretend that he was on the brink of starvation. He could only ward off attacks by stating with vague, convinced sadness that his expenses were much greater than any one could imagine.

In September, when the moon was red and full, and the sea glassy, he announced a series of nocturnal "Rocket Fêtes." The lifeboat, hung with Chinese lanterns, put out in the evening (charge five shillings) and, followed by half the harbour's fleet of rowing-boats and cutters, proceeded to the neighbourhood of the strip of beach, where a rocket apparatus had been installed by the help of the Lifeboat Secretary. The mortar was trained; there was a flash, a whizz, a line of fire, and a rope fell out of the sky across the lifeboat. The effect was thrilling and roused cheers. Never did the Lifeboat Institution receive such an advertisement as Denry gave it—gratis.

After the rocketing Denry stood alone on the slopes of the Little Orme and watched the lanterns floating home over the water, and heard the lusty mirth of his clients in the still air. It was an emotional experience for him.

"By Jove!" he said, "I've wakened this town up!"

VI

One morning, in the very last sad days of the dying season, when his receipts had dropped to the miserable figure of about fifty pounds a week, Denry had a great and pleasing surprise. He met Nellie on the Parade. It was a fact that the recognition of that innocent, childlike blushing face gave him joy. Nellie was with her father, Councillor Cotterill, and her mother. The Councillor was a speculative builder, who was erecting several streets of British homes in the new quarter above the new municipal park at Bursley. Denry had already encountered him once or twice in the way of business. He was a big and portly man of forty-five, with a thin face and a consciousness of prosperity. At one moment you would think him a jolly, bluff fellow, and at the next you would be disconcerted by a note of cunning or of harshness. Mrs Councillor Cotterill was one of these women who fail to live up to the ever-increasing height of their husbands. Afflicted with an eternal stage-fright, she never opened her close-pressed lips in society, though a few people knew that she could talk as fast and as effectively as any one. Difficult to set in motion, her vocal machinery was equally difficult to stop. She generally wore a low bonnet and a mantle. The Cotterills had been spending a fortnight in the Isle of Man, and they had come direct from Douglas to Llandudno by steamer, where they meant to pass two or three days. They were staying at Craig-y-don, at the eastern end of the Parade.

"Well, young man!" said Councillor Cotterill.

And he kept on young-manning Denry with an easy patronage which Denry could scarcely approve of. "I bet I've made more money this summer than you have with all your jerrying!" said Denry silently to the Councillor's back while the Cotterill family were inspecting the historic lifeboat on the beach. Councillor Cotterill said frankly that one reason for their calling at Llandudno was his desire to see this singular lifeboat, about which there had really been a very great deal of talk in the Five Towns. The admission comforted Denry. Then the Councillor recommenced his young-manning.

"Look here," said Demo, carelessly, "you must come and dine with me one night, all of you—will you?"

Nobody who has not passed at least twenty years in a district where people dine at one o'clock, and dining after dark is regarded as a wild idiosyncrasy of earls, can appreciate the effect of this speech.

The Councillor, when he had recovered himself, said that they would be pleased to dine with him; Mrs Cotterill's tight lips were seen to move, but not heard; and Nellie glowed.

"Yes," said Denry, "come and dine with me at the Majestic."

The name of the Majestic put an end to the young-manning. It was the new hotel by the pier, and advertised itself as the most luxurious hotel in the Principality. Which was bold of it, having regard to the magnificence of caravanserais at Cardiff. It had two hundred bedrooms, and waiters who talked English imperfectly; and its prices were supposed to be fantastic.

After all, the most startled and frightened person of the four was perhaps Denry. He had never given a dinner to anybody. He had never even dined at night. He had never been inside the Majestic. He had never had the courage to go inside the Majestic. He had no notion of the mysterious preliminaries to the offering of a dinner in a public place.

But the next morning he contracted to give away the lifeboat to a syndicate of boatmen, headed by John their leader, for thirty-five pounds. And he swore to himself that he would do that dinner properly, even if it cost him the whole price of the boat. Then he met Mrs Cotterill coming out of a shop. Mrs Cotterill, owing to a strange hazard of fate, began talking at once. And Denry, as an old shorthand writer, instinctively calculated that not Thomas Allen Reed himself could have taken Mrs Cotterill down verbatim. Her face tried to express pain, but pleasure shone out of it. For she found herself in an exciting contretemps which she could understand.

"Oh, Mr Machin," she said, "what *do* you think's happened? I don't know how to tell you, I'm sure. Here you've arranged for that dinner to-morrow and it's all settled, and now Miss Earp telegraphs to our Nellie to say she's coming to-morrow for a day or two with us. You know Ruth and Nellie are *such* friends. It's like as if what must be, isn't it? I don't know what to do, I do declare. What *ever* will Ruth say at us leaving her all alone the first night she comes? I really do think she might have——"

"You must bring her along with you," said Denry.

"But won't you—shan't you—won't she—won't it——"

"Not at all," said Denry. "Speaking for myself, I shall be delighted."

"Well, I'm sure you're very sensible," said Mrs Cotterill. "I was but saying to Mr Cotterill over breakfast—I said to him——"

"I shall ask Councillor Rhys-Jones to meet you," said Denry. "He's one of the principal members of the Town Council here; Local Secretary of the Lifeboat Institution. Great friend of mine."

"Oh!" exclaimed Mrs Cotterill, "it'll be quite an affair."

It was.

Denry found to his relief that the only difficult part of arranging a dinner at the Majestic was the steeling of yourself to enter the gorgeous portals of the hotel. After that, and after murmuring that you wished to fix up a little snack, you had nothing to do but listen to suggestions, each surpassing the rest in splendour, and say "Yes." Similarly with the greeting of a young woman who was once to you the jewel of the world. You simply said, "Good-afternoon, how are you?" And she said the same. And you shook hands. And there you were, still alive!

The one defect of the dinner was that the men were not in evening dress. (Denry registered a new rule of life: Never travel without your evening dress, because you never know what may turn up.) The girls were radiantly white. And after all there is nothing like white. Mrs Cotterill was in black silk and silence. And after all there is nothing like black silk. There was champagne. There were ices. Nellie, not being permitted champagne, took her revenge in ice. Denry had found an opportunity to relate to her the history of the Chocolate Remedy. She said,

"How wonderful you are!" And he said it was she who was wonderful. Denry gave no information about the Chocolate Remedy to her father. Neither did she. As for Ruth, indubitably she was responsible for the social success of the dinner. She seemed to have the habit of these affairs. She it was who loosed tongues. Nevertheless, Denry saw her now with different eyes, and it appeared incredible to him that he had once mistaken her for the jewel of the world.

At the end of the dinner Councillor Rhys-Jones produced a sensation by rising to propose the health of their host. He referred to the superb heroism of England's lifeboatmen, and in the name of the Institution thanked Denry for the fifty-three pounds which Denry's public had contributed to the funds. He said it was a noble contribution and that Denry was a philanthropist. And he called on Councillor Cotterill to second the toast. Which Councillor Cotterill did, in good set terms, the result of long habit. And Denry stammered that he was much obliged, and that really it was nothing.

But when the toasting was finished, Councillor Cotterill lapsed somewhat into a patronising irony, as if he were jealous of a youthful success. And he did not stop at "young man." He addressed Denry grandiosely as "my boy."

"This lifeboat—it was just an idea, my boy, just an idea," he said.

"Yes," said Denry, "but I thought of it."

"The question is," said the Councillor, "can you think of any more ideas as good?"

"Well," said Denry, "can *you*?"

With reluctance they left the luxury of the private dining-room, and Denry surreptitiously paid the bill with a pile of sovereigns, and Councillor Rhys-Jones parted from them with lively grief. The other five walked in a row along the Parade in the moonlight. And when they arrived in front of Craig-y-don, and the Cotterills were entering, Ruth, who loitered behind, said to Denry in a liquid voice:

"I don't feel a bit like going to sleep. I suppose you wouldn't care for a stroll?"

"Well——"

"I daresay you're very tired," she said.

"No," he replied, "it's this moonlight I'm afraid of."

And their eyes met under the door-lamp, and Ruth wished him pleasant dreams and vanished. It was exceedingly subtle.

VII

The next afternoon the Cotterills and Ruth Earp went home, and Denry with them. Llandudno was just settling into its winter sleep, and Denry's rather complex affairs had all been put in order. Though the others showed a certain lassitude, he himself was hilarious. Among his insignificant luggage was a new hat-box, which proved to be the origin of much gaiety.

"Just take this, will you?" he said to a porter on the platform at Llandudno Station, and held out the new hat-box with an air of calm. The porter innocently took it, and then, as the hat-box nearly jerked his arm out of the socket, gave vent to his astonishment after the manner of porters.

"By gum, mister!" said he, "that's heavy!"

It, in fact, weighed nearly two stone.

"Yes," said Denry, "it's full of sovereigns, of course."

And everybody laughed.

At Crewe, where they had to change, and again at Knype and at Bursley, he produced astonishment in porters by concealing the effort with which he handed them the hat-box, as though its weight was ten ounces. And each time he made the same witticism about sovereigns.

"What *have* you got in that hat-box?" Ruth asked.

"Don't I tell you?" said Denry, laughing. "Sovereigns!"

Lastly, he performed the same trick on his mother. Mrs Machin was working, as usual, in the cottage in Brougham Street. Perhaps the notion of going to Llandudno for a change had not occurred to her. In any case, her presence had been necessary in Bursley, for she had frequently collected Denry's rents for him, and collected them very well. Denry was glad to see her again, and she was glad to see him, but they concealed their feelings as much as possible. When he basely handed her the hat-box she dropped it, and roundly informed him that she was not going to have any of his pranks.

After tea, whose savouriness he enjoyed quite as much as his own state dinner, he gave her a key and asked her to open the hat-box, which he had placed on a chair.

"What is there in it?"

"A lot of jolly fine pebbles that I've been collecting on the beach," he said.

She got the hat-box on to her knee, and unlocked it, and came to a thick cloth, which she partly withdrew, and then there was a scream from Mrs Machin, and the hat-box rolled with a terrific crash to the tiled floor, and she was ankle-deep in sovereigns. She could see sovereigns running about all over the parlour. Gradually even the most active sovereigns decided to lie down and be quiet, and a great silence ensued. Denry's heart was beating.

Mrs Machin merely shook her head. Not often did her son deprive her of words, but this theatrical culmination of his home-coming really did leave her speechless.

Late that night rows of piles of sovereigns decorated the oval table in the parlour.

"A thousand and eleven," said Denry, at length, beneath the lamp. "There's fifteen missing yet. We'll look for 'em to-morrow."

For several days afterwards Mrs Machin was still picking up sovereigns. Two had even gone outside the parlour, and down the two steps into the backyard, and finding themselves unable to get back, had remained there.

And all the town knew that the unique Denry had thought of the idea of returning home to his mother with a hat-box crammed with sovereigns.

This was Denry's "latest," and it employed the conversation of the borough for I don't know how long.

CHAPTER VI

HIS BURGLARY

I

The fact that Denry Machin decided not to drive behind his mule to Sneyd Hall showed in itself that the enterprise of interviewing the Countess of Chell was not quite the simple daily trifling matter that he strove to pretend it was.

The mule was a part of his more recent splendour. It was aged seven, and it had cost Denry ten pounds. He had bought it off a farmer whose wife "stood" St Luke's Market. His excuse was that he needed help in getting about the Five Towns in pursuit of cottage rents, for his business of a rent-collector had grown. But for this purpose a bicycle would have served equally well, and would not have cost a shilling a day to feed, as the mule did, nor have shied at policemen, as the mule nearly always did. Denry had bought the mule simply because he had been struck all of a sudden with the idea of buying the mule. Some time previously Jos Curtenty (the Deputy-Mayor, who became Mayor of Bursley on the Earl of Chell being called away to govern an Australian colony) had made an enormous sensation by buying a flock of geese and driving them home himself. Denry did not like this. He was indeed jealous, if a large mind can be jealous. Jos Curtenty was old enough to be his grandfather, and had been a recognised "card" and "character" since before Denry's birth. But Denry, though so young, had made immense progress as a card, and had, perhaps justifiably, come to consider himself as the premier card, the very ace, of the town. He felt that some reply was needed to Curtenty's geese, and the mule was his reply. It served excellently. People were soon asking each other whether they had heard that Denry Machin's "latest" was to buy a mule. He obtained a little old victoria for another ten pounds, and a good set of harness for three guineas. The carriage was low, which enabled him, as he said, to nip in and out much more easily than in and out of a trap. In his business you did almost nothing but nip in and out. On the front seat he caused to be fitted a narrow box of japanned tin, with a formidable lock and slits on the top. This box was understood to receive the rents, as he collected them. It was always guarded on journeys by a cross between a mastiff and something unknown, whose growl would have terrorised a lion-tamer. Denry himself was afraid of Rajah, the dog, but he would not admit it. Rajah slept in the stable behind Mrs Machin's cottage, for which Denry paid a shilling a week. In the stable there was precisely room for Rajah, the mule and the carriage, and when Denry entered to groom or to harness, something had to go out.

The equipage quickly grew into a familiar sight in the streets of the district. Denry said that it was funny without being vulgar. Certainly it amounted to a continual advertisement for him; an infinitely more effective advertisement than, for instance, a sandwichman at eighteen-pence a day, and costing no more, even with the licence and the shoeing. Moreover, a sandwichman has this inferiority to a turnout: when you have done with him you cannot put him up to auction and sell him. Further, there are no sandwichmen in the Five Towns; in that democratic and independent neighbourhood nobody would deign to be a sandwichman.

The mulish vehicular display does not end the tale of Denry's splendour. He had an office in St Luke's Square, and in the office was an office-boy, small but genuine, and a real copying-press, and outside it was the little square signboard which in the days of his simplicity used to be screwed on to his mother's door. His mother's steely firmness of character had driven him into the extravagance of an office. Even after he had made over a thousand pounds out of the Llandudno lifeboat in less than three months, she would not listen to a proposal for going into a slightly larger house, of which one room might serve as an office. Nor would she abandon her own labours as a sempstress. She said that since her marriage she had always lived in that cottage and had always worked, and that she meant to die there, working: and that Denry could do what he chose. He was a bold youth, but not bold enough to dream of quitting his mother; besides, his share of household expenses in the cottage was only ten shillings a week. So he rented the office; and he hired an office-boy, partly to convey to his mother that he *should* do what he chose, and partly for his own private amusement.

He was thus, at an age when fellows without imagination are fraying their cuffs for the enrichment of their elders and glad if they can afford a cigar once a month, in possession of a business, business premises, a clerical staff, and a private carriage drawn by an animal unique in the Five Towns. He was living on less than his income; and in the course of about two years, to a small extent by economies and to a large extent by injudicious but happy investments, he had doubled the Llandudno thousand and won the deference of the manager of the bank at the top of St Luke's Square—one of the most unsentimental men that ever wrote "refer to drawer" on a cheque.

And yet Denry was not satisfied. He had a secret woe, due to the facts that he was gradually ceasing to be a card, and that he was not multiplying his capital by two every six months. He did not understand the money market, nor the stock market, nor even the financial article in the *Signal*; but he regarded himself as a financial genius, and deemed that as a financial genius he was vegetating. And as for setting the town on fire, or painting it scarlet, he seemed to have lost the trick of that.

II

And then one day the populace saw on his office door, beneath his name-board, another sign:

FIVE TOWNS UNIVERSAL THRIFT CLUB. *Secretary and Manager*—E.H. MACHIN.

An idea had visited him.

Many tradesmen formed slate-clubs—goose-clubs, turkey-clubs, whisky-clubs—in the autumn, for Christmas. Their humble customers paid so much a week to the tradesmen, who charged them nothing for keeping it, and at the end of the agreed period they took out the total sum in goods—dead or alive; eatable, drinkable, or wearable. Denry conceived a universal slate-club. He meant it to embrace each of the Five Towns. He saw forty thousand industrial families paying weekly instalments into his slate-club. He saw his slate-club entering into contracts with all the principal tradesmen of the entire district, so that the members of the slate-club could shop with slate-club tickets practically where they chose. He saw his slate-club so powerful that no tradesman could afford not to be in relations with it. He had induced all Llandudno to perform the same act daily for nearly a whole season, and he now wished to induce all the vast Five Towns to perform the same act to his profit for all eternity.

And he would be a philanthropist into the bargain. He would encourage thrift in the working-man and the working-man's wife. He would guard the working-man's money for him; and to save trouble to the working-man he would call at the working-man's door for the working-man's money. Further, as a special inducement and to prove superior advantages to ordinary slate-clubs, he would allow the working man to spend his full nominal subscription to the club as soon as he had actually paid only half of it. Thus, after paying ten shillings to Denry, the working-man could spend a pound in Denry's chosen shops, and Denry would settle with the shops at once, while collecting the balance weekly at the working-man's door. But this privilege of anticipation was to be forfeited or postponed if the working-man's earlier payments were irregular.

And Denry would bestow all these wondrous benefits on the working-man without any charge whatever. Every penny that members paid in, members would draw out. The affair was enormously philanthropic.

Denry's modest remuneration was to come from the shopkeepers upon whom his scheme would shower new custom. They were to allow him at least twopence in the shilling discount on all transactions, which would be more than 16 per cent. on his capital; and he would turn over his capital three times a year. He calculated that out of 50 per cent. per annum he would be able to cover working expenses and a little over.

Of course, he had to persuade the shopkeepers. He drove his mule to Hanbridge and began with Bostocks, the largest but not the most distinguished drapery house in the Five Towns. He succeeded in convincing them on every point except that of his own financial stability. Bostocks indicated their opinion that he looked far too much like a boy to be financially stable. His reply was to offer to deposit fifty pounds with them before starting business, and to renew the sum in advance as quickly as the members of his club should exhaust it. Cheques talk. He departed with Bostocks' name at the head of his list, and he used them as a clinching argument with other shops. But the prejudice against his youth was strong and general. "Yes," tradesmen would answer, "what you say is all right, but you are so young." As if to insinuate that a man must be either a rascal or a fool until he is thirty, just as he must be either a fool or a physician after he is forty. Nevertheless, he had soon compiled a list of several score shops.

His mother said:

"Why don't you grow a beard? Here you spend money on razors, strops, soaps and brushes, besides a quarter of an hour of your time every day, and cutting yourself—all to keep yourself from having something that would be the greatest help to you in business! With a beard you'd look at least thirty-one. Your father had a splendid beard, and so could you if you chose."

This was high wisdom. But he would not listen to it. The truth is, he was getting somewhat dandiacal.

At length his scheme lacked naught but what Denry called a "right-down good starting shove." In a word, a fine advertisement to fire it off. Now, he could have had the whole of the first page of the *Signal* (at that period) for five-and-twenty pounds. But he had been so accustomed to free advertisements of one sort or another that the notion of paying for one was loathsome to him. Then it was that he thought of the Countess of Chell, who happened to be staying at Knype. If he could obtain that great aristocrat, that ex-Mayoress, that lovely witch, that benefactor of the district, to honour his Thrift Club as patroness, success was certain. Everybody in the Five Towns sneered at the Countess and called her a busybody; she was even dubbed "Interfering Iris" (Iris being one of her eleven Christian names); the Five Towns was fiercely democratic—in theory. In practice the Countess was worshipped; her smile was worth at least five pounds, and her invitation to tea was priceless. She could not have been more sincerely adulated in the United States, the home of social equality.

Denry said to himself:

"And why *shouldn't* I get her name as patroness? I will have her name as patroness."

Hence the expedition to Sneyd Hall, one of the ancestral homes of the Earls of Chell.

III

He had been to Sneyd Hall before many times—like the majority of the inhabitants of the Five Towns—for, by the generosity of its owner, Sneyd Park was always open to the public. To picnic in Sneyd Park was one of the chief distractions of the Five Towns on Thursday and Saturday afternoons. But he had never entered the private gardens. In the midst of the private gardens stood the Hall, shut off by immense iron palisades, like a lion in a cage at the Zoo. On the autumn afternoon of his Historic visit, Denry passed with qualms through the double gates of the palisade, and began to crunch the gravel of the broad drive that led in a straight line to the overwhelming Palladian façade of the Hall.

Yes, he was decidedly glad that he had not brought his mule. As he approached nearer and nearer to the Countess's front-door his arguments in favour of the visit grew more and more ridiculous. Useless to remind himself that he had once danced with the Countess at the municipal ball, and amused her to the giggling point, and restored her lost fan to her. Useless to remind himself that he was a quite exceptional young man, with a quite exceptional renown, and the equal of any man or woman on earth. Useless to remind himself that the

Countess was notorious for her affability and also for her efforts to encourage the true welfare of the Five Towns. The visit was grotesque.

He ought to have written. He ought, at any rate, to have announced his visit by a note. Yet only an hour earlier he had been arguing that he could most easily capture the Countess by storm, with no warning or preparations of any kind.

Then, from a lateral path, a closed carriage and pair drove rapidly up to the Hall, and a footman bounced off the hammercloth. Denry could not see through the carriage, but under it he could distinguish the skirts of some one who got put of it. Evidently the Countess was just returning from a drive. He quickened his pace, for at heart he was an audacious boy.

"She can't eat me," he said.

This assertion was absolutely irrefutable, and yet there remained in his bold heart an irrational fear that after all she *could* eat him. Such is the extraordinary influence of a Palladian façade!

After what seemed several hours of torture entirely novel in his experience, he skirted the back of the carriage and mounted the steps to the portal. And, although the coachman was innocuous, being apparently carved in stone, Denry would have given a ten-pound note to find himself suddenly in his club or even in church. The masonry of the Hall rose up above him like a precipice. He was searching for the bell-knob in the face of the precipice when a lady suddenly appeared at the doors. At first he thought it was the Countess, and that heart of his began to slip down the inside of his legs. But it was not the Countess.

"Well?" demanded the lady. She was dressed in black.

"Can I see the Countess?" he inquired.

The lady stared at him. He handed her his professional card which lay waiting all ready in his waistcoat pocket.

"I will ask my lady," said the lady in black.

Denry perceived from her accent that she was not English.

She disappeared through a swinging door; and then Denry most clearly heard the Countess's own authentic voice saying in a pettish, disgusted tone:

"Oh! Bother!"

And he was chilled. He seriously wished that he had never thought of starting his confounded Universal Thrift Club.

After some time the carriage suddenly drove off, presumably to the stables. As he was now within the hollow of the porch, a sort of cave at the foot of the precipice, he could not see along the length of the façade. Nobody came to him. The lady who had promised to ask my lady whether the latter could see him did not return. He reflected that she had not promised to return; she had merely promised to ask a question. As the minutes passed he grew careless, or grew bolder, gradually dropping his correct attitude of a man-about-town paying an afternoon call, and peered through the glass of the doors that divided him from the Countess. He could distinguish nothing that had life. One of his preliminary tremors had been caused by a fanciful vision of multitudinous footmen, through a double line of whom he would be compelled to walk in order to reach the Countess.

But there was not even one footman. This complete absence of indoor footmen seemed to him remiss, not in accordance with centuries of tradition concerning life at Sneyd.

Then he caught sight, through the doors, of the back of Jock, the Countess's carriage footman and the son of his mother's old friend. Jock was standing motionless at a half-open door to the right of the space between Denry's double doors and the next pair of double doors. Denry tried to attract his attention by singular movements and strange noises of the mouth. But Jock, like his partner the coachman, appeared to be carven in stone. Denry decided that he would go in and have speech with Jock. They were on Christian-name terms, or had been a few years ago. He unobtrusively pushed at the doors, and at the very same moment Jock, with a start—as though released from some spell—vanished away from the door to the right.

Denry was now within.

"Jock!" He gave a whispering cry, rather conspiratorial in tone. And as Jock offered no response, he hurried after Jock through the door to the right. This door led to a large apartment which struck Denry as being an idealisation of a first-class waiting-room at a highly important terminal station. In a wall to the left was a small door, half open. Jock must have gone through that door. Denry hesitated—he had not properly been invited into the Hall. But in hesitating he was wrong; he ought to have followed his prey without qualms. When he had conquered qualms and reached the further door, his eyes were met, to their amazement, by an immense perspective of great chambers. Denry had once seen a Pullman car, which had halted at Knype Station with a French actress on board. What he saw now presented itself to him as a train of Pullman cars, one opening into the other, constructed for giants. Each car was about as large as the large hall in Bursley Town Hall, and, like that auditorium, had a ceiling painted to represent blue sky, milk-white clouds, and birds. But in the corners were groups of naked Cupids, swimming joyously on the ceiling; in Bursley Town Hall there were no naked Cupids. He understood now that he had been quite wrong in his estimate of the room by which he had come into this Versailles. Instead of being large it was tiny, and instead of being luxurious it was merely furnished with miscellaneous odds and ends left over from far more important furnishings. It was indeed naught but a nondescript box of a hole insignificantly wedged between the state apartments and the outer lobby.

For an instant he forgot that he was in pursuit of Jock. Jock was perfectly invisible and inaudible. He must, however, have gone down the vista of the great chambers, and therefore Denry went down the vista of the great chambers after him, curiously expecting to have a glimpse of his long salmon-tinted coat or his cockaded hat popping up out of some corner. He reached the other end of the vista, having traversed three enormous chambers, of which the middle one was the most enormous and the most gorgeous. There were high windows everywhere to his right, and to his left, in every chamber, double doors with gilt handles of a peculiar shape. Windows and doors, with equal splendour, were draped in hangings of brocade. Through the windows he had glimpses of the gardens in their autumnal colours, but no glimpse of a gardener. Then a carriage flew past the windows at the end of the suite, and he had a very clear though a transient view of two menials on the box-seat; one of those menials he knew must be Jock. Hence Jock must have escaped from the state suite by one of the numerous doors.

Denry tried one door after another, and they were all fastened firmly on the outside. The gilded handles would turn, but the lofty and ornate portals would not yield to pressure. Mystified and startled, he went back to the place from which he had begun his explorations, and was even more seriously startled, and more deeply mystified to find nothing but a blank wall where he had entered. Obviously he could not have penetrated through a solid wall. A careful perusal of the wall showed him that there was indeed a door in it, but that the door was artfully disguised by painting and other devices so as to look like part of the wall. He had never seen such a phenomenon before. A very small glass knob was the door's sole fitting. Denry turned this crystal, but with no useful result. In the brief space of time since his entrance, that door, and the door by which Jock had gone, had been secured by unseen hands. Denry imagined sinister persons bolting all the multitudinous doors, and inimical eyes staring at him through many keyholes. He imagined himself to be the victim of some fearful and incomprehensible conspiracy.

Why, in the sacred name of common-sense, should he have been imprisoned in the state suite? The only answer to the conundrum was that nobody was aware of his quite unauthorised presence in the state suite. But then why should the state suite be so suddenly locked up, since the Countess had just come in from a drive? It then occurred to him that, instead of just coming in, the Countess had been just leaving. The carriage must have driven round from some humbler part of the Hall, with the lady in black in it, and the lady in black—perhaps a lady's-maid—alone had stepped out from it. The Countess had been waiting for the carriage in the porch, and had fled to avoid being forced to meet the unfortunate Denry. (Humiliating thought!) The carriage had then taken her up at a side door. And now she was gone. Possibly she had left Sneyd Hall not to return for months, and that was why the doors had been locked. Perhaps everybody had departed from the Hall save one aged and deaf retainer—he knew, from historical novels which he had glanced at in his youth, that in every Hall that respected itself an aged and deaf retainer was invariably left solitary during the absences of the noble owner. He knocked on the small disguised door. His unique purpose in knocking was naturally to make a noise, but something prevented him from making a noise. He felt that he must knock decently, discreetly; he felt that he must not outrage the conventions.

No result to this polite summoning.

He attacked other doors; he attacked every door he could put his hands on; and gradually he lost his respect for decency and the conventions proper to Halls, knocking loudly and more loudly. He banged. Nothing but sheer solidity stopped his sturdy hands from going through the panels. He so far forgot himself as to shake the doors with all his strength furiously.

And finally he shouted: "Hi there! Hi! Can't you hear?"

Apparently the aged and deaf retainer could not hear. Apparently he was the deafest retainer that a peeress of the realm ever left in charge of a princely pile.

"Well, that's a nice thing!" Denry exclaimed, and he noticed that he was hot and angry. He took a certain pleasure in being angry. He considered that he had a right to be angry.

At this point he began to work himself up into the state of "not caring," into the state of despising Sneyd Hall, and everything for which it stood. As for permitting himself to be impressed or intimidated by the lonely magnificence of his environment, he laughed at the idea; or, more accurately, he snorted at it. Scornfully he tramped up and down those immense interiors, doing the caged lion, and cogitating in quest of the right dramatic, effective act to perform in the singular crisis. Unhappily, the carpets were very thick, so that though he could tramp, he could not stamp; and he desired to stamp. But in the connecting doorways there were expanses of bare, highly-polished oak floor, and here he did stamp.

The rooms were not furnished after the manner of ordinary rooms. There was no round or square table in the midst of each, with a checked cloth on it, and a plant in the centre. Nor in front of each window was there a small table with a large Bible thereupon. The middle parts of the rooms were empty, save for a group of statuary in the largest room. Great arm-chairs and double-ended sofas were ranged about in straight lines, and among these, here and there, were smaller chairs gilded from head to foot. Round the walls were placed long narrow tables with tops like glass-cases, and in the cases were all sorts of strange matters— such as coins, fans, daggers, snuff-boxes. In various corners white statues stood awaiting the day of doom without a rag to protect them from the winds of destiny. The walls were panelled in tremendous panels, and in each panel was a formidable dark oil-painting. The mantelpieces were so preposterously high that not even a giant could have sat at the fireplace and put his feet on them. And if they had held clocks, as mantelpieces do, a telescope would have been necessary to discern the hour. Above each mantelpiece, instead of a looking-glass, was a vast picture. The chandeliers were overpowering in glitter and in dimensions.

Near to a sofa Denry saw a pile of yellow linen things. He picked up the topmost article, and it assumed the form of a chair. Yes, these articles were furniture-covers. The Hall, then, was to be shut up. He argued from the furniture-covers that somebody must enter sooner or later to put the covers on the furniture.

Then he did a few more furlongs up and down the vista, and sat down at the far end, under a window. Anyhow, there were always the windows.

High though they were from the floor, he could easily open one, spring out, and slip unostentatiously away. But he thought he would wait until dusk fell. Prudence is seldom misplaced. The windows, however, held a disappointment for him. A mere bar, padlocked, prevented each one of them from being opened; it was a simple device. He would be under the necessity of breaking a plate-glass pane. For this enterprise he thought he would wait until black night. He sat down again. Then he made a fresh and noisy assault on all the doors. No result. He sat down a third time, and gazed info the gardens where the shadows were creeping darkly. Not a soul in the gardens. Then he felt a draught on the crown of his head, and looking aloft he saw that the summit of the window had a transverse glazed flap, for ventilation, and that this flap had been left open. If he could have climbed up, he might have fallen out on the other side into the gardens and liberty. But the summit of the window was at least sixteen feet from the floor. Night descended.

IV

At a vague hour in the evening a stout woman dressed in black, with a black apron, a neat violet cap on her head, and a small lamp in her podgy hand, unlocked one of the doors giving entry to the state rooms. She was on her nightly round of inspection. The autumn moon, nearly at full, had risen and was shining into the great windows. And in front of the furthest window she perceived in the radiance of the moonshine a pyramidal group, somewhat in the style of a family of acrobats, dangerously arranged on the stage of a music-hall. The base of the pyramid comprised two settees; upon these were several arm-chairs laid flat, and on the arm-chairs two tables covered with cushions and rugs; lastly, in the way of inanimate nature, two gilt chairs. On the gilt chairs was something that unmistakably moved, and was fumbling with the top of the window. Being a stout woman with a tranquil and sagacious mind, her first act was not to drop the lamp. She courageously clung to the lamp.

"Who's there?" said a voice from the apex of the pyramid.

Then a subsidence began, followed by a crash and a multitudinous splintering of glass. The living form dropped on to one of the settees, rebounding like a football from its powerful springs. There was a hole as big as a coffin in the window. The living form collected itself, and then jumped wildly through that hole into the gardens.

Denry ran. The moment had not struck him as a moment propitious for explanation. In a flash he had seen the ridiculousness of endeavouring to convince a stout lady in black that he was a gentleman paying a call on the Countess. He simply scrambled to his legs and ran. He ran aimlessly in the darkness and sprawled over a hedge, after crossing various flower-beds. Then he saw the sheen of the moon on Sneyd Lake, and he could take his bearings. In winter all the Five Towns skate on Sneyd Lake if the ice will bear, and the geography of it was quite familiar to Denry. He skirted its east bank, plunged into Great Shendon Wood, and emerged near Great Shendon Station, on the line from Stafford to Knype. He inquired for the next train in the tones of innocency, and in half an hour was passing through Sneyd Station itself. In another fifty minutes he was at home. The clock showed ten-fifteen. His mother's cottage seemed amazingly small. He said that he had been detained in Hanbridge on business, that he had had neither tea nor supper, and that he was hungry. Next morning he could scarcely be sure that his visit to Sneyd Hall was not a dream. In any event, it had been a complete failure.

V

It was on this untriumphant morning that one of the tenants under his control, calling at the cottage to pay some rent overdue, asked him when the Universal Thrift Club was going to commence its operations. He had talked of the enterprise to all his tenants, for it was precisely with his tenants that he hoped to make a beginning. He had there a *clientèle* ready to his hand, and as he was intimately acquainted with the circumstances of each, he could judge between those who would be reliable and those to whom he would be obliged to refuse membership. The tenants, conclaving together of an evening on doorsteps, had come to the conclusion that the Universal Thrift Club was the very contrivance which they had lacked for years. They saw in it a cure for all their economic ills, and the gate to Paradise. The dame who put the question to him on the morning after his defeat wanted to be the possessor of carpets, a new teapot, a silver brooch, and a cookery book; and she was evidently depending upon Denry. On consideration he saw no reason why the Universal Thrift Club should not be allowed to start itself by the impetus of its own intrinsic excellence. The dame was inscribed for three shares, paid eighteen-pence entrance fee, undertook to pay three shillings a week, and received a document entitling her to spend £3, 18s. in sixty-five shops as soon as she had paid £1, 19s. to Denry. It was a marvellous scheme. The rumour of it spread; before dinner Denry had visits from other aspirants to membership, and he had posted a cheque to Bostocks', but more from ostentation than necessity; for no member could possibly go into Bostocks' with his coupons until at least two months had elapsed.

But immediately after dinner, when the posters of the early edition of the *Signal* waved in the streets, he had material for other thought. He saw a poster as he was walking across to his office. The awful legend ran:

ASTOUNDING ATTEMPTED BURGLARY AT SNEYD HALL.

In buying the paper he was afflicted with a kind of ague. And the description of events at Sneyd Hall was enough to give ague to a negro. The account had been taken from the lips of Mrs Gater, housekeeper at Sneyd Hall. She had related to a reporter how, upon going into the state suite before retiring for the night, she had surprised a burglar of Herculean physique and Titanic proportions. Fortunately she knew her duty, and did not blench. The burglar had threatened her with a revolver, and then, finding such bluff futile, had deliberately jumped through a large plate-glass window and vanished. Mrs Gater could not conceive how the fellow had "effected an entrance." (According to the reporter, Mrs Gater said "effected an entrance," not "got in." And here it may be mentioned that in the columns of the *Signal* burglars never get into a residence; without exception they invariably effect an entrance.) Mrs Gater explained further how the plans of the burglar must have been laid with the most diabolic skill; how he must have studied the daily life of the Hall patiently for weeks, if not months; how he must have known the habits and plans of every soul in the place, and the exact instant at which the Countess had arranged to drive to Stafford to catch the London express.

It appeared that save for four maidservants, a page, two dogs, three gardeners, and the kitchen-clerk, Mrs Gater was alone in the Hall. During the late afternoon and early evening they had all been to assist at a rat-catching in the stables, and the burglar must have been aware of this. It passed Mrs Gater's comprehension how the criminal had got clear away out of the gardens and park, for to set up a hue and cry had been with her the work of a moment. She could not be sure whether he had taken any valuable property, but the inventory was being checked. Though surely for her an inventory was scarcely necessary, as she had been housekeeper at Sneyd Hall for six-and-twenty years, and might be said to know the entire contents of the mansion by heart! The police were at work. They had studied footprints and *débris*. There was talk of obtaining detectives from London. Up to the time of going to press, no clue had been discovered, but Mrs Gater was confident that a clue would be discovered, and of her ability to recognise the burglar when he should be caught. His features, as seen in the moonlight, were imprinted on her mind for ever. He was a young man, well dressed. The Earl had telegraphed, offering a reward of £20 for the fellow's capture. A warrant was out.

So it ran on.

Denry saw clearly all the errors of tact which he had committed on the previous day. He ought not to have entered uninvited. But having entered, he ought to have held firm in quiet dignity until the housekeeper came, and then he ought to have gone into full details with the housekeeper, producing his credentials and showing her unmistakably that he was offended by the experience which somebody's gross carelessness had forced upon him.

Instead of all that, he had behaved with simple stupidity, and the result was that a price was upon his head. Far from acquiring moral impressiveness and influential aid by his journey to Sneyd Hall, he had utterly ruined himself as a founder of a Universal Thrift Club. You cannot conduct a thrift club from prison, and a sentence of ten years does not inspire confidence in the ignorant mob. He trembled at the thought of what would happen when the police learned from the Countess that a man with a card on which was the name of Machin had called at Sneyd just before her departure.

However, the police never did learn this from the Countess (who had gone to Rome for the autumn). It appeared that her maid had merely said to the Countess that "a man" had called, and also that the maid had lost the card. Careful research showed that the burglar had been disturbed before he had had opportunity to burgle. And the affair, after raising a terrific bother in the district, died down.

Then it was that an article appeared in the *Signal*, signed by Denry, and giving a full picturesque description of the state apartments at Sneyd Hall. He had formed a habit of occasional contributions to the *Signal*. This article began:—

"The recent sensational burglary at Sneyd Hall has drawn attention to the magnificent state apartments of that unique mansion. As very few

but the personal friends of the family are allowed a glimpse of these historic rooms, they being of course quite closed to the public, we have thought that some account of them might interest the readers of the *Signal*. On the occasion of our last visit...," etc.

He left out nothing of their splendour.

The article was quoted as far as Birmingham in the Midlands Press. People recalled Denry's famous waltz with the Countess at the memorable dance in Bursley Town Hall. And they were bound to assume that the relations thus begun had been more or less maintained. They were struck by Denry's amazing discreet self-denial in never boasting of them. Denry rose in the market of popular esteem. Talking of Denry, people talked of the Universal Thrift Club, which went quietly ahead, and they admitted that Denry was of the stuff which succeeds and deserves to succeed.

But only Denry himself could appreciate fully how great Denry was, to have snatched such a wondrous victory out of such a humiliating defeat!

His chin slowly disappeared from view under a quite presentable beard. But whether the beard was encouraged out of respect for his mother's sage advice, or with the object of putting the housekeeper of Sneyd Hall off the scent, if she should chance to meet Denry, who shall say?

CHAPTER VII

THE RESCUER OF DAMES

I

It next happened that Denry began to suffer from the ravages of a malady which is almost worse than failure—namely, a surfeit of success. The success was that of his Universal Thrift Club. This device, by which members after subscribing one pound in weekly instalments could at once get two pounds' worth of goods at nearly any large shop in the district, appealed with enormous force to the democracy of the Five Towns. There was no need whatever for Denry to spend money on advertising. The first members of the club did all the advertising and made no charge for doing it. A stream of people anxious to deposit money with Denry in exchange for a card never ceased to flow Into his little office in St Luke's Square. The stream, indeed, constantly thickened. It was a wonderful invention, the Universal Thrift Club. And Denry ought to have been happy, especially as his beard was growing strongly and evenly, and giving him the desired air of a man of wisdom and stability. But he was not happy. And the reason was that the popularity of the Thrift Club necessitated much book-keeping, which he hated.

He was an adventurer, in the old honest sense, and no clerk. And he found himself obliged not merely to buy large books of account, but to fill them with figures; and to do addition sums from page to page; and to fill up hundreds of cards; and to write out lists of shops, and to have long interviews with printers whose proofs made him dream of lunatic asylums; and to reckon innumerable piles of small coins; and to assist his small office-boy in the great task of licking envelopes and stamps. Moreover, he was worried by shopkeepers; every shopkeeper in the district now wanted to allow him twopence in the shilling on the purchases of club members. And he had to collect all the subscriptions, in addition to his rents; and also to make personal preliminary inquiries as to the reputation of intending members. If he could have risen every day at 4 A.M. and stayed up working every night till 4 A.M. he might have got through most of the labour. He did, as a fact, come very near to this ideal. So near that one morning his mother said to him, at her driest:

"I suppose I may as well sell your bedstead. Denry?"

And there was no hope of improvement; instead of decreasing, the work multiplied.

What saved him was the fortunate death of Lawyer Lawton. The aged solicitor's death put the town into mourning and hung the church with black. But Denry as a citizen bravely bore the blow because he was able to secure the services of Penkethman, Lawyer Lawton's eldest clerk, who, after keeping the Lawton books and writing the Lawton letters for thirty-five years, was dismissed by young Lawton for being over fifty and behind the times. The desiccated bachelor was grateful to Denry. He called Denry "Sir," or rather he called Denry's suit of clothes "Sir," for he had a vast respect for a well-cut suit. On the other hand, he maltreated the little office-boy, for he had always been accustomed to maltreating little office-boys, not seriously, but just enough to give them an interest in life. Penkethman enjoyed desks, ledgers, pens, ink, rulers, and blotting-paper. He could run from bottom to top of a column of figures more quickly than the fire-engine could run up Oldcastle Street; and his totals were never wrong. His gesture with a piece of blotting-paper as he blotted off a total was magnificent. He liked long hours; he was thoroughly used to overtime, and his boredom in his lodgings was such that he would often arrive at the office before the appointed hour. He asked thirty shillings a week, and Denry in a mood of generosity gave him thirty-one. He gave Denry his whole life, and put a meticulous order into the establishment. Denry secretly thought him a miracle, but up at the club at Porthill he was content to call him "the human machine." "I wind him up every Saturday night with a sovereign, half a sovereign, and a shilling," said Denry, "and he goes for a week. Compensated balance adjusted for all temperatures. No escapement. Jewelled in every hole. Ticks in any position. Made in England."

This jocularity of Denry's was a symptom that Denry's spirits were rising. The bearded youth was seen oftener in the streets behind his mule and his dog. The adventurer had, indeed, taken to the road again. After an emaciating period he began once more to stouten. He was the image of success. He was the picturesque card, whom everybody knew and everybody had pleasure in greeting.

In some sort he was rather like the flag on the Town Hall.

And then a graver misfortune threatened.

It arose out of the fact that, though Denry was a financial genius, he was in no sense qualified to be a Fellow of the Institute of Chartered Accountants. The notion that an excess of prosperity may bring ruin had never presented itself to him, until one day he discovered that out of over two thousand pounds there remained less than six hundred to his credit at the bank. This was at the stage of the Thrift Club when the founder of the Thrift Club was bound under the rules to give credit. When the original lady member had paid in her two pounds or so, she was entitled to spend four pounds or so at shops. She did spend four pounds or so at shops. And Denry had to pay the shops. He was thus temporarily nearly two pounds out of pocket, and he had to collect that sum by trifling instalments. Multiply this case by five hundred, and you will understand the drain on Denry's capital. Multiply it by a thousand, and you will understand the very serious peril which overhung Denry. Multiply it by fifteen hundred and you will understand that Denry had been culpably silly to inaugurate a mighty scheme like the Universal Thrift Club on a paltry capital of two thousand pounds. He had. In his simplicity he had regarded two thousand pounds as boundless wealth.

Although new subscriptions poured in, the drain grew more distressing. Yet he could not persuade himself to refuse new members. He stiffened his rules, and compelled members to pay at his office instead of on their own doorsteps; he instituted fines for irregularity. But nothing could stop the progress of the

Universal Thrift Club. And disaster approached. Denry felt as though he were being pushed nearer and nearer to the edge of a precipice by a tremendous multitude of people. At length, very much against his inclination, he put up a card in his window that no new members could be accepted until further notice, pending the acquisition of larger offices and other arrangements. For the shrewd, it was a confession of failure, and he knew it.

Then the rumour began to form, and to thicken, and to spread, that Denry's famous Universal Thrift Club was unsound at the core, and that the teeth of those who had bitten the apple would be set on edge.

And Denry saw that something great, something decisive, must be done and done with rapidity.

II

His thoughts turned to the Countess of Chell. The original attempt to engage her moral support in aid of the Thrift Club had ended in a dangerous fiasco. Denry had been beaten by circumstances. And though he had emerged from the defeat with credit, he had no taste for defeat. He disliked defeat even when it was served with jam. And his indomitable thoughts turned to the Countess again. He put it to himself in this way, scratching his head:

"I've got to get hold of that woman, and that's all about it!"

The Countess at this period was busying herself with the policemen of the Five Towns. In her exhaustless passion for philanthropy, bazaars, and platforms, she had already dealt with orphans, the aged, the blind, potter's asthma, crèches, churches, chapels, schools, economic cookery, the smoke-nuisance, country holidays, Christmas puddings and blankets, healthy musical entertainments, and barmaids. The excellent and beautiful creature was suffering from a dearth of subjects when the policemen occurred to her. She made the benevolent discovery that policemen were over-worked, underpaid, courteous and trustworthy public servants, and that our lives depended on them. And from this discovery it naturally followed that policemen deserved her energetic assistance. Which assistance resulted in the erection of a Policemen's Institute at Hanbridge, the chief of the Five Towns. At the Institute policemen would be able to play at draughts, read the papers, and drink everything non-alcoholic at prices that defied competition. And the Institute also conferred other benefits on those whom all the five Mayors of the Five Towns fell into the way of describing as "the stalwart guardians of the law." The Institute, having been built, had to be opened with due splendour and ceremony. And naturally the Countess of Chell was the person to open it, since without her it would never have existed.

The solemn day was a day in March, and the hour was fixed for three o'clock, and the place was the large hall of the Institute itself, behind Crown Square, which is the Trafalgar Square of Hanbridge. The Countess was to drive over from Sneyd. Had the epoch been ten years later she would have motored over. But probably that would not have made any difference to what happened.

In relating what did happen, I confine myself to facts, eschewing imputations. It is a truism that life is full of coincidences, but whether these events comprised a coincidence, or not, each reader must decide for himself, according to his cynicism or his faith in human nature.

The facts are: First, that Denry called one day at the house of Mrs Kemp a little lower down Brougham Street, Mrs Kemp being friendly with Mrs Machin, and the mother of Jock, the Countess's carriage-footman, whom Denry had known from boyhood. Second, that a few days later, when Jock came over to see his mother, Denry was present, and that subsequently Denry and Jock went for a stroll together in the cemetery, the principal resort of strollers in Bursley. Third, that on the afternoon of the opening ceremony the Countess's carriage broke down in Sneyd Vale, two miles from Sneyd and three miles from Hanbridge. Fourth, that five minutes later Denry, all in his best clothes, drove up behind his mule. Fifth, that Denry drove right past the breakdown, apparently not noticing it. Sixth, that Jock, touching his hat to Denry as if to a stranger (for, of course, while on duty a footman must be dead to all humanities), said:

"Excuse me, sir," and so caused Denry to stop.

These are the simple facts.

Denry looked round with that careless half-turn of the upper part of the body which drivers of elegant equipages affect when their attention is called to something trifling behind them. The mule also looked round—it was a habit of the mule's—and if the dog had been there the dog would have shown an even livelier inquisitiveness; but Denry had left the faithful animal at home.

"Good-afternoon, Countess," he said, raising his hat, and trying to express surprise, pleasure, and imperturbability all at once.

The Countess of Chell, who was standing in the road, raised her lorgnon, which was attached to the end of a tortoiseshell pole about a foot long, and regarded Denry. This lorgnon was a new device of hers, and it was already having the happy effect of increasing the sale of long-handled lorgnons throughout the Five Towns.

"Oh! it's you, is it?" said the Countess. "I see you've grown a beard."

It was just this easy familiarity that endeared her to the district. As observant people put it, you never knew what she would say next, and yet she never compromised her dignity.

"Yes," said Denry. "Have you had an accident?"

"No," said the Countess, bitterly: "I'm doing this for idle amusement."

The horses had been taken out, and were grazing by the roadside like common horses. The coachman was dipping his skirts in the mud as he bent down in front of the carriage and twisted the pole to and fro and round about and round about. The footman, Jock, was industriously watching him.

"It's the pole-pin, sir," said Jock.

Denry descended from his own hammercloth. The Countess was not smiling. It was the first time that Denry had ever seen her without an efficient smile on her face.

"Have you got to be anywhere particular?" he asked. Many ladies would not have understood what he meant. But the Countess was used to the Five Towns.

"Yes," said she. "I have got to be somewhere particular. I've got to be at the Police Institute at three o'clock particular, Mr Machin. And I shan't be. I'm late now. We've been here ten minutes."

The Countess was rather too often late for public ceremonies. Nobody informed her of the fact. Everybody, on the contrary, assiduously pretended that she had arrived to the very second. But she was well aware that she had a reputation for unpunctuality. Ordinarily, being too hurried to invent a really clever excuse, she would assert lightly that something had happened to her carriage. And now something in truth had happened to her carriage—but who would believe it at the Police Institute?

"If you'll come with me I'll guarantee to get you there by three o'clock," said Denry.

The road thereabouts was lonely. A canal ran parallel with it at a distance of fifty yards, and on the canal a boat was moving in the direction of Hanbridge at the rate of a mile an hour. Such was the only other vehicle in sight. The outskirts of Knype, the nearest town, did not begin until at least a mile further on; and the Countess, dressed for the undoing of mayors and other unimpressionable functionaries, could not possibly have walked even half a mile in that rich dark mud. She thanked him, and without a word to her servants took the seat beside him.

III

Immediately the mule began to trot the Countess began to smile again. Relief and content were painted upon her handsome features. Denry soon learnt that she knew all about mules—or almost all. She told him how she had ridden hundreds of miles on mules in the Apennines, where there were no roads, and only mules, goats and flies could keep their feet on the steep, stony paths. She said that a good mule was worth forty pounds in the Apennines, more than a horse of similar quality. In fact, she was very sympathetic about mules. Denry saw that he must drive with as much style as possible, and he tried to remember all that he had picked up from a book concerning the proper manner of holding the reins. For in everything that appertained to riding and driving the Countess was an expert. In the season she hunted once or twice a week with the North Staffordshire Hounds, and the *Signal* had stated that she was a fearless horsewoman. It made this statement one day when she had been thrown and carried to Sneyd senseless.

The mule, too, seemingly conscious of its responsibilities and its high destiny, put its best foot foremost and behaved in general like a mule that knew the name of its great-grandfather. It went through Knype in admirable style, not swerving at the steam-cars nor exciting itself about the railway bridge. A photographer who stood at his door manoeuvring a large camera startled it momentarily, until it remembered that it had seen a camera before. The Countess, who wondered why on earth a photographer should be capering round a tripod in a doorway, turned to inspect the man with her lorgnon.

They were now coursing up the Cauldon Bank towards Hanbridge. They were already within the boundaries of Hanbridge, and a pedestrian here and there recognised the Countess. You can hide nothing from the quidnunc of Hanbridge. Moreover, when a quidnunc in the streets of Hanbridge sees somebody famous or striking, or notorious, he does not pretend that he has seen nobody. He points unmistakably to what he has observed, if he has a companion, and if he has no companion he stands still and stares with such honest intensity that the entire street stands and stares too. Occasionally you may see an entire street standing and staring without any idea of what it is staring at. As the equipage dashingly approached the busy centre of Hanbridge, the region of fine shops, public-houses, hotels, halls, and theatres, more and more of the inhabitants knew that Iris (as they affectionately called her) was driving with a young man in a tumble-down little victoria behind a mule whose ears flapped like an elephant's. Denry being far less renowned in Hanbridge than in his native Bursley, few persons recognised him. After the victoria had gone by people who had heard the news too late rushed from shops and gazed at the Countess's back as at a fading dream until the insistent clang of a car-bell made them jump again to the footpath.

At length Denry and the Countess could see the clock of the Old Town Hall in Crown Square and it was a minute to three. They were less than a minute off the Institute.

"There you are!" said Denry, proudly. "Three miles if it's a yard, in seventeen minutes. For a mule it's none so dusty."

And such was the Countess's knowledge of the language of the Five Towns that she instantly divined the meaning of even that phrase, "none so dusty."

They swept into Crown Square grandly.

And then, with no warning, the mule suddenly applied all the automatic brakes which a mule has, and stopped.

"Oh Lor!" sighed Denry. He knew the cause of that arresting.

A large squad of policemen, a perfect regiment of policemen, was moving across the north side of the square in the direction of the Institute. Nothing could have seemed more reassuring, less harmful, than that band of policemen, off duty for the afternoon and collected together for the purpose of giving a hearty and policemanly welcome to their benefactress the Countess. But the mule had his own views about policemen. In the early days of Denry's ownership of him he had nearly always shied at the spectacle of a policemen. He would tolerate steam-rollers, and even falling kites, but a policeman had ever been antipathetic to him. Denry, by patience and punishment, had gradually brought him round almost to the Countess's views of policemen—namely, that they were a courteous and trustworthy body of public servants, not to be treated as scarecrows or the dregs of society. At any rate, the mule had of late months practically ceased to set his face against the policing of the Five Towns. And when he was on his best behaviour he would ignore a policeman completely.

But there were several hundreds of policemen in that squad, the majority of all the policemen in the Five Towns. And clearly the mule considered that Denry, in confronting him with several hundred policemen simultaneously, had been presuming upon his good-nature.

The mule's ears were saying agitatedly:

"A line must be drawn somewhere, and I have drawn it where my forefeet now are."

The mule's ears soon drew together a little crowd.

It occurred to Denry that if mules were so wonderful in the Apennines the reason must be that there are no policemen in the Apennines. It also occurred to him that something must be done to this mule.

"Well?" said the Countess, inquiringly.

It was a challenge to him to prove that he and not the mule was in charge of the expedition.

He briefly explained the mule's idiosyncrasy, as it were apologising for its bad taste in objecting to public servants whom the Countess cherished.

"They'll be out of sight in a moment," said the Countess. And both she and Demo tried to look as if the victoria had stopped in that special spot for a special reason, and that the mule was a pattern of obedience. Nevertheless, the little crowd was growing a little larger.

"Now," said the Countess, encouragingly. The tail of the regiment of policemen had vanished towards the Institute.

"Tchk! Tchk!" Denry persuaded the mule.

No response from those forefeet!

"Perhaps I'd better get out and walk," the Countess suggested. The crowd was becoming inconvenient, and had even begun to offer unsolicited hints as to the proper management of mules. The crowd was also saying to itself: "It's her! It's her! It's her!" Meaning that it was the Countess.

"Oh no," said Denry, "it's all right."

And he caught the mule "one" over the head with his whip.

The mule, stung into action, dashed away, and the crowd scattered as if blown to pieces by the explosion of a bomb. Instead of pursuing a right line the mule turned within a radius of its own length, swinging the victoria round after it as though the victoria had been a kettle attached to it with string. And Countess, Denry, and victoria were rapt with miraculous swiftness away—not at all towards the Policemen's Institute, but down Longshaw Road, which is tolerably steep. They were pursued, but ineffectually. For the mule had bolted and was winged. They fortunately came into contact with nothing except a large barrow of carrots, turnips, and cabbages which an old woman was wheeling up Longshaw Road. The concussion upset the barrow, half filled the victoria with vegetables, and for a second stayed the mule; but no real harm seemed to have been done, and the mule proceeded with vigour. Then the Countess noticed that Denry was not using his right arm, which swung about rather uselessly.

"I must have knocked my elbow against the barrow," he muttered. His face was pale.

"Give me the reins," said the Countess.

"I think I can turn the brute up here," he said.

And he did in fact neatly divert the mule up Birches Street, which is steeper even than Longshaw Road. The mule for a few instants pretended that all gradients, up or down, were equal before its angry might. But Birches Street has the slope of a house-roof. Presently the mule walked, and then it stood still. And half Birches Street emerged to gaze, for the Countess's attire was really very splendid.

"I'll leave this here, and we'll walk back," said Denry. "You won't be late— that is, nothing to speak of. The Institute is just round the top here."

"You don't mean to say you're going to let that mule beat you?" exclaimed the Countess.

"I was only thinking of your being late."

"Oh, bother!" said she. "Your mule may be ruined." The horse-trainer in her was aroused.

"And then my arm?" said Denry.

"Shall I drive back?" the Countess suggested.

"Oh, do," said Denry. "Keep on up the street, and then to the left."

They changed places, and two minutes later she brought the mule to an obedient rest in front of the Police Institute, which was all newly red with terra-cotta. The main body of policemen had passed into the building, but two remained at the door, and the mule haughtily tolerated them. The Countess despatched one to Longshaw Road to settle with the old woman whose vegetables they had brought away with them. The other policeman, who, owing to the Countess's philanthropic energy, had received a course of instruction in first aid, arranged a sling for Denry's arm. And then the Countess said that Denry ought certainly to go with her to the inauguration ceremony. The policeman whistled a boy to hold the mule. Denry picked a carrot out of the complex folds of the Countess's rich costume. And the Countess and her saviour entered the portico and were therein met by an imposing group of important male personages, several of whom wore mayoral chains. Strange tales of what had happened to the Countess had already flown up to the Institute, and the chief expression on the faces of the group seemed to be one of astonishment that she still lived.

IV

Denry observed that the Countess was now a different woman. She had suddenly put on a manner to match her costume, which in certain parts was stiff with embroidery. From the informal companion and the tamer of mules she had miraculously developed into the public celebrity, the peeress of the realm, and the inaugurator-general of philanthropic schemes and buildings. Not one of the important male personages but would have looked down on Denry!

And yet, while treating Denry as a jolly equal, the Countess with all her embroidered and stiff politeness somehow looked down on the important male personages—and they knew it. And the most curious thing was that they seemed rather to enjoy it. The one who seemed to enjoy it the least was Sir Jehoshophat Dain, a white-bearded pillar of terrific imposingness.

Sir Jee—as he was then beginning to be called—had recently been knighted, by way of reward for his enormous benefactions to the community. In the *rôle* of philanthropist he was really much more effective than the Countess. But he was not young, he was not pretty, he was not a woman, and his family had not helped to rule England for generations—at any rate, so far as anybody knew. He had made more money than had ever before been made by a single brain in the manufacture of earthenware, and he had given more money to public causes than a single pocket had ever before given in the Five Towns. He had never sought municipal honours, considering himself to be somewhat above such trifles. He was the first purely local man to be knighted in the Five Towns. Even before the bestowal of the knighthood his sense of humour had been deficient, and immediately afterwards it had vanished entirely. Indeed, he did not miss it. He divided the population of the kingdom into two classes—the titled and the untitled. With Sir Jee, either you were titled, or you weren't. He lumped all the untitled together; and to be just to his logical faculty, he lumped all the titled together. There were various titles—Sir Jee admitted that—but a title was a title, and therefore all titles were practically equal. The Duke of Norfolk was one titled individual, and Sir Jee was another. The fine difference between them might be perceptible to the titled, and might properly be recognised by the titled when the titled were among themselves, but for the untitled such a difference ought not to exist and could not exist.

Thus for Sir Jee there were two titled beings in the group—the Countess and himself. The Countess and himself formed one caste in the group, and the rest another caste. And although the Countess, in her punctilious demeanour towards him, gave due emphasis to his title (he returning more than due emphasis to hers), he was not precisely pleased by the undertones of suave condescension that characterised her greeting of him as well as her greeting of the others. Moreover, he had known Denry as a clerk of Mr Duncalf's, for Mr Duncalf had done a lot of legal work for him in the past. He looked upon Denry as an upstart, a capering mountebank, and he strongly resented Denry's familiarity with the Countess. He further resented Denry's sling, which gave to Denry an interesting romantic aspect (despite his beard), and he more than all resented that Denry should have rescued the Countess from a carriage accident by means of his preposterous mule. Whenever the Countess, in the preliminary chatter, referred to Denry or looked at Denry, in recounting the history of her adventures, Sir Jee's soul squirmed, and his body sympathised with his soul. Something in him that was more powerful than himself compelled him to do his utmost to reduce Denry to a moral pulp, to flatten him, to ignore him, or to exterminate him by the application of ice. This tactic was no more lost on the Countess than it was on Denry. And the Countess foiled it at every instant. In truth, there existed between the Countess and Sir Jee a rather hot rivalry in philanthropy and the cultivation of the higher welfare of the district. He regarded himself, and she regarded herself, as the most brightly glittering star of the Five Towns.

When the Countess had finished the recital of her journey, and the faces of the group had gone through all the contortions proper to express terror, amazement, admiration, and manly sympathy, Sir Jee took the lead, coughed, and said in his elaborate style:

"Before we adjourn to the hall, will not your ladyship take a little refreshment?"

"Oh no, thanks," said the Countess. "I'm not a bit upset." Then she turned to the enslinged Denry and with concern added: "But will *you* have something?"

If she could have foreseen the consequences of her question, she might never have put it. Still, she might have put it just the same.

Denry paused an instant, and an old habit rose up in him.

"Oh no, thanks," he said, and turning deliberately to Sir Jee, he added: "Will *you?*"

This, of course, was mere crude insolence to the titled philanthropic white-beard. But it was by no means the worst of Denry's behaviour. The group—every member of the group—distinctly perceived a movement of Denry's left hand towards Sir Jee. It was the very slightest movement, a wavering, a nothing. It would have had no significance whatever, but for one fact. Denry's left hand still held the carrot.

Everybody exhibited the most marvellous self-control. And everybody except Sir Jee was secretly charmed, for Sir Jee had never inspired love. It is remarkable how local philanthropists are unloved, locally. The Countess, without blenching, gave the signal for what Sir Jee called the "adjournment" to the hall. Nothing might have happened, yet everything had happened.

V

Next, Denry found himself seated on the temporary platform which had been erected in the large games hall of the Policemen's Institute.

The Mayor of Hanbridge was in the chair, and he had the Countess on his right and the Mayoress of Bursley on his left. Other mayoral chains blazed in the centre of the platform, together with fine hats of mayoresses and uniforms of police-superintendents and captains of fire-brigades. Denry's sling also contributed to the effectiveness; he was placed behind the Countess. Policemen (looking strange without helmets) and their wives, sweethearts, and friends, filled the hall to its fullest; enthusiasm was rife and strident; and there was only one little sign that the untoward had occurred. That little sign was an empty chair in the first row near the Countess. Sir Jee, a prey to a sudden indisposition, had departed. He had somehow faded away, while the personages were climbing the stairs. He had faded away amid the expressed regrets of those few who by chance saw him in the act of fading. But even these bore up manfully. The high humour of the gathering was not eclipsed.

Towards the end of the ceremony came the votes of thanks, and the principal of these was the vote of thanks to the Countess, prime cause of the Institute. It was proposed by the Superintendent of the Hanbridge Police. Other personages had wished to propose it, but the stronger right of the Hanbridge Superintendent, as chief officer of the largest force of constables in the Five Towns, could not be disputed. He made a few facetious references to the episode of the Countess's arrival, and brought the house down by saying that if he did his duty he would arrest both the Countess and Denry for driving to the common danger. When he sat down, amid tempestuous applause, there was a hitch. According to the official programme Sir Jehoshophat Dain was to have seconded the vote, and Sir Jee was not there. All that remained of Sir Jee was his chair. The Mayor of Hanbridge looked round about, trying swiftly to make up his mind what was to be done, and Denry heard him whisper to another mayor for advice.

"Shall I do it?" Denry whispered, and by at once rising relieved the Mayor from the necessity of coming to a decision.

Impossible to say why Denry should have risen as he did, without any warning. Ten seconds before, five seconds before, he himself had not the dimmest idea that he was about to address the meeting. All that can be said is that he was subject to these attacks of the unexpected.

Once on his legs he began to suffer, for he had never before been on his legs on a platform, or even on a platform at all. He could see nothing whatever except a cloud that had mysteriously and with frightful suddenness filled the room. And through this cloud he could feel that hundreds and hundreds of eyes were piercingly fixed upon him. A voice was saying inside him—"What a fool you are! What a fool you are! I always told you you were a fool!" And his heart was beating as it had never beat, and his forehead was damp, his throat distressingly dry, and one foot nervously tap-tapping on the floor. This condition lasted for something like ten hours, during which time the eyes continued to pierce the cloud and him with patient, obstinate cruelty.

Denry heard some one talking. It was himself.

The Superintendent had said: "I have very great pleasure in proposing the vote of thanks to the Countess of Chell."

And so Denry heard himself saying: "I have very great pleasure in seconding the vote of thanks to the Countess of Chell."

He could not think of anything else to say. And there was a pause, a real pause, not a pause merely in Denry's sick imagination.

Then the cloud was dissipated. And Denry himself said to the audience of policemen, with his own natural tone, smile and gesture, colloquially, informally, comically:

"Now then! Move along there, please! I'm not going to say any more!"

And for a signal he put his hands in the position for applauding. And sat down.

He had tickled the stout ribs of every bobby in the place. The applause surpassed all previous applause. The most staid ornaments of the platform had to laugh. People nudged each other and explained that it was "that chap Machin from Bursley," as if to imply that that chap Machin from Bursley never let a day pass without doing something striking and humorous. The Mayor was still smiling when he put the vote to the meeting, and the Countess was still smiling when she responded.

Afterwards in the portico, when everything was over, Denry exercised his right to remain in charge of the Countess. They escaped from the personages by going out to look for her carriage and neglecting to return. There was no sign of the Countess's carriage, but Denry's mule and victoria were waiting in a quiet corner.

"May I drive you home?" he suggested.

But she would not. She said that she had a call to pay before dinner, and that her brougham would surely arrive the very next minute.

"Will you come and have tea at the Sub Rosa?" Denry next asked.

"The Sub Rosa?" questioned the Countess.

"Well," said Denry, "that's what we call the new tea-room that's just been opened round here." He indicated a direction. "It's quite a novelty in the Five Towns."

The Countess had a passion for tea.

"They have splendid China tea," said Denry.

"Well," said the Countess, "I suppose I may as well go through with it."

At the moment her brougham drove up. She instructed her coachman to wait next to the mule and victoria. Her demeanour had cast off all its similarity to her dress: it appeared to imply that, as she had begun with a mad escapade, she ought to finish with another one.

Thus the Countess and Denry went to the tea-shop, and Denry ordered tea and paid for it. There was scarcely a customer in the place, and the few who were fortunate enough to be present had not the wit to recognise the Countess. The proprietress did not recognise the Countess. (Later, when it became known that the Countess had actually patronised the Sub Rosa, half the ladies of Hanbridge were almost ill from sheer disgust that they had not heard of it in time. It would have been so easy for them to be there, taking tea at the next table to the Countess, and observing her choice of cakes, and her manner of holding a spoon, and whether she removed her gloves or retained them in the case of a meringue. It was an opportunity lost that would in all human probability never occur again.)

And in the discreet corner which she had selected the Countess fired a sudden shot at Denry.

"How did you get all those details about the state rooms at Sneyd?" she asked.

Upon which opening the conversation became lively.

The same evening Denry called at the *Signal* office and gave an order for a half-page advertisement of the Five Towns Universal Thrift Club—"Patroness, the Countess of Chell." The advertisement informed the public that the club had now made arrangements to accept new members. Besides the order for a half-page advertisement, Denry also gave many interesting and authentic details about the historic drive from Sneyd Vale to Hanbridge. The next day the *Signal* was simply full of Denry and the Countess. It had a large photograph, taken by a photographer on Cauldon Bank, which showed Denry actually driving the Countess, and the Countess's face was full in the picture. It presented, too, an excellently appreciative account of Denry's speech, and it congratulated Denry on his first appearance in the public life of the Five Towns. (In parenthesis it sympathised with Sir Jee in his indisposition.) In short, Denry's triumph obliterated the memory of his previous triumphs. It obliterated, too, all rumours adverse to the Thrift Club. In a few days he had a thousand new members. Of course, this addition only increased his liabilities; but now he could obtain capital on fair terms, and he did obtain it. A company was formed. The Countess had a few shares in this company. So (strangely) had Jock and his companion the coachman. Not the least of the mysteries was that when Denry reached his mother's cottage on the night of the tea with the Countess, his arm was not in a sling, and showed no symptom of having been damaged.

CHAPTER VIII

RAISING A WIGWAM

I

A still young man—his age was thirty—with a short, strong beard peeping out over the fur collar of a vast overcoat, emerged from a cab at the snowy corner of St Luke's Square and Brougham Street, and paid the cabman with a gesture that indicated both wealth and the habit of command. And the cabman, who had driven him over from Hanbridge through the winter night, responded accordingly. Few people take cabs in the Five Towns. There are few cabs to take. If you are going to a party you may order one in advance by telephone, reconciling yourself also in advance to the expense, but to hail a cab in the street without forethought and jump into it as carelessly as you would jump into a tram—this is by very few done. The young man with the beard did it frequently, which proved that he was fundamentally ducal.

He was encumbered with a large and rather heavy parcel as he walked down Brougham Street, and, moreover, the footpath of Brougham Street was exceedingly dirty. And yet no one acquainted with the circumstances of his life would have asked why he had dismissed the cab before arriving at his destination, because every one knew. The reason was that this ducal person, with the gestures of command, dared not drive up to his mother's door in a cab oftener than about once a month. He opened that door with a latch-key (a modern lock was almost the only innovation that he had succeeded in fixing on his mother), and stumbled with his unwieldy parcel into the exceedingly narrow lobby.

"Is that you, Denry?" called a feeble voice from the parlour.

"Yes," said he, and went into the parlour, hat, fur coat, parcel, and all.

Mrs Machin, in a shawl and an antimacassar over the shawl, sat close to the fire and leaning towards it. She looked cold and ill. Although the parlour was very tiny and the fire comparatively large, the structure of the grate made it impossible that the room should be warm, as all the heat went up the chimney. If Mrs Machin had sat on the roof and put her hands over the top of the chimney, she would have been much warmer than at the grate.

"You aren't in bed?" Denry queried.

"Can't ye see?" said his mother. And, indeed, to ask a woman who was obviously sitting up in a chair whether she was in bed, did seem somewhat absurd. She added, less sarcastically: "I was expecting ye every minute. Where have ye had your tea?"

"Oh!" he said lightly, "in Hanbridge."

An untruth! He had not had his tea anywhere. But he had dined richly at the new Hôtel Métropole, Hanbridge.

"What have ye got there?" asked his mother.

"A present for you," said Denry. "It's your birthday to-morrow."

"I don't know as I want reminding of that," murmured Mrs Machin.

But when he had undone the parcel and held up the contents before her, she exclaimed:

"Bless us!"

The staggered tone was an admission that for once in a way he had impressed her.

It was a magnificent sealskin mantle, longer than sealskin mantles usually are. It was one of those articles the owner of which can say: "Nobody can have a better than this—I don't care who she is." It was worth in monetary value all the plain, shabby clothes on Mrs Machin's back, and all her very ordinary best clothes upstairs, and all the furniture in the entire house, and perhaps all Denry's dandiacal wardrobe too, except his fur coat. If the entire contents of the cottage, with the aforesaid exception, had been put up to auction, they would not have realised enough to pay for that sealskin mantle.

Had it been anything but a sealskin mantle, and equally costly, Mrs Machin would have upbraided. But a sealskin mantle is not "showy." It "goes with" any and every dress and bonnet. And the most respectable, the most conservative, the most austere woman may find legitimate pleasure in wearing it. A sealskin mantle is the sole luxurious ostentation that a woman of Mrs Machin's temperament— and there are many such in the Five Towns and elsewhere—will conscientiously permit herself.

"Try it on," said Denry.

She rose weakly and tried it on. It fitted as well as a sealskin mantle can fit.

"My word—it's warm!" she said. This was her sole comment.

"Keep it on," said Denry.

His mother's glance withered the suggestion.

"Where are you going?" he asked, as she left the room.

"To put it away," said she. "I must get some moth-powder to-morrow."

He protested with inarticulate noises, removed his own furs, which he threw down on to the old worn-out sofa, and drew a Windsor chair up to the fire. After a while his mother returned, and sat down in her rocking-chair, and began to shiver again under the shawl and the antimacassar. The lamp on the table lighted up the left side of her face and the right side of his.

"Look here, mother," said he, "you must have a doctor."

"I shall have no doctor."

"You've got influenza, and it's a very tricky business—influenza is; you never know where you are with it."

"Ye can call it influenza if ye like," said Mrs Machin. "There was no influenza in my young days. We called a cold a cold."

"Well," said Denry, "you aren't well, are you?"

"I never said I was," she answered grimly.

"No," said Denry, with the triumphant ring of one who is about to devastate an enemy. "And you never will be in this rotten old cottage."

"This was reckoned a very good class of house when your father and I came into it. And it's always been kept in repair. It was good enough for your father, and it's good enough for me. I don't see myself flitting. But some folks have gotten so grand. As for health, old Reuben next door is ninety-one. How many people over ninety are there in those gimcrack houses up by the Park, I should like to know?"

Denry could argue with any one save his mother. Always, when he was about to reduce her to impotence, she fell on him thus and rolled him in the dust. Still, he began again.

"Do we pay four-and-sixpence a week for this cottage, or don't we?" he demanded.

"And always have done," said Mrs Machin. "I should like to see the landlord put it up," she added, formidably, as if to say: "I'd landlord him, if he tried to put *my* rent up!"

"Well," said Denry, "here we are living in a four-and-six-a-week cottage, and do you know how much I'm making? I'm making two thousand pounds a year. That's what I'm making."

A second wilful deception of his mother! As Managing Director of the Five Towns Universal Thrift Club, as proprietor of the majority of its shares, as its absolute autocrat, he was making very nearly four thousand a year. Why could he not as easily have said four as two to his mother? The simple answer is that he was afraid to say four. It was as if he ought to blush before his mother for being so plutocratic, his mother who had passed most of her life in hard toil to gain a few shillings a week. Four thousand seemed so fantastic! And in fact the Thrift Club, which he had invented in a moment, had arrived at a prodigious success, with its central offices in Hanbridge and its branch offices in the other four towns, and its scores of clerks and collectors presided over by Mr Penkethman. It had met with opposition. The mighty said that Denry was making an unholy fortune under the guise of philanthropy. And to be on the safe side the Countess of Chell had resigned her official patronage of the club and given her shares to the Pirehill Infirmary, which had accepted the high dividends on them without the least protest. As for Denry, he said that he had never set out to be a philanthropist nor posed as one, and that his unique intention was to grow rich by supplying a want, like the rest of them, and that anyhow there was no compulsion to belong to his Thrift Club. Then letters in his defence from representatives of the thousands and thousands of members of the club rained into the columns of the *Signal*, and Denry was the most discussed personage in the county. It was stated that such thrift clubs, under various names, existed in several large towns in Yorkshire and Lancashire. This disclosure rehabilitated Denry completely in general esteem, for whatever obtains in Yorkshire and Lancashire must be right for Staffordshire; but it rather dashed Denry, who was obliged to admit to himself that after all he had not invented the Thrift Club. Finally the hundreds of tradesmen who had bound themselves to allow a discount of twopence in the shilling to the club (sole source of the club's dividends) had endeavoured to revolt. Denry effectually cowed them by threatening to establish co-operative stores—there was not a single co-operative store in the Five Towns. They knew he would have the wild audacity to do it.

Thenceforward the progress of the Thrift Club had been unruffled. Denry waxed amazingly in importance. His mule died. He dared not buy a proper horse and dogcart, because he dared not bring such an equipage to the front door of his mother's four-and-sixpenny cottage. So he had taken to cabs. In all exterior magnificence and lavishness he equalled even the great Harold Etches, of whom he had once been afraid; and like Etches he became a famous *habitué* of Llandudno pier. But whereas Etches lived with his wife in a superb house at Bleakridge, Denry lived with his mother in a ridiculous cottage in ridiculous Brougham Street. He had a regiment of acquaintances and he accepted a lot of hospitality, but he could not return it at Brougham Street. His greatness fizzled into nothing in Brougham Street. It stopped short and sharp at the corner of St Luke's Square, where he left his cabs. He could do nothing with his mother. If she was not still going out as a sempstress the reason was, not that she was not ready to go out, but that her old clients had ceased to send for her. And could they be blamed for not employing at three shillings a day the mother of a young man who wallowed in thousands sterling? Denry had essayed over and over again to instil reason into his mother, and he had invariably failed. She was too independent, too profoundly rooted in her habits; and her character had more force than his. Of course, he might have left her and set up a suitably gorgeous house of his own.

But he would not.

In fact, they were a remarkable pair.

On this eve of her birthday he had meant to cajole her into some step, to win her by an appeal, basing his argument on her indisposition. But he was being beaten off once more. The truth was that a cajoling, caressing tone could not be long employed towards Mrs Machin. She was not persuasive herself, nor; favourable to persuasiveness in others.

"Well," said she, "if you're making two thousand a year, ye can spend it or save it as ye like, though ye'd better save it. Ye never know what may happen in these days. There was a man dropped half-a-crown down a grid opposite only the day before yesterday."

Denry laughed.

"Ay!" she said; "ye can laugh."

"There's no doubt about one thing," he said, "you ought to be in bed. You ought to stay in bed for two or three days at least."

"Yes," she said. "And who's going to look after the house while I'm moping between blankets?"

"You can have Rose Chudd in," he said.

"No," said she. "I'm not going to have any woman rummaging about my house, and me in bed."

"You know perfectly well she's been practically starving since her husband died, and as she's going out charing, why can't you have her and put a bit of bread into her mouth?"

"Because I won't have her! Neither her nor any one. There's naught to prevent you giving her some o' your two thousand a year if you've a mind. But I

96

see no reason for my house being turned upside down by her, even if I *have* got a bit of a cold."

"You're an unreasonable old woman," said Denry.

"Happen I am!" said she. "There can't be two wise ones in a family. But I'm not going to give up this cottage, and as long as I am standing on my feet I'm not going to pay any one for doing what I can do better myself." A pause. "And so you needn't think it! You can't come round me with a fur mantle." She retired to rest. On the following morning he was very glum.

"You needn't be so glum," she said.

But she was rather pleased at his glumness. For in him glumness was a sign that he recognised defeat.

II

The next episode between them was curiously brief. Denry had influenza. He said that naturally he had caught hers.

He went to bed and stayed there. She nursed him all day, and grew angry in a vain attempt to force him to eat. Towards night he tossed furiously on the little bed in the little bedroom, complaining of fearful headaches. She remained by his side most of the night. In the morning he was easier. Neither of them mentioned the word "doctor." She spent the day largely on the stairs. Once more towards night he grew worse, and she remained most of the second night by his side.

In the sinister winter dawn Denry murmured in a feeble tone:

"Mother, you'd better send for him."

"Doctor?" she said. And secretly she thought that she *had* better send for the doctor, and that there must be after all some difference between influenza and a cold.

"No," said Denry; "send for young Lawton."

"Young Lawton!" she exclaimed. "What do you want young Lawton to come *here* for?"

"I haven't made my will," Denry answered.

"Pooh!" she retorted.

Nevertheless she was the least bit in the world frightened. And she sent for Dr Stirling, the aged Harrop's Scotch partner.

Dr Stirling, who was full-bodied and left little space for anybody else in the tiny, shabby bedroom of the man with four thousand a year, gazed at Mrs Machin, and he gazed also at Denry.

"Ye must go to bed this minute," said he.

"But he's *in* bed," cried Mrs Machin.

"I mean yerself," said Dr Stirling.

She was very nearly at the end of her resources. And the proof was that she had no strength left to fight Dr Stirling. She did go to bed. And shortly afterwards Denry got up. And a little later, Rose Chudd, that prim and efficient young widow from lower down the street, came into the house and controlled it as if it had been her own. Mrs Machin, whose constitution was hardy, arose in about a week, cured, and duly dismissed Rose with wages and without thanks. But Rose had been. Like the *Signal's* burglars, she had "effected an entrance." And the house had not been turned upside down. Mrs Machin, though she tried, could not find fault with the result of Rose's uncontrolled activities.

III

One morning—and not very long afterwards, in such wise did Fate seem to favour the young at the expense of the old—Mrs Machin received two letters which alarmed and disgusted her. One was from her landlord, announcing that he had sold the house in which she lived to a Mr Wilbraham of London, and that in future she must pay the rent to the said Mr Wilbraham or his legal representatives. The other was from a firm of London solicitors announcing that their client, Mr Wilbraham, had bought the house, and that the rent must be paid to their agent, whom they would name later.

Mrs Machin gave vent to her emotion in her customary manner: "Bless us!"

And she showed the impudent letters to Denry.

"Oh!" said Denry. "So he has bought them, has he? I heard he was going to."

"Them?" exclaimed Mrs Machin. "What else has he bought?"

"I expect he's bought all the five—this and the four below, as far as Downes's. I expect you'll find that the other four have had notices just like these. You know all this row used to belong to the Wilbrahams. You surely must remember that, mother?"

"Is he one of the Wilbrahams of Hillport, then?"

"Yes, of course he is."

"I thought the last of 'em was Cecil, and when he'd beggared himself here he went to Australia and died of drink. That's what I always heard. We always used to say as there wasn't a Wilbraham left."

"He did go to Australia, but he didn't die of drink. He disappeared, and when he'd made a fortune he turned up again in Sydney, so it seems. I heard he's thinking of coming back here to settle. Anyhow, he's buying up a lot of the Wilbraham property. I should have thought you'd have heard of it. Why, lots of people have been talking about it."

"Well," said Mrs Machin, "I don't like it."

She objected to a law which permitted a landlord to sell a house over the head of a tenant who had occupied it for more than thirty years. In the course of the morning she discovered that Denry was right—the other tenants had received notices exactly similar to hers.

Two days later Denry arrived home for tea with a most surprising article of news. Mr Cecil Wilbraham had been down to Bursley from London, and had visited him, Denry. Mr Cecil Wilbraham's local information was evidently quite out of date, for he had imagined Denry to be a rent-collector and estate agent, whereas the fact was that Denry had abandoned this minor vocation years ago. His desire had been that Denry should collect his rents and watch over his growing interests in the district.

"So what did you tell him?" asked Mrs Machin.

"I told him I'd do it." said Denry.

"Why?"

"I thought it might be safer for *you*," said Denry, with a certain emphasis. "And, besides, it looked as if it might be a bit of a lark. He's a very peculiar chap."

"Peculiar?"

"For one thing, he's got the largest moustaches of any man I ever saw. And there's something up with his left eye. And then I think he's a bit mad."

"Mad?"

"Well, touched. He's got a notion about building a funny sort of a house for himself on a plot of land at Bleakridge. It appears he's fond of living alone, and he's collected all kind of dodges for doing without servants and still being comfortable."

"Ay! But he's right there!" breathed Mrs Machin in deep sympathy. As she said about once a week, "She never could abide the idea of servants." "He's not married, then?" she added.

"He told me he'd been a widower three times, but he'd never had any children," said Denry.

"Bless us!" murmured Mrs Machin.

Denry was the one person in the town who enjoyed the acquaintance and the confidence of the thrice-widowed stranger with long moustaches. He had descended without notice on Bursley, seen Denry (at the branch office of the Thrift Club), and then departed. It was understood that later he would permanently settle in the district. Then the wonderful house began to rise on the plot of land at Bleakridge. Denry had general charge of it, but always subject to erratic and autocratic instructions from London. Thanks to Denry, who, since the historic episode at Llandudno, had remained very friendly with the Cotterill family, Mr Cotterill had the job of building the house; the plans came from London. And though Mr Cecil Wilbraham proved to be exceedingly watchful against any form of imposition, the job was a remunerative one for Mr Cotterill, who talked a great deal about the originality of the residence. The town judged of the wealth and importance of Mr Cecil Wilbraham by the fact that a person so wealthy and important as Denry should be content to act as his agent. But then the Wilbrahams had been magnates in the Bursley region for generations, up till the final Wilbraham smash in the late seventies. The town hungered to see those huge moustaches and that peculiar eye. In addition to Denry, only one person had seen the madman, and that person was Nellie Cotterill, who had been viewing the half-built house with Denry one Sunday morning when the madman had most astonishingly arrived upon the scene, and after a few minutes vanished. The building of the house strengthened greatly the friendship between Denry and the Cotterills. Yet Denry neither liked Mr Cotterill nor trusted him. The next incident in these happening was that Mrs Machin received notice from the London firm to quit her four-and-sixpence-a-week cottage. It seemed to her that not merely Brougham Street, but the world, was coming to an end. She was very angry with Denry for not protecting her more successfully. He was Mr Wilbraham's agent, he collected the rent, and it was his duty to guard his mother from unpleasantness. She observed, however, that he was remarkably disturbed by the notice, and he assured her that Mr Wilbraham had not consulted him in the matter at all. He wrote a letter to London, which she signed, demanding the reason of this absurd notice flung at an ancient and perfect tenant. The reply was that Mr Wilbraham intended to pull the houses down, beginning with Mrs Machin's, and rebuild.

"Pooh!" said Denry. "Don't you worry your head, mother; I shall arrange it. He'll be down here soon to see his new house—it's practically finished, and the furniture is coming in—and I'll just talk to him."

But Mr Wilbraham did not come, the explanation doubtless being that he was mad. On the other hand, fresh notices came with amazing frequency. Mrs Machin just handed them over to Denry. And then Denry received a telegram to say that Mr Wilbraham would be at his new house that night and wished to see Denry there. Unfortunately, on the same day, by the afternoon post, while Denry was at his offices, there arrived a sort of supreme and ultimate notice from London to Mrs Machin, and it was on blue paper. It stated, baldly, that as Mrs Machin had failed to comply with all the previous notices, had, indeed, ignored them, she and her goods would now be ejected into the street, according to the law. It gave her twenty-four hours to flit. Never had a respectable dame been so insulted as Mrs Machin was insulted by that notice. The prospect of camping out in Brougham Street confronted her. When Denry reached home that evening, Mrs Machin, as the phrase is, "gave it him."

Denry admitted frankly that he was nonplussed, staggered and outraged. But the thing was simply another proof of Mr Wilbraham's madness. After tea he decided that his mother must put on her best clothes, and go up with him to see Mr Wilbraham and firmly expostulate—in fact, they would arrange the situation between them; and if Mr Wilbraham was obstinate they would defy Mr Wilbraham. Denry explained to his mother that an Englishwoman's cottage was her castle, that a landlord's minions had no right to force an entrance, and that the one thing that Mr Wilbraham could do was to begin unbuilding the cottage from the top outside.... And he would like to see Mr Wilbraham try it on!

So the sealskin mantle (for it was spring again) went up with Denry to Bleakridge.

IV

The moon shone in the chill night. The house stood back from Trafalgar Road in the moonlight—a squarish block of a building.

"Oh!" said Mrs Machin, "it isn't so large."

"No! He didn't want it large. He only wanted it large enough," said Denry, and pushed a button to the right of the front door. There was no reply, though they heard the ringing of the bell inside. They waited. Mrs Machin was very nervous, but thanks to her sealskin mantle she was not cold.

"This is a funny doorstep," she remarked, to kill time.

"It's of marble," said Denry.

"What's that for?" asked his mother.

"So much easier to keep clean," said Denry.

"Well," said Mrs Machin, "it's pretty dirty now, anyway."

It was.

"Quite simple to clean," said Denry, bending down. "You just turn this tap at the side. You see, it's so arranged that it sends a flat jet along the step. Stand off a second."

He turned the tap, and the step was washed pure in a moment.

"How is it that that water steams?" Mrs Machin demanded.

"Because it's hot," said Denry. "Did you ever know water steam for any other reason?"

"Hot water outside?"

"Just as easy to have hot water outside as inside, isn't it?" said Denry.

"Well, I never!" exclaimed Mrs Machin. She was impressed.

"That's how everything's dodged up in this house," said Denry. He shut off the water.

And he rang once again. No answer! No illumination within the abode!

"I'll tell you what I shall do," said Denry at length. "I shall let myself in. I've got a key of the back door."

"Are you sure it's all right?"

"I don't care if it isn't all right," said Denry, defiantly. "He asked me to be up here, and he ought to be here to meet me. I'm not going to stand any nonsense from anybody."

In they went, having skirted round the walls of the house.

Denry closed the door, pushed a switch, and the electric light shone. Electric light was then quite a novelty in Bursley. Mrs Machin had never seen it in action. She had to admit that it was less complicated than oil-lamps. In the kitchen the electric light blazed upon walls tiled in grey and a floor tiled in black and white. There was a gas range and a marble slopstone with two taps. The woodwork was dark. Earthenware saucepans stood on a shelf. The cupboards were full of gear chiefly in earthenware. Denry began to exhibit to his mother a tank provided with ledges and shelves and grooves, in which he said that everything except knives could be washed and dried automatically.

"Hadn't you better go and find your Mr Wilbraham?" she interrupted.

"So I had," said Denry; "I was forgetting him."

She heard him wandering over the house and calling in divers tones upon Mr Wilbraham. But she heard no other voice. Meanwhile she examined the kitchen in detail, appreciating some of its devices and failing to comprehend others.

"I expect he's missed the train," said Denry, coming back. "Anyhow, he isn't here. I may as well show you the rest of the house now."

He led her into the hall, which was radiantly lighted.

"It's quite warm here," said Mrs Machin.

"The whole house is heated by steam," said Denry. "No fireplaces."

"No fireplaces!"

"No! No fireplaces. No grates to polish, ashes to carry down, coals to carry up, mantelpieces to dust, fire-irons to clean, fenders to polish, chimneys to sweep."

"And suppose he wants a bit of fire all of a sudden in summer?"

"Gas stove in every room for emergencies," said Denry.

She glanced into a room.

"But," she cried, "it's all complete, ready! And as warm as toast."

"Yes," said Denry, "he gave orders. I can't think why on earth he isn't here."

At that moment an electric bell rang loud and sharp, and Mrs Machin jumped.

"There he is!" said Denry, moving to the door.

"Bless us! What will he think of us being here like?" Mrs Machin mumbled.

"Pooh!" said Denry, carelessly. And he opened the door.

V

Three persons stood on the newly-washed marble step—Mr and Mrs Cotterill and their daughter.

"Oh! Come in! Come in! Make yourselves quite at home. That's what *we're* doing," said Demo in blithe greeting; and added, "I suppose he's invited you too?"

And it appeared that Mr Cecil Wilbraham had indeed invited them too. He had written from London saying that he would be glad if Mr and Mrs Cotterill would "drop in" on this particular evening. Further, he had mentioned that, as be had already had the pleasure of meeting Miss Cotterill, perhaps she would accompany her parents.

"Well, he isn't here," said Denry, shaking hands. "He must have missed his train or something. He can't possibly be here now till to-morrow. But the house seems to be all ready for him...."

"Yes, my word! And how's yourself, Mrs Cotterill?" put in Mrs Machin.

"So we may as well look over it in its finished state. I suppose that's what he asked us up for," Denry concluded.

Mrs Machin explained quickly and nervously that she had not been comprised in any invitation; that her errand was pure business.

"Come on upstairs," Denry called out, turning switches and adding radiance to radiance.

"Denry!" his mother protested, "I'm sure I don't know what Mr and Mrs Cotterill will think of you! You carry on as if you owned everything in the place. I wonder *at* you!"

"Well," said Denry, "if anybody in this town is the owner's agent I am. And Mr Cotterill has built the blessed house. If Wilbraham wanted to keep his old shanty to himself, he shouldn't send out invitations. It's simple enough not to send out invitations. Now, Nellie!"

He was hanging over the balustrade at the curve of the stairs.

The familiar ease with which he said, "Now, Nellie," and especially the spontaneity of Nellie's instant response, put new thoughts into the mind of Mrs Machin. But she neither pricked up her ears, nor started back, nor accomplished any of the acrobatic feats which an ordinary mother of a wealthy son would have performed under similar circumstances. Her ears did not even tremble. And she just said:

"I like this balustrade knob being of black china."

"Every knob in the house is of black china," said Denry. "Never shows dirt. But if you should take it into your head to clean it, you can do it with a damp cloth in a second."

Nellie now stood beside him. Nellie had grown up since the Llandudno episode. She did not blush at a glance. When spoken to suddenly she could answer without torture to herself. She could, in fact, maintain a conversation without breaking down for a much longer time than, a few years ago, she had been able to skip without breaking down. She no longer imagined that all the people in the street were staring at her, anxious to find faults in her appearance. She had temporarily ruined the lives of several amiable and fairly innocent young men by refusing to marry them. (For she was pretty, and her father cut a figure in the town, though her mother did not.) And yet, despite the immense accumulation of her experiences and the weight of her varied knowledge of human nature, there was something very girlish and timidly roguish about her as she stood on the stairs near Denry, waiting for the elder generation to follow. The old Nellie still lived in her.

The party passed to the first floor.

And the first floor exceeded the ground floor in marvels. In each bedroom two aluminium taps poured hot and cold water respectively into a marble basin, and below the marble basin was a sink. No porterage of water anywhere in the house. The water came to you, and every room consumed its own slops. The bedsteads were of black enamelled iron and very light. The floors were covered with linoleum, with a few rugs that could be shaken with one hand. The walls were painted with grey enamel. Mrs Cotterill, with her all-seeing eye, observed a detail that Mrs Machin had missed. There were no sharp corners anywhere. Every corner, every angle between wall and floor or wall and wall, was rounded, to facilitate cleaning. And every wall, floor, ceiling, and fixture could be washed, and all the furniture was enamelled and could be wiped with a cloth in a moment instead of having to be polished with three cloths and many odours in a day and a half. The bath-room was absolutely waterproof; you could spray it with a hose, and by means of a gas apparatus you could produce an endless supply of hot water independent of the general supply. Denry was apparently familiar with each detail of Mr Wilbraham's manifold contrivances, and he explained them with an enormous gusto.

"Bless us!" said Mrs Machin.

"Bless us!" said Mrs Cotterill (doubtless the force of example).

They descended to the dining-room, where a supper-table had been laid by order of the invisible Mr Cecil Wilbraham. And there the ladies lauded Mr Wilbraham's wisdom in eschewing silver. Everything of the table service that could be of earthenware was of earthenware. The forks and spoons were electro-plate.

"Why," Mrs Cotterill said, "I could run this house without a servant and have myself tidy by ten o'clock in a morning."

And Mrs Machin nodded.

"And then when you want a regular turn-out, as you call it," said Denry, "there's the vacuum-cleaner."

The vacuum-cleaner was at that period the last word of civilisation, and the first agency for it was being set up in Bursley. Denry explained the vacuum-cleaner to the housewives, who had got no further than a Ewbank. And they again called down blessings on themselves.

"What price this supper?" Denry exclaimed. "We ought to eat it. I'm sure he'd like us to eat it. Do sit down, all of you. I'll take the consequences."

Mrs Machin hesitated even more than the other ladies.

"It's really very strange, him not being here." She shook her head.

"Don't I tell you he's quite mad," said Denry.

"I shouldn't think he was so mad as all that," said Mrs Machin, dryly. "This is the most sensible kind of a house I've ever seen."

"Oh! Is it?" Denry answered. "Great Scott! I never noticed those three bottles of wine on the sideboard."

At length he succeeded in seating them at the table. Thenceforward there was no difficulty. The ample and diversified cold supper began to disappear steadily, and the wine with it. And as the wine disappeared so did Mr Cotterill (who had been pompous and taciturn) grow talkative, offering to the company the exact figures of the cost of the house, and so forth. But ultimately the sheer joy of life killed arithmetic.

Mrs Machin, however, could not quite rid herself of the notion that she was in a dream that outraged the proprieties. The entire affair, for an unromantic spot like Bursley, was too fantastically and wickedly romantic.

"We must be thinking about home, Denry," said she.

"Plenty of time," Denry replied. "What! All that wine gone! I'll see if there's any more in the sideboard."

He emerged, with a red face, from bending into the deeps of the enamelled sideboard, and a wine-bottle was in his triumphant hand. It had already been opened.

"Hooray!" he proclaimed, pouring a white wine into his glass and raising the glass: "here's to the health of Mr Cecil Wilbraham."

He made a brave tableau in the brightness of the electric light.

Then he drank. Then he dropped the glass, which broke.

"Ugh! What's that?" he demanded, with the distorted features of a gargoyle.

His mother, who was seated next to him, seized the bottle. Denry's hand, in clasping the bottle, had hidden a small label, which said:

"*POISON—Nettleship's Patent Enamel-Cleaning Fluid. One wipe does it.*"

Confusion! Only Nellie Cotterill seemed to be incapable of realising that a grave accident had occurred. She had laughed throughout the supper, and she still laughed, hysterically, though she had drunk scarcely any wine. Her mother silenced her.

Denry was the first to recover.

"It'll be all right," said he, leaning back in his chair. "They always put a bit of poison in those things. It can't hurt me, really. I never noticed the label."

Mrs Machin smelt at the bottle. She could detect no odour, but the fact that she could detect no odour appeared only to increase her alarm.

"You must have an emetic instantly," she said.

"Oh no!" said Denry. "I shall be all right." And he did seem to be suddenly restored.

"You must have an emetic instantly," she repeated.

"What can I have?" he grumbled. "You can't expect to find emetics here."

"Oh yes, I can," said she. "I saw a mustard tin in a cupboard in the kitchen. Come along now, and don't be silly."

Nellie's hysteric mirth surged up again.

Denry objected to accompanying his mother into the kitchen. But he was forced to submit. She shut the door on both of them. It is probable that during the seven minutes which they spent mysteriously together in the kitchen, the practicability of the kitchen apparatus for carrying off waste products was duly tested. Denry came forth, very pale and very cross, on his mother's arm.

"There's no danger now," said his mother, easily.

Naturally the party was at an end. The Cotterills sympathised, and prepared to depart, and inquired whether Denry could walk home.

Denry replied, from a sofa, in a weak, expiring voice, that he was perfectly incapable of walking home, that his sensations were in the highest degree disconcerting, that he should sleep in that house, as the bedrooms were ready for occupation, and that he should expect his mother to remain also.

And Mrs Machin had to concur. Mrs Machin sped the Cotterills from the door as though it had been her own door. She was exceedingly angry and agitated. But she could not impart her feelings to the suffering Denry. He moaned on a bed for about half-an-hour, and then fell asleep. And in the middle of the night, in the dark, strange house, she also fell asleep.

VI

The next morning she arose and went forth, and in about half-an-hour returned. Denry was still in bed, but his health seemed to have resumed its normal excellence. Mrs Machin burst upon him in such a state of complicated excitement as he had never before seen her in.

"Denry," she cried, "what do you think?"

"What?" said he.

"I've just been down home, and they're—they're pulling the house down. All the furniture's out, and they've got all the tiles off the roof, and the windows out. And there's a regular crowd watching."

Denry sat up.

"And I can tell you another piece of news," said he. "Mr Cecil Wilbraham is dead."

"Dead!" she breathed.

"Yes," said Denry. "*I think he's served his purpose.* As we're here, we'll stop here. Don't forget it's the most sensible kind of a house you've ever seen. Don't forget that Mrs Cotterill could run it without a servant and have herself tidy by ten o'clock in a morning."

Mrs Machin perceived then, in a flash of terrible illumination, that there never had been any Cecil Wilbraham; that Denry had merely invented him and his long moustaches and his wall eye for the purpose of getting the better of his mother. The whole affair was an immense swindle upon her. Not a Mr Cecil Wilbraham, but her own son had bought her cottage over her head and jockeyed her out of it beyond any chance of getting into it again. And to defeat his mother the rascal had not simply perverted the innocent Nellie Cotterill to some co-operation in his scheme, but he had actually bought four other cottages, because the landlord would not sell one alone, and he was actually demolishing property to the sole end of stopping her from re-entering it!

Of course, the entire town soon knew of the upshot of the battle, of the year-long battle, between Denry and his mother, and the means adopted by Denry to win. The town also had been hoodwinked, but it did not mind that. It loved its Denry the more, and seeing that he was now properly established in the most remarkable house in the district, it soon afterwards made him a Town Councillor as some reward for his talent in amusing it.

And Denry would say to himself:

"Everything went like clockwork, except the mustard and water. I didn't bargain for the mustard and water. And yet, if I was clever enough to think of putting a label on the bottle and to have the beds prepared, I ought to have been clever enough to keep mustard out of the house." It would be wrong to mince the unpleasant fact that the sham poisoning which he had arranged to the end that he and his mother should pass the night in the house had finished in a manner much too realistic for Denry's pleasure. Mustard and water, particularly when mixed by Mrs Machin, is mustard and water. She had that consolation.

CHAPTER IX

THE GREAT NEWSPAPER WAR

I

When Denry and his mother had been established a year and a month in the new house at Bleakridge, Denry received a visit one evening which perhaps flattered him more than anything had ever flattered him. The visitor was Mr Myson. Now Mr Myson was the founder, proprietor and editor of the *Five Towns Weekly*, a new organ of public opinion which had been in existence about a year; and Denry thought that Mr Myson had popped in to see him in pursuit of an advertisement of the Thrift Club, and at first he was not at all flattered.

But Mr Myson was not hunting for advertisements, and Denry soon saw him to be the kind of man who would be likely to depute that work to others. Of middle height, well and quietly dressed, with a sober, assured deportment, he spoke in a voice and accent that were not of the Five Towns; they were superior to the Five Towns. And in fact Mr Myson originated in Manchester and had seen London. He was not provincial, and he beheld the Five Towns as part of the provinces; which no native of the Five Towns ever succeeds in doing. Nevertheless, his manner to Denry was the summit of easy and yet deferential politeness.

He asked permission "to put something before" Denry. And when, rather taken aback by such smooth phrases, Denry had graciously accorded the permission, he gave a brief history of the *Five Towns Weekly*, showing how its circulation had grown, and definitely stating that at that moment it was yielding a profit. Then he said:

"Now my scheme is to turn it into a daily."

"Very good notion," said Denry, instinctively.

"I'm glad you think so," said Mr Myson. "Because I've come here in the hope of getting your assistance. I'm a stranger to the district, and I want the co-operation of some one who isn't. So I've come to you. I need money, of course, though I have myself what most people would consider sufficient capital. But what I need more than money is—well—moral support."

"And who put you on to me?" asked Denry.

Mr Myson smiled. "I put myself on to you," said he. "I think I may say I've got my bearings in the Five Towns, after over a year's journalism in it, and it appeared to me that you were the best man I could approach. I always believe in flying high."

Therein was Denry flattered. The visit seemed to him to seal his position in the district in a way in which his election to the Bursley Town Council had failed to do. He had been somehow disappointed with that election. He had desired to display his interest in the serious welfare of the town, and to answer his opponent's arguments with better ones. But the burgesses of his ward appeared to have no passionate love of logic. They just cried "Good old Denry!" and elected him—with a majority of only forty-one votes. He had expected to feel a different Denry when he could put "Councillor" before his name. It was not so. He had been solemnly in the mayoral procession to church, he had attended meetings of the council, he had been nominated to the Watch Committee. But he was still precisely the same Denry, though the youngest member of the council. But now he was being recognised from the outside. Mr Myson's keen Manchester eye, ranging over the quarter of a million inhabitants of the Five Towns in search of a representative individual force, had settled on Denry Machin. Yes, he was flattered. Mr Myson's choice threw a rose-light on all Denry's career: his wealth and its origin; his house and stable, which were the astonishment and the admiration of the town; his Universal Thrift Club; yea, and his councillorship! After all, these *were* marvels. (And possibly the greatest marvel was the resigned presence of his mother in that wondrous house, and the fact that she consented to employ Rose Chudd, the incomparable Sappho of charwomen, for three hours every day.)

In fine, he perceived from Mr Myson's eyes that his position was unique.

And after they had chatted a little, and the conversation had deviated momentarily from journalism to house property, he offered to display Machin House (as he had christened it) to Mr Myson, and Mr Myson was really impressed beyond the ordinary. Mr Myson's homage to Mrs Machin, whom they chanced on in the paradise of the bath-room, was the polished mirror of courtesy. How Denry wished that he could behave like that when he happened to meet countesses.

Then, once more in the drawing-room, they resumed the subject of newspapers.

"You know," said Mr Myson, "it's really a very bad thing indeed for a district to have only one daily newspaper. I've nothing myself to say against *The Staffordshire Signal*, but you'd perhaps be astonished"—this in a confidential tone—"at the feeling there is against the *Signal* in many quarters."

"Really!" said Denry.

"Of course its fault is that it isn't sufficiently interested in the great public questions of the district. And it can't be. Because it can't take a definite side. It must try to please all parties. At any rate it must offend none. That is the great evil of a journalistic monopoly.... Two hundred and fifty thousand people—why! there is an ample public for two first-class papers. Look at Nottingham! Look at Bristol! Look at Leeds! Look at Sheffield!...and *their* newspapers."

And Denry endeavoured to look at these great cities! Truly the Five Towns was just about as big.

The dizzy journalistic intoxication seized him. He did not give Mr Myson an answer at once, but he gave himself an answer at once. He would go into the immense adventure. He was very friendly with the *Signal* people—certainly; but business was business, and the highest welfare of the Five Towns was the highest welfare of the Five Towns.

Soon afterwards all the hoardings of the district spoke with one blue voice, and said that the *Five Towns Weekly* was to be transformed into the *Five Towns Daily*, with four editions, beginning each day at noon, and that the new organ would be conducted on the lines of a first-class evening paper.

The inner ring of knowing ones knew that a company entitled "The Five Towns Newspapers, Limited," had been formed, with a capital of ten thousand pounds, and that Mr Myson held three thousand pounds' worth of shares, and the great Denry Machin one thousand five hundred, and that the remainder were to be sold and allotted as occasion demanded. The inner ring said that nothing would ever be able to stand up against the *Signal*. On the other hand, it admitted that Denry, the most prodigious card ever born into the Five Towns, had never been floored by anything. The inner ring anticipated the future with glee. Denry and Mr Myson anticipated the future with righteous confidence. As for the *Signal*, it went on its august way, blind to sensational hoardings.

II

On the day of the appearance of the first issue of the *Five Towns Daily*, the offices of the new paper at Hanbridge gave proof of their excellent organisation, working in all details with an admirable smoothness. In the basement a Marinoni machine thundered like a sucking dove to produce fifteen thousand copies an hour. On the ground floor ingenious arrangements had been made for publishing the paper; in particular, the iron railings to keep the boys in order in front of the publishing counter had been imitated from the *Signal*. On the first floor was the editor and founder with his staff, and above that the composing department. The number of stairs that separated the composing department from the machine-room was not a positive advantage, but bricks and mortar are inelastic, and one does what one can. The offices looked very well from the outside, and they compared passably with the offices of the *Signal* close by. The posters were duly in the ground-floor windows, and gold signs, one above another to the roof, produced an air of lucrative success.

Denry happened to be in the *Daily* offices that afternoon. He had had nothing to do with the details of organisation, for details of organisation were not his speciality. His speciality was large, leading ideas. He knew almost nothing of the agreements with correspondents and Press Association and Central News, and the racing services and the fiction syndicates, nor of the difficulties with the Compositors' Union, nor of the struggle to lower the price of paper by the twentieth of a penny per pound, nor of the awful discounts allowed to certain advertisers, nor of the friction with the railway company, nor of the sickening adulation that had been lavished on quite unimportant newsagents, nor—worst of all—of the dearth of newsboys. These matters did not attract him. He could not stoop to them. But when Mr Myson, calm and proud, escorted him down to the machine-room, and the Marinoni threw a folded pink *Daily* almost into his hands, and it looked exactly like a real newspaper, and he saw one of his own descriptive articles in it, and he reflected that he was an owner of it—then Denry was attracted and delighted, and his heart beat. For this pink thing was the symbol and result of the whole affair, and had the effect of a miracle on him.

And he said to himself, never guessing how many thousands of men had said it before him, that a newspaper was the finest toy in the world.

About four o'clock the publisher, in shirt sleeves and an apron, came up to Mr Myson and respectfully asked him to step into the publishing office. Mr Myson stepped into the publishing office and Denry with him, and they there beheld a small ragged boy with a bleeding nose and a bundle of *Dailys* in his wounded hand.

"Yes," the boy sobbed; "and they said they'd cut my eyes out and plee [play] marbles wi' 'em, if they cotched me in Crown Square agen," And he threw down the papers with a final yell.

The two directors learnt that the delicate threat had been uttered by four *Signal* boys, who had objected to any fellow-boys offering any paper other than the *Signal* for sale in Crown Square or anywhere else.

Of course, it was absurd.

Still, absurd as it was, it continued. The central publishing offices of the *Daily* at Hanbridge, and its branch offices in the neighbouring towns, were like military hospitals, and the truth appeared to the directors that while the public was panting to buy copies of the *Daily*, the sale of the *Daily* was being prevented by means of a scandalous conspiracy on the part of *Signal* boys. For it must be understood that in the Five Towns people prefer to catch their newspaper in the street as it flies and cries. The *Signal* had a vast army of boys, to whom every year it gave a great *fête*. Indeed, the *Signal* possessed nearly all the available boys, and assuredly all the most pugilistic and strongest boys. Mr Myson had obtained boys only after persistent inquiry and demand, and such as he had found were not the fittest, and therefore were unlikely to survive. You would have supposed that in a district that never ceases to grumble about bad trade and unemployment, thousands of boys would have been delighted to buy the *Daily* at fourpence a dozen and sell it at sixpence. But it was not so.

On the second day the dearth of boys at the offices of the *Daily* was painful. There was that magnificent, enterprising newspaper waiting to be sold, and there was the great enlightened public waiting to buy; and scarcely any business could be done because the *Signal* boys had established a reign of terror over their puny and upstart rivals!

The situation was unthinkable.

Still, unthinkable as it was, it continued. Mr Myson had thought of everything except this. Naturally it had not occurred to him that an immense and serious effort for the general weal was going to be blocked by a gang of tatterdemalions.

He complained with dignity to the *Signal*, and was informed with dignity by the *Signal* that the *Signal* could not be responsible for the playful antics of its boys in the streets; that, in short, the Five Towns was a free country. In the latter proposition Mr Myson did not concur.

After trouble in the persuasion of parents—astonishing how indifferent the Five Towns' parent was to the loss of blood by his offspring!—a case reached the police-court. At the hearing the *Signal* gave a solicitor a watching brief, and that solicitor expressed the *Signal's* horror of carnage. The evidence was excessively contradictory, and the Stipendiary dismissed the summons with a good joke. The sole definite result was that the boy whose father had ostensibly brought the summons, got his ear torn within a quarter of an hour of leaving the court. Boys will be boys.

Still, the *Daily* had so little faith in human nature that it could not believe that the *Signal* was not secretly encouraging its boys to be boys. It could not believe that the *Signal*, out of a sincere desire for fair play and for the highest welfare of the district, would willingly sacrifice nearly half its circulation and a portion of its advertisement revenue. And the hurt tone of Mr Myson's leading articles seemed to indicate that in Mr Myson's opinion his older rival *ought* to do everything in its power to ruin itself. The *Signal* never spoke of the fight. The *Daily* gave shocking details of it every day.

The struggle trailed on through the weeks.

Then Denry had one of his ideas. An advertisement was printed in the *Daily* for two hundred able-bodied men to earn two shillings for working six hours a day. An address different from the address of the *Daily* was given. By a ruse Denry procured the insertion of the advertisement in the *Signal* also.

"We must expend our capital on getting the paper on to the streets," said Denry. "That's evident. We'll have it sold by men. We'll soon see if the *Signal* ragamuffins will attack *them*. And we won't pay 'em by results; we'll pay 'em a fixed wage; that'll fetch 'em. And a commission on sales into the bargain. Why! I wouldn't mind engaging *five* hundred men. Swamp the streets! That's it! Hang expense. And when we've done the trick, then we can go back to the boys; they'll have learnt their lesson."

And Mr Myson agreed and was pleased that Denry was living up to his reputation.

The state of the earthenware trade was supposed that summer to be worse than it had been since 1869, and the grumblings of the unemployed were prodigious, even seditious. Mr Myson therefore, as a measure of precaution, engaged a couple of policemen to ensure order at the address, and during the hours, named in the advertisement as a rendezvous for respectable men in search of a well-paid job. Having regard to the thousands of perishing families in the Five Towns, he foresaw a rush and a crush of eager breadwinners. Indeed, the arrangements were elaborate.

Forty minutes after the advertised time for the opening of the reception of respectable men in search of money, four men had arrived. Mr Myson, mystified, thought that there had been a mistake in the advertisement, but there was no mistake in the advertisement. A little later two more men came. Of the six, three were tipsy, and the other three absolutely declined to be seen selling papers in the streets. Two were abusive, one facetious. Mr Myson did not know his Five Towns; nor did Denry. A Five Towns' man, when he can get neither bread nor beer, will keep himself and his family on pride and water. The policemen went off to more serious duties.

III

Then came the announcement of the thirty-fifth anniversary of the *Signal*, and of the processional *fête* by which the *Signal* was at once to give itself a splendid spectacular advertisement and to reward and enhearten its boys. The *Signal* meant to liven up the streets of the Five Towns on that great day by means of a display of all the gilt chariots of Snape's Circus in the main thoroughfare. Many of the boys would be in the gilt chariots. Copies of the anniversary number of the *Signal* would be sold from the gilt chariots. The idea was excellent, and it showed that after all the *Signal* was getting just a little more afraid of its young rival than it had pretended to be.

For, strange to say, after a trying period of hesitation, the *Five Towns Daily* was slightly on the upward curve—thanks to Denry. Denry did not mean to be beaten by the puzzle which the *Daily* offered to his intelligence. There the *Daily* was, full of news, and with quite an encouraging show of advertisements, printed on real paper with real ink—and yet it would not "go." Notoriously the *Signal* earned a net profit of at the very least five thousand a year, whereas the *Daily* earned a net loss of at the very least sixty pounds a week—and of that sixty quite a third was Denry's money. He could not explain it. Mr Myson tried to rouse the public by passionately stirring up extremely urgent matters—such as the smoke nuisance, the increase of the rates, the park question, German competition, technical education for apprentices; but the public obstinately would not be roused concerning its highest welfare to the point of insisting on a regular supply of the *Daily*. If a mere five thousand souls had positively demanded daily a copy of the *Daily* and not slept till boys or agents had responded to their wish, the troubles of the *Daily* would soon have vanished. But this ridiculous public did not seem to care which paper was put into its hand in exchange for its halfpenny, so long as the sporting news was put there. It simply was indifferent. It failed to see the importance to such an immense district of having two flourishing and mutually-opposing daily organs. The fundamental boy difficulty remained ever present.

And it was the boy difficulty that Denry perseveringly and ingeniously attacked, until at length the *Daily* did indeed possess some sort of a brigade of its own, and the bullying and slaughter in the streets (so amusing to the inhabitants) grew a little less one-sided.

A week or more before the *Signal's* anniversary day, Denry heard that the *Signal* was secretly afraid lest the *Daily's* brigade might accomplish the marring of its gorgeous procession, and that the *Signal* was ready to do anything to smash the *Daily's* brigade. He laughed; he said he did not mind. About that time hostilities were rather acute; blood was warming, and both papers, in the excitation of rivalry, had partially lost the sense of what was due to the dignity of great organs. By chance a tremendous local football match—Knype *v.* Bursley—fell on the very Saturday of the procession. The rival arrangements for the reporting of the match were as tremendous as the match itself, and somehow the match seemed to add keenness to the journalistic struggle, especially as the *Daily* favoured Bursley and the *Signal* was therefore forced to favour Knype.

By all the laws of hazard there ought to have been a hitch on that historic Saturday. Telephone or telegraph ought to have broken down, or rain ought to have made play impossible, but no hitch occurred. And at five-thirty o'clock of a glorious afternoon in earliest November the *Daily* went to press with a truly brilliant account of the manner in which Bursley (for the first and last time in its history) had defeated Knype by one goal to none. Mr Myson was proud. Mr Myson defied the *Signal* to beat his descriptive report. As for the *Signal's* procession—well, Mr Myson and the chief sub-editor of the *Daily* glanced at each other and smiled.

And a few minutes later the *Daily* boys were rushing out of the publishing room with bundles of papers—assuredly in advance of the *Signal*.

It was at this juncture that the unexpected began to occur to the *Daily* boys. The publishing door of the *Daily* opened into Stanway Rents, a narrow alley in a maze of mean streets behind Crown Square. In Stanway Rents was a small warehouse in which, according to rumours of the afternoon, a free soup kitchen was to be opened. And just before the football edition of the *Daily* came off the Marinoni, it emphatically was opened, and there issued from its inviting gate an odour—not, to be sure, of soup, but of toasted cheese and hot jam—such an odour as had never before tempted the nostrils of a *Daily* boy; a unique and omnipotent odour. Several boys (who, I may state frankly, were traitors to the *Daily* cause, spies and mischief-makers from elsewhere) raced unhesitatingly in, crying that toasted cheese sandwiches and jam tarts were to be distributed like lightning to all authentic newspaper lads.

The entire gang followed—scores, over a hundred—inwardly expecting to emerge instantly with teeth fully employed, followed like sheep into a fold.

And the gate was shut.

Toasted cheese and hot jammy pastry were faithfully served to the ragged host—but with no breathless haste. And when, loaded, the boys struggled to depart, they were instructed by the kind philanthropist who had fed them to depart by another exit, and they discovered themselves In an enclosed yard, of which the double doors were apparently unyielding. And the warehouse door was shut also. And as the cheese and jam disappeared, shouts of fury arose on the air. The yard was so close to the offices of the *Daily* that the chimneypots of those offices could actually be seen. And yet the shouting brought no answer from the lords of the *Daily*, congratulating themselves up there on their fine account of the football match, and on their celerity in going to press and on the loyalty of their brigade.

The *Signal*, it need not be said, disavowed complicity in this extraordinary entrapping of the *Daily* brigade by means of an odour. Could it be held responsible for the excesses of its disinterested sympathisers?... Still, the appalling trick showed the high temperature to which blood had risen in the genial battle between great rival organs. Persons in the inmost ring whispered that Denry Machin had at length been bested on this critically important day.

IV

Snape's Circus used to be one of the great shining institutions of North Staffordshire, trailing its magnificence on sculptured wheels from town to town, and occupying the dreams of boys from one generation to another. Its headquarters were at Axe, in the Moorlands, ten miles away from Hanbridge, but the riches of old Snape had chiefly come from the Five Towns. At the time of the struggle between the *Signal* and the *Daily* its decline had already begun. The aged proprietor had recently died, and the name, and the horses, and the chariots, and the carefully-repaired tents had been sold to strangers. On the Saturday of the anniversary and the football match (which was also Martinmas Saturday) the circus was set up at Oldcastle, on the edge of the Five Towns, and was giving its final performances of the season. Even boys will not go to circuses in the middle of a Five Towns' winter. The *Signal* people had hired the processional portion of Snape's for the late afternoon and early evening. And the instructions were that the entire *cortège* should be round about the *Signal* offices, in marching order, not later than five o'clock.

But at four o'clock several gentlemen with rosettes in their button-holes and *Signal* posters in their hands arrived important and panting at the fair-ground at Oldcastle, and announced that the programme had been altered at the last moment, in order to defeat certain feared machinations of the unscrupulous *Daily*. The cavalcade was to be split into three groups, one of which, the chief, was to enter Hanbridge by a "back road," and the other two were to go to Bursley and Longshaw respectively. In this manner the forces of advertisement would be distributed, and the chief parts of the district equally honoured.

The special linen banners, pennons, and ribbons—bearing the words—
"*SIGNAL:* THIRTY-FIFTH ANNIVERSARY," &c.
had already been hung and planted and draped about the gilded summits of the chariots. And after some delay the processions were started, separating at the bottom of the Cattle Market. The head of the Hanbridge part of the procession consisted of an enormous car of Jupiter, with six wheels and thirty-six paregorical figures (as the clown used to say), and drawn by six piebald steeds guided by white reins. This coach had a windowed interior (at the greater fairs it sometimes served as a box-office) and in the interior one of the delegates of the *Signal* had fixed himself; from it he directed the paths of the procession.

It would be futile longer to conceal that the delegate of the *Signal* in the bowels of the car of Jupiter was not honestly a delegate of the *Signal* at all. He was, indeed, Denry Machin, and none other. From this single fact it will be seen to what extent the representatives of great organs had forgotten what was due to their dignity and to public decency. Ensconced in his lair Denry directed the main portion of the *Signal's* advertising procession by all manner of discreet lanes round the skirts of Hanbridge and so into the town from the hilly side. And ultimately the ten vehicles halted in Crapper Street, to the joy of the simple inhabitants.

Denry emerged and wandered innocently towards the offices of his paper, which were close by. It was getting late. The first yelling of the imprisoned *Daily* boys was just beginning to rise on the autumn air.

Suddenly Denry was accosted by a young man.

"Hello, Machin!" cried the young man. "What have you shaved your beard off, for? I scarcely knew you."

"I just thought I would, Swetnam," said Denry, who was obviously discomposed.

It was the youngest of the Swetnam boys; he and Denry had taken a sort of curt fancy to one another.

"I say," said Swetnam, confidentially, as if obeying a swift impulse, "I did hear that the *Signal* people meant to collar all your chaps this afternoon, and I believe they have done. Hear that now?" (Swetnam's father was intimate with the *Signal* people.)

"I know," Denry replied.

"But I mean—papers and all."

"I know," said Denry.

"Oh!" murmured Swetnam.

"But I'll tell you a secret," Denry added. "They aren't to-day's papers. They're yesterday's, and last week's and last month's. We've been collecting them specially and keeping them nice and new-looking."

"Well, you're a caution!" murmured Swetnam.

"I am," Denry agreed.

A number of men rushed at that instant with bundles of the genuine football edition from the offices of the *Daily*.

"Come on!" Denry cried to them. "Come on! This way! By-by, Swetnam."

And the whole file vanished round a corner. The yelling of imprisoned cheese-fed boys grew louder.

V

In the meantime at the *Signal* office (which was not three hundred yards away, but on the other side of Crown Square) apprehension had deepened into anxiety as the minutes passed and the Snape Circus procession persisted in not appearing on the horizon of the Oldcastle Road. The *Signal* would have telephoned to Snape's, but for the fact that a circus is never on the telephone. It then telephoned to its Oldcastle agent, who, after a long delay, was able to reply that the cavalcade had left Oldcastle at the appointed hour, with every sign of health and energy. Then the *Signal* sent forth scouts all down the Oldcastle Road to put spurs into the procession, and the scouts returned, having seen nothing. Pessimists glanced at the possibility of the whole procession having fallen into the canal at Cauldon Bridge. The paper was printed, the train-parcels for Knype, Longshaw, Bursley, and Turnhill were despatched; the boys were waiting; the fingers of the clock in the publishing department were simply flying. It had been arranged that the bulk of the Hanbridge edition, and in particular the first copies of it, should be sold by boys from the gilt chariots themselves. The publisher hesitated for an awful moment, and then decided that he could wait no more, and that the boys must sell the papers in the usual way from the pavements and gutters. There was no knowing what the *Daily* might not be doing.

And then *Signal* boys in dozens rushed forth paper-laden, but they were disappointed boys; they had thought to ride in gilt chariots, not to paddle in mud. And almost the first thing they saw in Crown Square was the car of Jupiter in its glory, flying all the *Signal* colours; and other cars behind. They did not rush now; they sprang, as from a catapult; and alighted like flies on the vehicles. Men insisted on taking their papers from them and paying for them on the spot. The boys were startled; they were entirely puzzled; but they had not the habit of refusing money. And off went the procession to the music of its own band down the road to Knype, and perhaps a hundred boys on board, cheering. The men in charge then performed a curious act: they tore down all the *Signal* flagging, and replaced it with the emblem of the *Daily*.

So that all the great and enlightened public wandering home in crowds from the football match at Knype, had the spectacle of a *Daily* procession instead of a *Signal* procession, and could scarce believe their eyes. And *Dailys* were sold in quantities from the cars. At Knype Station the procession curved and returned to Hanbridge, and finally, after a multitudinous triumph, came to a stand with all its *Daily* bunting in front of the *Signal* offices; and Denry appeared from his lair. Denry's men fled with bundles.

"They're an hour and a half late," said Denry calmly to one of the proprietors of the *Signal*, who was on the pavement. "But I've managed to get them here. I thought I'd just look in to thank you for giving such a good feed to our lads."

The telephones hummed with news of similar *Daily* processions in Longshaw and Bursley. And there was not a high-class private bar in the district that did not tinkle with delighted astonishment at the brazen, the inconceivable effrontery of that card, Denry Machin. Many people foresaw law-suits, but it was agreed that the *Signal* had begun the game of impudence in trapping the *Daily* lads so as to secure a holy calm for its much-trumpeted procession.

And Denry had not finished with the *Signal*.

In the special football edition of the *Daily* was an announcement, the first, of special Martinmas *fêtes* organised by the *Five Towns Daily*. And on the same morning every member of the Universal Thrift Club had received an invitation to the said *fêtes*. They were three—held on public ground at Hanbridge, Bursley, and Longshaw. They were in the style of the usual Five Towns "wakes"; that is to say, roundabouts, shows, gingerbread stalls, swings, cocoanut shies. But at each *fête* a new and very simple form of "shy" had been erected. It consisted of a row of small railway signals.

"March up! March up!" cried the shy-men. "Knock down the signal! Knock down the signal! And a packet of Turkish delight is yours. Knock down the signal!"

And when you had knocked down the signal the men cried:

"We wrap it up for you in the special Anniversary Number of the *Signal*."

And they disdainfully tore into suitable fragments copies of the *Signal* which had cost Denry & Co. a halfpenny each, and enfolded the Turkish delight therein, and handed it to you with a smack.

And all the fair-grounds were carpeted with draggled and muddy *Signals*. People were up to the ankles in *Signals*.

The affair was the talk of Sunday. Few matters in the Five Towns have raised more gossip than did that enormous escapade which Denry invented and conducted. The moral damage to the *Signal* was held to approach the disastrous. And now not the possibility but the probability of law-suits was incessantly discussed.

On the Monday both papers were bought with anxiety. Everybody was frothing to know what the respective editors would say.

But in neither sheet was there a single word as to the affair. Both had determined to be discreet; both were afraid. The *Signal* feared lest it might not, if the pinch came, be able to prove its innocence of the crime of luring boys into confinement by means of toasted cheese and hot jam. The *Signal* had also to consider its seriously damaged dignity; for such wounds silence is the best dressing. The *Daily* was comprehensively afraid. It had practically driven its gilded chariots through the entire Decalogue. Moreover, it had won easily in the grand altercation. It was exquisitely conscious of glory.

Denry went away to Blackpool, doubtless to grow his beard.

The proof of the *Daily's* moral and material victory was that soon afterwards there were four applicants, men of substance, for shares in the *Daily* company. And this, by the way, was the end of the tale. For these applicants, who secured options on a majority of the shares, were emissaries of the *Signal*. Armed with the options, the *Signal* made terms with its rival, and then by mutual agreement killed it. The price of its death was no trifle, but it was less than a year's profits of the *Signal*. Denry considered that he had been "done." But in the depths of his heart he was glad that he had been done. He had had too disconcerting a glimpse of the rigours and perils of journalism to wish to continue it. He had scored supremely and, for him, to score was life itself. His reputation as a card was far, far higher than ever. Had he so desired, he could have been elected to the House of Commons on the strength of his procession and *fête*.

Mr Myson, somewhat scandalised by the exuberance of his partner, returned to Manchester.

And the *Signal*, subsequently often referred to as "The Old Lady," resumed its monopolistic sway over the opinions of a quarter of a million of people, and has never since been attacked.

CHAPTER X

HIS INFAMY

I

When Denry at a single stroke "wherreted" his mother and proved his adventurous spirit by becoming the possessor of one of the first motor-cars ever owned in Bursley, his instinct naturally was to run up to Councillor Cotterill's in it. Not that he loved Councillor Cotterill, and therefore wished to make him a partaker in his joy; for he did not love Councillor Cotterill. He had never been able to forgive Nellie's father for those patronising airs years and years before at Llandudno, airs indeed which had not even yet disappeared from Cotterill's attitude towards Denry. Though they were Councillors on the same Town Council, though Denry was getting richer and Cotterill was assuredly not getting richer, the latter's face and tone always seemed to be saying to Denry: "Well, you are not doing so badly for a beginner." So Denry did not care to lose an opportunity of impressing Councillor Cotterill. Moreover, Denry had other reasons for going up to the Cotterills. There existed a sympathetic bond between him and Mrs Cotterill, despite her prim taciturnity and her exasperating habit of sitting with her hands pressed tight against her body and one over the other. Occasionally he teased her—and she liked being teased. He had glimpses now and then of her secret soul; he was perhaps the only person in Bursley thus privileged. Then there was Nellie. Denry and Nellie were great friends. For the rest of the world she had grown up, but not for Denry, who treated her as the chocolate child; while she, if she called him anything, called him respectfully "Mr."

The Cotterills had a fairly large old house with a good garden "up Bycars Lane," above the new park and above all those red streets which Mr Cotterill had helped to bring into being. Mr Cotterill built new houses with terra-cotta facings for others, but preferred an old one in stucco for himself. His abode had been saved from the parcelling out of several Georgian estates. It was dignified. It had a double entrance gate, and from this portal the drive started off for the house door, but deliberately avoided reaching the house door until it had wandered in curves over the entire garden. That was the Georgian touch! The modern touch was shown in Councillor Cotterill's bay windows, bath-room and garden squirter. There was stabling, in which were kept a Victorian dogcart and a Georgian horse, used by the Councillor in his business. As sure as ever his wife or daughter wanted the dogcart, it was either out or just going out, or the Georgian horse was fatigued and needed repose. The man who groomed the Georgian also ploughed the flowerbeds, broke the windows in cleaning them, and put blacking on brown boots. Two indoor servants had differing views as to the frontier between the kingdom of his duties and the kingdom of theirs, in fact, it was the usual spacious household of successful trade in a provincial town.

Denry got to Bycars Lane without a breakdown. This was in the days, quite thirteen years ago, when automobilists made their wills and took food supplies when setting forth. Hence Denry was pleased. The small but useful fund of prudence in him, however, forbade him to run the car along the unending sinuous drive. The May night was fine, and he left the loved vehicle with his new furs in the shadow of a monkey-tree near the gate.

As he was crunching towards the door, he had a beautiful idea: "I'll take 'em all out for a spin. There'll just be room!" he said.

Now even to-day, when the very cabman drives his automobile, a man who buys a motor cannot say to a friend: "I've bought a motor. Come for a spin," in the same self-unconscious accents as he would say: "I've bought a boat. Come for a sail," or "I've bought a house. Come and look at it." Even to-day and in the centre of London there is still something about a motor—well something.... Everybody who has bought a motor, and everybody who has dreamed of buying a motor, will comprehend me. Useless to feign that a motor is the most banal thing imaginable. It is not. It remains the supreme symbol of swagger. If such is the effect of a motor in these days and in Berkeley Square, what must it have been in that dim past, and in that dim town three hours by the fastest express from Euston? The imagination must be forced to the task of answering this question. Then will it be understood that Denry was simply tingling with pride.

"Master in?" he demanded of the servant, who was correctly starched, but unkempt in detail.

"No, sir. He ain't been in for tea."

("I shall take the women out then," said Denry to himself.)

"Come in! Come in!" cried a voice from the other side of the open door of the drawing-room, Nellie's voice! The manners and state of a family that has industrially risen combine the spectacular grandeur of the caste to which it has climbed with the ease and freedom of the caste which it has quitted.

"Such a surprise!" said the voice. Nellie appeared, rosy.

Denry threw his new motoring cap hastily on to the hall-stand. No! He did not hope that Nellie would see it. He hoped that she would not see it. Now that the moment was really come to declare himself the owner of a motor-car, he grew timid and nervous. He would have liked to hide his hat. But then Denry was quite different from our common humanity. He was capable even of feeling awkward in a new suit of clothes. A singular person.

"Hello!" she greeted him.

"Hello!" he greeted her.

Their hands touched.

"Father hasn't come yet," she added. He fancied she was not quite at ease.

"Well," he said, "what's this surprise."

She motioned him into the drawing-room.

The surprise was a wonderful woman, brilliant in black—not black silk, but a softer, delicate stuff. She reclined in an easy-chair with surpassing grace and self-possession. A black Egyptian shawl, spangled with silver, was slipping off her shoulders. Her hair was dressed—that is to say, it was *dressed*; it was obviously and thrillingly a work of elaborate art. He could see her two feet and one of her ankles. The boots, the open-work stocking—such boots, such an open-work stocking, had never been seen in Bursley, not even at a ball! She was in mourning, and wore scarcely any jewellery, but there was a gleaming tint of gold here and there among the black, which resulted in a marvellous effect of richness.

The least experienced would have said, and said rightly: "This must be a woman of wealth and fashion." It was the detail that finished the demonstration. The detail was incredible. There might have been ten million stitches in the dress. Ten sempstresses might have worked on the dress for ten years. An examination of it under a microscope could but have deepened one's amazement at it.

She was something new in the Five Towns, something quite new.

Denry was not equal to the situation. He seldom was equal to a small situation. And although he had latterly acquired a considerable amount of social *savoir*, he was constantly mislaying it, so that he could not put his hand on it at the moment when he most required it, as now.

"Well, Denry!" said the wondrous creature in black, softly.

And he collected himself as though for a plunge, and said:

"Well, Ruth!"

This was the woman whom he had once loved, kissed, and engaged himself to marry. He was relieved that she had begun with Christian names, because he could not recall her surname. He could not even remember whether he had ever heard it. All he knew was that, after leaving Bursley to join her father in Birmingham, she had married somebody with a double name, somebody well off, somebody older than herself; somebody apparently of high social standing; and that this somebody had died.

She made no fuss. There was no implication in her demeanour that she expected to be wept over as a lone widow, or that because she and he had on a time been betrothed, therefore they could never speak naturally to each other again. She just talked as if nothing had ever happened to her, and as if about twenty-four hours had elapsed since she had last seen him. He felt that she must have picked up this most useful diplomatic calmness in her contacts with her late husband's class. It was a valuable lesson to him: "Always behave as if nothing had happened —no matter what has happened."

To himself he was saying:

"I'm glad I came up in my motor."

He seemed to need something in self-defence against the sudden attack of all this wealth and all this superior social tact, and the motor-car served excellently.

"I've been hearing a great deal about you lately," said she with a soft smile, unobtrusively rearranging a fold of her skirt.

"Well," he replied, "I'm sorry I can't say the same of you."

Slightly perilous perhaps, but still he thought it rather neat.

"Oh!" she said. "You see I've been so much out of England. We were just talking about holidays. I was saying to Mrs Cotterill they certainly ought to go to Switzerland this year for a change."

"Yes, Mrs Capron-Smith was just saying—" Mrs Cotterill put in.

(So that was her name.)

"It would be something too lovely!" said Nellie in ecstasy.

Switzerland! Astonishing how with a single word she had marked the gulf between Bursley people and herself. The Cotterills had never been out of England. Not merely that, but the Cotterills had never dreamt of going out of England. Denry had once been to Dieppe, and had come back as though from Timbuctoo with a traveller's renown. And she talked of Switzerland easily!

"I suppose it is very jolly," he said.

"Yes," she said, "it's splendid in summer. But, of course, *the* time is winter, for the sports. Naturally, when you aren't free to take a bit of a holiday in winter, you must be content with summer, and very splendid it is. I'm sure you'd enjoy it frightfully, Nell."

"I'm sure I should—frightfully!" Nellie agreed. "I shall speak to father. I shall make him—"

"Now, Nellie—" her mother warned her.

"Yes, I shall, mother," Nellie insisted.

"There *is* your father!" observed Mrs Cotterill, after listening.

Footsteps crossed the hall, and died away into the dining-room.

"I wonder why on earth father doesn't come in here. He must have heard us talking," said Nellie, like a tyrant crossed in some trifle.

A bell rang, and then the servant came into the drawing-room and remarked: "If you please, mum," at Mrs Cotterill, and Mrs Cotterill disappeared, closing the door after her.

"What are they up to, between them?" Nellie demanded, and she, too, departed, with wrinkled brow, leaving Denry and Ruth together. It could be perceived on Nellie's brow that her father was going "to catch it."

"I haven't seen Mr Cotterill yet," said Mrs Capron-Smith.

"When did you come?" Denry asked.

"Only this afternoon."

She continued to talk.

As he looked at her, listening and responding intelligently now and then, he saw that Mrs Capron-Smith was in truth the woman that Ruth had so cleverly imitated ten years before. The imitation had deceived him then; he had accepted it for genuine. It would not have deceived him now—he knew that. Oh yes! This was the real article that could hold its own anywhere.... Switzerland! And not simply Switzerland, but a refinement on Switzerland! Switzerland in winter! He divined that in her opinion Switzerland in summer was not worth doing—in the way of correctness. But in winter...

II

Nellie had announced a surprise for Denry as he entered the house, but Nellie's surprise for Denry, startling and successful though it proved, was as naught to the surprise which Mr Cotterill had in hand for Nellie, her mother, Denry, the town of Bursley, and various persons up and down the country.

Mrs Cotterill came hysterically in upon the duologue between Denry and Ruth in the drawing-room. From the activity of her hands, which, instead of being decently folded one over the other, were waving round her head in the strangest way, it was clear that Mrs Cotterill was indeed under the stress of a very unusual emotion.

"It's those creditors—at last! I knew it would be! It's all those creditors! They won't let him alone, and now they've *done* it."

So Mrs Cotterill! She dropped into a chair. She had no longer any sense of shame, of what was due to her dignity. She seemed to have forgotten that certain matters are not proper to be discussed in drawing-rooms. She had left the room Mrs Councillor Cotterill; she returned to it nobody in particular, the personification of defeat. The change had operated in five minutes.

Mrs Capron-Smith and Denry glanced at each other, and even Mrs Capron-Smith was at a loss for a moment. Then Ruth approached Mrs Cotterill and took her hand. Perhaps Mrs Capron-Smith was not so astonished after all. She and Nellie's mother had always been "very friendly." And in the Five Towns "very friendly" means a lot.

"Perhaps if you were to leave us," Ruth suggested, twisting her head to glance at Denry.

It was exactly what he desired to do. There could be no doubt that Ruth was supremely a woman of the world. Her tact was faultless.

He left them, saying to himself: "Well, here's a go!"

In the hall, through an open door, he saw Councillor Cotterill standing against the dining-room mantelpiece.

When Cotterill caught sight of Denry he straightened himself into a certain uneasy perkiness.

"Young man," he said in a counterfeit of his old patronising tone, "come in here. You may as well hear about it. You're a friend of ours. Come in and shut the door."

Nellie was not in view.

Denry went in and shut the door.

"Sit down," said Cotterill.

And it was just as if he had said: "Now, you're a fairly bright sort of youth, and you haven't done so badly in life; and as a reward I mean to admit you to the privilege of hearing about our ill-luck, which for some mysterious reason reflects more credit on me than your good luck reflects on you, young man."

And he stroked his straggling grey beard.

"I'm going to file my petition to-morrow," said he, and gave a short laugh.

"Really!" said Denry, who could think of nothing else to say. His name was not Capron-Smith.

"Yes; they won't leave me any alternative," said Mr Cotterill.

Then he gave a brief history of his late commercial career to the young man. And he seemed to figure it as a sort of tug-of-war between his creditors and his debtors, he himself being the rope. He seemed to imply that he had always done his sincere best to attain the greatest good of the greatest number, but that those wrong-headed creditors had consistently thwarted him.

However, he bore them no grudge. It was the fortune of the tug-of-war. He pretended, with shabby magnificence of spirit, that a bankruptcy at the age of near sixty, in a community where one has cut a figure, is a mere passing episode.

"Are you surprised?" he asked foolishly, with a sheepish smile.

Denry took vengeance for all the patronage that he had received during a decade.

"No!" he said. "Are you?"

Instead of kicking Denry out of the house for an impudent young jackanapes, Mr Cotterill simply resumed his sheepish smile.

Denry had been surprised for a moment, but he had quickly recovered. Cotterill's downfall was one of those events which any person of acute intelligence can foretell after they have happened. Cotterill had run the risks of the speculative builder, built and mortgaged, built and mortgaged, sold at a profit, sold without profit, sold at a loss, and failed to sell; given bills, second mortgages, and third mortgages; and because he was a builder and could do nothing but build, he had continued to build in defiance of Bursley's lack of enthusiasm for his erections. If rich gold deposits had been discovered in Bursley Municipal Park, Cotterill would have owned a mining camp and amassed immense wealth; but unfortunately gold deposits were not discovered in the Park. Nobody knew his position; nobody ever does know the position of a speculative builder. He did not know it himself. There had been rumours, but they had been contradicted in an adequate way. His recent refusal of the mayoral chain, due to lack of spare coin, had been attributed to prudence. His domestic existence had always been conducted on the same moderately lavish scale. He had always paid the baker, the butcher, the tailor, the dressmaker.

And now he was to file his petition in bankruptcy, and to-morrow the entire town would have "been seeing it coming" for years.

"What shall you do?" Denry inquired in amicable curiosity.

"Well," said Cotterill, "that's the point. I've got a brother a builder in Toronto, you know. He's doing very well; building *is* building over there. I wrote to him a bit since, and he replied by the next mail —by the next mail—that what he wanted was just a man like me to overlook things. He's getting an old man now, is John. So, you see, there's an opening waiting for me."

As if to say, "The righteous are never forsaken."

"I tell you all this as you're a friend of the family like," he added.

Then, after an expanse of vagueness, he began hopefully, cheerfully, undauntedly:

"Even *now* if I could get hold of a couple of thousand I could pull through handsome—and there's plenty of security for it."

"Bit late now, isn't it?"

"Not it. If only some one who really knows the town, and has faith in the property market, would come down with a couple of thousand—well, he might double it in five years."

"Really!"

"Yes," said Cotterill. "Look at Clare Street."

Clare Street was one of his terra-cotta masterpieces.

"You, now," said Cotterill, insinuating. "I don't expect anyone can teach *you* much about the value o' property in this town. You know as well as I do. If you happened to have a couple of thousand loose—by gosh! it's a chance in a million."

"Yes," said Denry. "I should say that was just about what it was."

"I put it before you," Cotterill proceeded, gathering way, and missing the flavour of Denry's remark. "Because you're a friend of the family. You're so often here. Why, it's pretty near ten years...."

Denry sighed: "I expect I come and see you all about once a fortnight fairly regular. That makes two hundred and fifty times in ten years. Yes...."

"A couple of thou'," said Cotterill, reflectively.

"Two hundred and fifty into two thousand—eight. Eight pounds a visit. A shade thick, Cotterill, a shade thick. You might be half a dozen fashionable physicians rolled into one."

Never before had he called the Councillor "Cotterill" unadorned. Me Cotterill flushed and rose.

Denry does not appear to advantage in this interview. He failed in magnanimity. The only excuse that can be offered for him is that Mr Cotterill had called him "young man" once or twice too often in the course of ten years. It is subtle.

III

"No," whispered Ruth, in all her wraps. "Don't bring it up to the door. I'll walk down with you to the gate, and get in there."

He nodded.

They were off, together. Ruth, it had appeared, was actually staying at the Five Towns Hotel at Knype, which at that epoch was the only hotel in the Five Towns seriously pretending to be "first-class" in the full-page advertisement sense. The fact that Ruth was staying at the Five Towns Hotel impressed Denry anew. Assuredly she did things in the grand manner. She had meant to walk down by the Park to Bursley Station and catch the last loop-line train to Knype, and when Denry suddenly disclosed the existence of his motor-car, and proposed to see her to her hotel in it, she in her turn had been impressed. The astonishment in her tone as she exclaimed: "Have you got a *motor*?" was the least in the world naïve.

Thus they departed together from the stricken house, Ruth saying brightly to Nellie, who had reappeared in a painful state of demoralisation, that she should return on the morrow.

And Denry went down the obscure drive with a final vision of the poor child, Nellie, as she stood at the door to speed them. It was extraordinary how that child had remained a child. He knew that she must be more than half-way through her twenties, and yet she persisted in being the merest girl. A delightful little thing;

but no *savoir vivre*, no equality to a situation, no spectacular pride. Just a nice, bright girl, strangely girlish.... The Cotterills had managed that bad evening badly. They had shown no dignity, no reserve, no discretion; and old Cotterill had been simply fatuous in his suggestion. As for Mrs Cotterill, she was completely overcome, and it was due solely to Ruth's calm, managing influence that Nellie, nervous and whimpering, had wound herself up to come and shut the front door after the guests.

It was all very sad.

When he had successfully started the car, and they were sliding down the Moorthorne hill together, side by side, their shoulders touching, Denry threw off the nightmarish effect of the bankrupt household. After all, there was no reason why he should be depressed. He was not a bankrupt. He was steadily adding riches to riches. He acquired wealth mechanically now. Owing to the habits of his mother, he never came within miles of living up to his income. And Ruth—she, too, was wealthy. He felt that she must be wealthy in the strict significance of the term. And she completed wealth by experience of the world. She was his equal. She understood things in general. She had lived, travelled, suffered, reflected—in short, she was a completed article of manufacture. She was no little, clinging, raw girl. Further, she was less hard than of yore. Her voice and gestures had a different quality. The world had softened her. And it occurred to him suddenly that her sole fault—extravagance— had no importance now that she was wealthy.

He told her all that Mr Cotterill had said about Canada. And she told him all that Mrs Cotterill had said about Canada. And they agreed that Mr Cotterill had got his deserts, and that, in its own interest, Canada was the only thing for the Cotterill family; and the sooner the better. People must accept the consequences of bankruptcy. Nothing could be done.

"I think it's a pity Nellie should have to go," said Denry.

"Oh! *Do* you?" replied Ruth.

"Yes; going out to a strange country like that. She's not what you may call the Canadian kind of girl. If she could only get something to do here. ...If something could be found for her."

"Oh, I don't agree with you at *all*," said Ruth. "Do you really think she ought to leave her parents just *now*? Her place is with her parents. And besides, between you and me, she'll have a much better chance of marrying there than in *this* town—after all this. Of course I shall be very sorry to lose her—and Mrs Cotterill, too. But...."

"I expect you're right," Denry concurred.

And they sped on luxuriously through the lamp-lit night of the Five Towns. And Denry pointed out his house as they passed it. And they both thought much of the security of their positions in the world, and of their incomes, and of the honeyed deference of their bankers; and also of the mistake of being a failure.... You could do nothing with a failure.

IV

On a frosty morning in early winter you might have seen them together in a different vehicle—a first-class compartment of the express from Knype to Liverpool. They had the compartment to themselves, and they were installed therein with every circumstance of luxury. Both were enwrapped in furs, and a fur rug united their knees in its shelter. Magazines and newspapers were scattered about to the value of a labourer's hire for a whole day; and when Denry's eye met the guard's it said "shilling." In short, nobody could possibly be more superb than they were on that morning in that compartment.

The journey was the result of peculiar events.

Mr Cotterill had made himself a bankrupt, and cast away the robe of a Town Councillor. He had submitted to the inquisitiveness of the Official Receiver, and to the harsh prying of those rampant baying beasts, his creditors. He had laid bare his books, his correspondence, his lack of method, his domestic extravagance, and the distressing fact that he had continued to trade long after he knew himself to be insolvent. He had for several months, in the interests of the said beasts, carried on his own business as manager at a nominal salary. And gradually everything that was his had been sold. And during the final weeks the Cotterill family had been obliged to quit their dismantled house and exist in lodgings. It had been arranged that they should go to Canada by way of Liverpool, and on the day before the journey of Denry and Ruth to Liverpool they had departed from the borough of Bursley (which Mr Cotterill had so extensively faced with terra-cotta) unhonoured and unsung. Even Denry, though he had visited them in their lodgings to say good-bye, had not seen them off at the station; but Ruth Capron-Smith had seen them off at the station. She had interrupted a sojourn to Southport in order to come to Bursley, and despatch them therefrom with due friendliness. Certain matters had to be attended to after their departure, and Ruth had promised to attend to them.

Now immediately after seeing them off Ruth had met Denry in the street.

"Do you know," she said brusquely, "those people are actually going steerage? I'd no idea of it. Mr and Mrs Cotterill kept it from me, and I should not have heard of it only from something Nellie said. That's why they've gone to-day. The boat doesn't sail till to-morrow afternoon."

"Steerage?" and Denry whistled.

"Yes," said Ruth. "Nothing but pride, of course. Old Cotterill wanted to have every penny he could scrape, so as to be able to make the least tiny bit of a show when he gets to Toronto, and so—steerage! Just think of Mrs Cotterill and Nellie in the steerage. If I'd known of it I should have altered that, I can tell you, and pretty quickly too; and now it's too late."

"No, it isn't," Denry contradicted her flatly.

"But they've gone."

"I could telegraph to Liverpool for saloon berths—there's bound to be plenty at this time of year—and I could run over to Liverpool to-morrow and catch 'em on the boat, and make 'em change."

She asked him whether he really thought he could, and he assured her.

"Second-cabin berths would be better," said she.

"Why?"

"Well, because of dressing for dinner, and so on. They haven't got the clothes, you know."

"Of course," said Denry.

"Listen," she said, with an enchanting smile. "Let's halve the cost, you and I. And let's go to Liverpool together, and—er—make the little gift, and arrange things. I'm leaving for Southport to-morrow, and Liverpool's on my way."

Denry was delighted by the suggestion, and telegraphed to Liverpool with success.

Thus they found themselves on that morning in the Liverpool express together. The work of benevolence in which they were engaged had a powerful influence on their mood, which grew both intimate and tender. Ruth made no concealment of her regard for Denry; and as he gazed across the compartment at her, exquisitely mature (she was slightly older than himself), dressed to a marvel, perfect in every detail of manner, knowing all that was to be known about life, and secure in a handsome fortune—as he gazed, Denry reflected, joyously, victoriously:

"I've got the dibs, of course. But she's got 'em too—perhaps more. Therefore she must like me for myself alone. This brilliant creature has been everywhere and seen everything, and she comes back to the Five Towns and comes back to *me*."

It was his proudest moment. And in it he saw his future far more glorious than he had dreamt.

"When shall you be out of mourning?" he inquired.

"In two months," said she.

This was not a proposal and acceptance, but it was very nearly one. They were silent, and happy.

Then she said:

"Do you ever have business at Southport?"

And he said, in a unique manner:

"I shall have."

Another silence. This time he felt he *would* marry her.

V

The White Star liner, *Titubic*, stuck out of the water like a row of houses against the landing-stage. There was a large crowd on her promenade-deck, and a still larger crowd on the landing-stage. Above the promenade-deck officers paced on the navigating deck, and above that was the airy bridge, and above that the funnels, smoking, and somewhere still higher a flag or two fluttering in the icy breeze. And behind the crowd on the landing-stage stretched a row of four-wheeled cabs and rickety horses. The landing-stage swayed ever so slightly on the tide. Only the ship was apparently solid, apparently cemented in foundations of concrete.

On the starboard side of the promenade-deck, among a hundred other small groups, was a group consisting of Mr and Mrs Cotterill and Ruth and Denry.

Nellie stood a few feet apart, Mrs Cotterill was crying. People naturally thought she was crying because of the adieux; but she was not. She wept because Denry and Ruth, by sheer force of will, had compelled them to come out of the steerage and occupy beautiful and commodious berths in the second cabin, where the manner of the stewards was quite different. She wept because they had been caught in the steerage. She wept because she was ashamed, and because people were too kind. She was at once delighted and desolated. She wanted to outpour psalms of gratitude, and also she wanted to curse.

Mr Cotterill said stiffly that he should repay—and that soon.

An immense bell sounded impatiently.

"We'd better be shunting," said Denry. "That's the second."

In exciting crises he sometimes employed such peculiar language as this. And he was very excited. He had done a great deal of rushing about. The upraising of the Cotterill family from the social Hades of the steerage to the respectability of the second cabin had demanded all his energy, and a lot of Ruth's.

Ruth kissed Mrs Cotterill and then Nellie. And Mrs Cotterill and Nellie acquired rank and importance for the whole voyage by reason of being kissed in public by a woman so elegant and aristocratic as Ruth Capron-Smith.

And Denry shook hands. He looked brightly at the parents, but he could not look at Nellie; nor could she look at him; their handshaking was perfunctory. For months their playful intimacy had been in abeyance.

"Good-bye."

"Good luck."

"Thanks. Good-bye."

"Good-bye."

The horrible bell continued to insist.

"All non-passengers ashore! All ashore!"

The numerous gangways were thronged with people obeying the call, and handkerchiefs began to wave. And there was a regular vibrating tremor through the ship.

Mr and Mrs Cotterill turned away.

Ruth and Denry approached the nearest gangway, and Denry stood aside, and made a place for her to pass. And, as always, a number of women pushed into the gangways immediately after her, and Denry had to wait, being a perfect gentleman.

His eye caught Nellie's. She had not moved.

He felt then as he had never felt in his life. No, absolutely never. Her sad, her tragic glance rendered him so uncomfortable, and yet so deliciously uncomfortable, that the symptoms startled him. He wondered what would happen to his legs. He was not sure that he had legs.

However, he demonstrated the existence of his legs by running up to Nellie. Ruth was by this time swallowed in the crowd on the landing-stage. He looked at Nellie. Nellie looked at him. Her lips twitched.

"What am I doing here?" he asked of his soul.

She was not at all well dressed. She was indeed shabby—in a steerage style. Her hat was awry; her gloves miserable. No girlish pride in her distraught face. No determination to overcome Fate. No consciousness of ability to meet a bad situation. Just those sad eyes and those twitching lips.

"Look here," Denry whispered, "you must come ashore for a second. I've something I want to give you, and I've left it in the cab."

"But there's no time. The bell's..."

"Bosh!" he exclaimed gruffly, extinguishing her timid, childish voice. "You won't go for at least a quarter of an hour. All that's only a dodge to get people off in plenty of time. Come on, I tell you."

And in a sort of hysteria he seized her thin, long hand and dragged her along the deck to another gangway, down whose steep slope they stumbled together. The crowd of sightseers and handkerchief-wavers jostled them. They could see nothing but heads and shoulders, and the great side of the ship rising above. Denry turned her back on the ship.

"This way." He still held her hand.

He struggled to the cab-rank.

"Which one is it?" she asked.

"Any one. Never mind which. Jump in." And to the first driver whose eye met his, he said: "Lime Street Station."

The gangways were being drawn away. A hoarse boom filled the air, and then a cheer.

"But I shall miss the boat," the dazed girl protested.

"Jump in."

He pushed her in.

"But I shall miss the..."

"I know you will," he replied, as if angrily. "Do you suppose I was going to let you go by that steamer? Not much."

"But mother and father..."

"I'll telegraph. They'll get it on landing."

"And where's Ruth?"

"*Be hanged to Ruth!*" he shouted furiously.

As the cab rattled over the cobbles the *Titubic* slipped away from the landing-stage. The irretrievable had happened.

Nellie burst into tears.

"Look here," Denry said savagely. "If you don't dry up, I shall have to cry myself."

"What are you going to do with me?" she whimpered.

"Well, what do *you* think? I'm going to marry you, of course."

His aggrieved tone might have been supposed to imply that people had tried to thwart him, but that he had no intention of being thwarted, nor of asking permissions, nor of conducting himself as anything but a fierce tyrant.

As for Nellie, she seemed to surrender.

Then he kissed her—also angrily. He kissed her several times—yes, even in Lord Street itself—less and less angrily.

"Where are you taking me to?" she inquired humbly, as a captive.

"I shall take you to my mother's," he said.

"Will she like it?"

"She'll either like it or lump it," said Denry. "It'll take a fortnight."

"What?"

"The notice, and things."

In the train, in the midst of a great submissive silence, she murmured:

"It'll be simply awful for father and mother."

"That can't be helped," said he. "And they'll be far too sea-sick to bother their heads about you."

"You can't think how you've staggered me," said she.

"You can't think how I've staggered myself," said he.

"When did you decide to..."

"When I was standing at the gangway, and you looked at me," he answered.

"But..."

"It's no use butting," he said. "I'm like that.... That's me, that is."

It was the bare truth that he had staggered himself. But he had staggered himself into a miraculous, ecstatic happiness. She had no money, no clothes, no style, no experience, no particular gifts. But she was she. And when he looked at her, calmed, he knew that he had done well for himself. He knew that if he had not yielded to that terrific impulse he would have done badly for himself. Mrs Machin had what she called a ticklish night of it.

VI

The next day he received a note from Ruth, dated Southport, inquiring how he came to lose her on the landing-stage, and expressing concern. It took him three days to reply, and even then the reply was a bad one. He had behaved infamously to Ruth; so much could not be denied. Within three hours of practically proposing to her, he had run off with a simple girl, who was not fit to hold a candle to her. And he did not care. That was the worst of it; he did not care.

Of course the facts reached her. The facts reached everybody; for the singular reappearance of Nellie in the streets of Bursley immediately after her departure for Canada had to be explained. Moreover, the infamous Denry was rather proud of the facts. And the town inevitably said: "Machin all over, that! Snatching the girl off the blooming lugger. Machin all over." And Denry agreed privately that it was Machin all over.

"What other chap," he demanded of the air, "would have thought of it? Or had the pluck?..."

It was mere malice on the part of destiny that caused Denry to run across Mrs Capron-Smith at Euston some weeks later. Happily they both had immense nerve.

"Dear me," said she. "What are *you* doing here?"

"Only honeymooning," he said.

CHAPTER XI

IN THE ALPS

I

Although Denry was extremely happy as a bridegroom, and capable of the most foolish symptoms of affection in private, he said to himself, and he said to Nellie (and she sturdily agreed with him): "We aren't going to be the ordinary silly honeymooners." By which, of course, he meant that they would behave so as to be taken for staid married persons. They failed thoroughly in this enterprise as far as London, where they spent a couple of nights, but on leaving Charing Cross they made a new and a better start, in the light of experience.

Their destination, it need hardly be said, was Switzerland. After Mrs Capron-Smith's remarks on the necessity of going to Switzerland in winter if one wished to respect one's self, there was really no alternative to Switzerland. Thus it was announced in the *Signal* (which had reported the wedding in ten lines, owing to the excessive quietude of the wedding) that Mr and Mrs Councillor Machin were spending a month at Mont Pridoux, sur Montreux, on the Lake of Geneva. And the announcement looked very well.

At Dieppe they got a through carriage. There were several through carriages for Switzerland on the train. In walking through the corridors from one to another Denry and Nellie had their first glimpse of the world which travels and which runs off for a holiday whenever it feels in the mood. The idea of going for a holiday in any month but August seemed odd to both of them. Denry was very bold and would insist on talking in a naturally loud voice. Nellie was timid and clinging. "What do you say?" Denry would roar at her when she half-whispered something, and she had to repeat it so that all could hear. It was part of their plan to address each other curtly, brusquely, and to frown, and to pretend to be slightly bored by each other.

They were outclassed by the world which travels. Try as they might, even Denry was morally intimidated. He had managed his clothes fairly correctly; he was not ashamed of them; and Nellie's were by no means the worst in the compartments; indeed, according to the standard of some of the most intimidating women, Nellie's costume erred in not being quite sufficiently negligent, sufficiently "anyhow." And they had plenty, and ten times plenty of money, and the consciousness of it. Expense was not being spared on that honeymoon. And yet.... Well, all that can be said is that the company was imposing. The company, which was entirely English, seemed to be unaware that any one ever did anything else but travel luxuriously to places mentioned in second-year geographies. It astounded Nellie that there should be so many people in the world with nothing to do but spend. And they were constantly saying the strangest things with an air of perfect calm.

"How much did you pay for the excess luggage?" an untidy young woman asked of an old man.

"Oh! Thirteen pounds," answered the old man, carelessly.

And not long before Nellie had scarcely escaped ten days in the steerage of an Atlantic liner.

After dinner in the restaurant car—no champagne, because it was vulgar, but a good sound, expensive wine—they felt more equal to the situation, more like part-owners of the train. Nellie prudently went to bed ere the triumphant feeling wore off. But Denry stayed up smoking in the corridor. He stayed up very late, being too proud and happy and too avid of new sensations to be able to think of sleep. It was a match which led to a conversation between himself and a thin, drawling, overbearing fellow with an eyeglass. Denry had hated this lordly creature all the way from Dieppe. In presenting him with a match he felt that he was somehow getting the better of him, for the match was precious in the nocturnal solitude of the vibrating corridor. The mere fact that two people are alone together and awake, divided from a sleeping or sleepy population only by a row of closed, mysterious doors, will do much to break down social barriers. The excellence of Denry's cigar also helped. It atoned for the breadth of his accent.

He said to himself:

"I'll have a bit of a chat with this johnny."

And then he said aloud:

"Not a bad train this!"

"No!" the eyeglass agreed languidly. "Pity they give you such a beastly dinner!"

And Denry agreed hastily that it was.

Soon they were chatting of places, and somehow it came out of Denry that he was going to Montreux. The eyeglass professed its indifference to Montreux in winter, but said the resorts above Montreux were all right, such as Caux or Pridoux.

And Denry said:

"Well, of course, shouldn't think of stopping *in* Montreux. Going to try Pridoux."

The eyeglass said it wasn't going so far as Switzerland yet; it meant to stop in the Jura.

"Geneva's a pretty deadly place, ain't it?" said the eyeglass after a pause.

"Ye-es," said Denry.

"Been there since that new esplanade was finished?"

"No," said Denry. "I saw nothing of it."

"When were you there?"

"Oh! A couple of years ago."

"Ah! It wasn't started then. Comic thing! Of course they're awfully proud in Geneva of the view of Mont Blanc."

"Yes," said Denry.

"Ever noticed how queer women are about that view? They're no end keen on it at first, but after a day or two it gets on their nerves."

"Yes," said Denry. "I've noticed that myself. My wife...."

He stopped, because he didn't know what he was going to say. The eyeglass nodded understandingly.

"All alike," it said. "Odd thing!"

When Denry introduced himself into the two-berth compartment which he had managed to secure at the end of the carriage for himself and Nellie, the poor tired child was as wakeful as an owl.

"Who have you been talking to?" she yawned.

"The eyeglass johnny."

"Oh! Really," Nellie murmured, interested and impressed. "With him, have you? I could hear voices. What sort of a man is he?"

"He seems to be an ass," said Denry. "Fearfully haw-haw. Couldn't stand him for long. I've made him believe we've been married for two years."

II

They stood on the balcony of the Hôtel Beau-Site of Mont Pridoux. A little below, to the right, was the other hotel, the Métropole, with the red-and-white Swiss flag waving over its central tower. A little below that was the terminal station of the funicular railway from Montreux. The railway ran down the sheer of the mountain into the roofs of Montreux, like a wire. On it, two toy trains crawled towards each other, like flies climbing and descending a wall. Beyond the fringe of hotels that constituted Montreux was a strip of water, and beyond the water a range of hills white at the top.

"So these are the Alps!" Nellie exclaimed.

She was disappointed; he also. But when Denry learnt from the guide-book and by inquiry that the strip of lake was seven miles across, and the highest notched peaks ten thousand feet above the sea and twenty-five miles off, Nellie gasped and was content.

They liked the Hôtel Beau-Site. It had been recommended to Denry, by a man who knew what was what, as the best hotel in Switzerland. "Don't you be misled by prices," the man had said. And Denry was not. He paid sixteen francs a day for the two of them at the Beau-Site, and was rather relieved than otherwise by the absence of finger-bowls. Everything was very good, except sometimes the hot water. The hot-water cans bore the legend "hot water," but these two words were occasionally the only evidence of heat in the water. On the other hand, the bedrooms could be made sultry by merely turning a handle; and the windows were double. Nellie was wondrously inventive. They breakfasted in bed, and she would save butter and honey from the breakfast to furnish forth afternoon tea, which was not included in the terms. She served the butter freshly with ice by the simple expedient of leaving it outside the window of a night. And Denry was struck by this house-wifery.

The other guests appeared to be of a comfortable, companionable class, with, as Denry said, "no frills." They were amazed to learn that a chattering little woman of thirty-five, who gossiped with everybody, and soon invited Denry and Nellie to have tea in her room, was an authentic Russian Countess, inscribed in the visitors' lists as "Comtesse Ruhl (with maid), Moscow." Her room was the untidiest that Nellie had ever seen, and the tea a picnic. Still, it was thrilling to have had tea with a Russian Countess.... (Plots! Nihilism! Secret police! Marble palaces!).... Those visitors' lists were breath-taking. Pages and pages of them; scores of hotels, thousands of names, nearly all English—and all people who came to Switzerland in winter, having naught else to do. Denry and Nellie bathed in correctness as in a bath.

The only persons in the hotel with whom they did not "get on" nor "hit it off" were a military party, chiefly named Clutterbuck, and presided over by a Major Clutterbuck and his wife. They sat at a large table in a corner—father, mother, several children, a sister-in-law, a sister, a governess—eight heads in all; and while utterly polite they seemed to draw a ring round themselves. They grumbled at the hotel; they played bridge (then a newish game); and once, when Denry and the Countess played with them (Denry being an adept card-player) for shilling points, Denry overheard the sister-in-law say that she was sure Captain Deverax wouldn't play for shilling points. This was the first rumour of the existence of Captain Deverax; but afterwards Captain Deverax began to be mentioned several times a day. Captain Deverax was coming to join them, and it seemed that he was a very particular man. Soon all the rest of the hotel had got its back up against this arriving Captain Deverax. Then a Clutterbuck cousin came, a smiling, hard, fluffy woman, and pronounced definitely that the Hôtel Beau-Site would never do for Captain Deverax. This cousin aroused Denry's hostility in a strange way. She imparted to the Countess (who united all sects) her opinion that Denry and Nellie were on their honeymoon. At night in a corner of the drawing-room the Countess delicately but bluntly asked Nellie if she had been married long. "No," said Nellie. "A month?" asked the Countess, smiling. "N-no," said Nellie.

The next day all the hotel knew. The vast edifice of make-believe that Denry and Nellie had laboriously erected crumbled at a word, and they stood forth, those two, blushing for the criminals they were.

The hotel was delighted. There is more rejoicing in a hotel over one honeymoon couple than over fifty families with children.

But the hotel had a shock the same day. The Clutterbuck cousin had proclaimed that owing to the inadequacy of the bedroom furniture she had been obliged to employ a sofa as a wardrobe. Then there were more references to Captain Deverax. And then at dinner it became known— Heaven knows how!— that the entire Clutterbuck party had given notice and was seceding to the Hotel Métropole. Also they had tried to carry the Countess with them, but had failed.

Now, among the guests of the Hôtel Beau-Site there had always been a professed scorn of the rival Hotel Métropole, which was a franc a day dearer, and famous for its new and rich furniture. The Métropole had an orchestra twice a week, and the English Church services were held in its drawing-room; and it was larger than the Beau-Site. In spite of these facts the clients of the Beau-Site affected to despise it, saying that the food was inferior and that the guests were snobbish. It was an article of faith in the Beau-Site that the Beau-Site was the best hotel on the mountain-side, if not in Switzerland.

The insolence of this defection on the part of the Clutterbucks! How on earth *could* people have the face to go to a landlord and say to him that they meant to desert him in favour of his rival?

Another detail: the secession of nine or ten people from one hotel to the other meant that the Métropole would decidedly be more populous than the Beau-Site, and on the point of numbers the emulation was very keen. "Well," said the Beau-Site, "let 'em go! With their Captain Deverax! We shall be better without 'em!" And that deadliest of all feuds sprang up —a rivalry between the guests of rival hotels. The Métropole had issued a general invitation to a dance, and after the monstrous conduct of the Clutterbucks the question arose whether the Beau-Site should not boycott the dance. However, it was settled that the truly effective course would be to go with critical noses in the air, and emit unfavourable comparisons with the Beau-Site. The Beau-Site suddenly became perfect in the esteem of its patrons. Not another word was heard on the subject of hot water being coated with ice. And the Clutterbucks, with incredible assurance, slid their luggage off in a sleigh to the Métropole, in the full light of day, amid the contempt of the faithful.

III

Under the stars the dancing section of the Beau-Site went off in jingling sleighs over the snow to the ball at the Métropole. The distance was not great, but it was great enough to show the inadequacy of furs against twenty degrees of mountain frost, and it was also great enough to allow the party to come to a general final understanding that its demeanour must be cold and critical in the gilded halls of the Métropole. The rumour ran that Captain Deverax had arrived, and every one agreed that he must be an insufferable booby, except the Countess Ruhl, who never used her fluent exotic English to say ill of anybody.

The gilded halls of the Métropole certainly were imposing. The hotel was incontestably larger than the Beau-Site, newer, more richly furnished. Its occupants, too, had a lordly way with them, trying to others, but inimitable. Hence the visitors from the Beau-Site, as they moved to and fro beneath those crystal chandeliers from Tottenham Court Road, had their work cut out to maintain the mien of haughty indifference. Nellie, for instance, frankly could not do it. And Denry did not do it very well. Denry, nevertheless, did score one point over Mrs Clutterbuck's fussy cousin.

"Captain Deverax has come," said this latter. "He was very late. He'll be downstairs in a few minutes. We shall get him to lead the cotillon."

"Captain Deverax?" Denry questioned.

"Yes. You've heard us mention him," said the cousin, affronted.

"Possibly," said Denry. "I don't remember."

On hearing this brief colloquy the cohorts of the Beau-Site felt that in Denry they possessed the making of a champion.

There was a disturbing surprise, however, waiting for Denry.

The lift descended; and with a peculiar double action of his arms on the doors, like a pantomime fairy emerging from an enchanted castle, a tall thin man stepped elegantly out of the lift and approached the company with a certain mincingness. But before he could reach the company several young women had rushed towards him, as though with the intention of committing suicide by hanging themselves from his neck. He was in an evening suit so perfect in detail that it might have sustained comparison with the costume of the head waiter. And he wore an eyeglass in his left eye. It was the eyeglass that made Denry jump. For two seconds he dismissed the notion.... But another two seconds of examination showed beyond doubt that this eyeglass was the eyeglass of the train. And Denry had apprehensions....

"Captain Deverax!" exclaimed several voices.

The manner in which the youthful and the mature fair clustered around this Captain, aged forty (and not handsome) was really extraordinary, to the males of the Hôtel Beau-Site. Even the little Russian Countess attached herself to him at once. And by reason of her title, her social energy, and her personal distinction, she took natural precedence of the others.

"Recognise him?" Denry whispered to his wife.

Nellie nodded. "He seems rather nice," she said diffidently.

"Nice!" Denry repeated the adjective. "The man's an ass!"

And the majority of the Beau-Site party agreed with Denry's verdict either by word or gesture.

Captain Deverax stared fixedly at Denry; then smiled vaguely and drawled, "Hullo! How d' do?"

And they shook hands.

"So you know him?" some one murmured to Denry.

"Know him?... Since infancy."

The inquirer scented facetiousness, but he was somehow impressed. The remarkable thing was that though he regarded Captain Deverax as a popinjay, he could not help feeling a certain slight satisfaction in the fact that they were in some sort acquaintances.... Mystery of the human heart!... He wished sincerely that he had not, in his conversation with the Captain in the train, talked about previous visits to Switzerland. It was dangerous.

The dance achieved that brightness and joviality which entitle a dance to call itself a success. The cotillon reached brilliance, owing to the captaincy of Captain Deverax. Several score opprobrious epithets were applied to the Captain in the course of the night, but it was agreed *nemine contradicente* that, whatever he would have done in front of a Light Brigade at Balaclava, as a leader of cotillons he was terrific. Many men, however, seemed to argue that if a man who *was* a man led a cotillon, he ought not to lead it too well, on pain of being considered a cox-comb.

At the close, during the hot soup, the worst happened. Denry had known that it would.

Captain Deverax was talking to Nellie, who was respectfully listening, about the scenery, when the Countess came up, plate in hand.

"No, no," the Countess protested. "As for me, I hate your mountains. I was born in the steppe where it is all level—level! Your mountains close me in. I am only here by order of my doctor. Your mountains get on my nerves." She shrugged her shoulders.

Captain Deverax smiled.

"It is the same with you, isn't it?" he said turning to Nellie.

"Oh, no," said Nellie, simply.

"But your husband told me the other day that when you and he were in Geneva a couple of years ago, the view of Mont Blanc used to—er—upset you."

"View of Mont Blanc?" Nellie stammered.

Everybody was aware that she and Denry had never been in Switzerland before, and that their marriage was indeed less than a month old.

"You misunderstood me," said Denry, gruffly. "My wife hasn't been to Geneva."

"Oh!" drawled Captain Deverax.

His "Oh!" contained so much of insinuation, disdain, and lofty amusement that Denry blushed, and when Nellie saw her husband's cheek she blushed in competition and defeated him easily. It was felt that either Denry had been romancing to the Captain, or that he had been married before, unknown to his Nellie, and had been "carrying on" at Geneva. The situation, though it dissolved of itself in a brief space, was awkward. It discredited the Hôtel Beau-Site. It was in the nature of a repulse for the Hôtel Beau-Site (franc a day cheaper than the Métropole) and of a triumph for the popinjay. The fault was utterly Denry's. Yet he said to himself:

"I'll be even with that chap."

On the drive home he was silent. The theme of conversation in the sleighs which did not contain the Countess was that the Captain had flirted tremendously with the Countess, and that it amounted to an affair.

IV

Captain Deverax was equally salient in the department of sports. There was a fair sheet of ice, obtained by cutting into the side of the mountain, and a very good tobogganing track, about half a mile in length and full of fine curves, common to the two hotels. Denry's predilection was for the track. He would lie on his stomach on the little contrivance which the Swiss call a luge, and which consists of naught but three bits of wood and two steel-clad runners, and would course down the perilous curves at twenty miles an hour. Until the Captain came, this was regarded as dashing, because most people were content to sit on the luge and travel legs-foremost instead of head-foremost. But the Captain, after a few eights on the ice, intimated that for the rest no sport was true sport save the sport of ski-running. He allowed it to be understood that luges were for infants. He had brought his skis, and these instruments of locomotion, some six feet in length, made a sensation among the inexperienced. For when he had strapped them to his feet the Captain, while stating candidly that his skill was as nothing to that of the Swedish professionals at St Moritz, could assuredly slide over snow in manner prodigious and beautiful. And he was exquisitely clothed for the part. His knickerbockers, in the elegance of their lines, were the delight of beholders. Skiing became the rage. Even Nellie insisted on hiring a pair. And the pronunciation of the word "ski" aroused long discussions and was never definitely settled by anybody. The Captain said "skee," but he did not object to "shee," which was said to be the more strictly correct by a lady who knew some one who had been to Norway. People with no shame and no feeling for correctness said brazenly, "sky." Denry, whom nothing could induce to desert his luge, said that obviously "s-k-i" could only spell "planks." And thanks to his inspiration this version was adopted by the majority.

On the second day of Nellie's struggle with her skis she had more success than she either anticipated or desired. She had been making experiments at the summit of the track, slithering about, falling, and being restored to uprightness by as many persons as happened to be near. Skis seemed to her to be the most ungovernable and least practical means of travel that the madness of man had ever concocted. Skates were well-behaved old horses compared to these long, untamed fiends, and a luge was like a tricycle. Then suddenly a friendly starting push drove her a yard or two, and she glided past the level on to the first imperceptible slope of the track. By some hazard her two planks were exactly parallel, as they ought to be, and she glided forward miraculously. And people heard her say:

"How lovely!"

And then people heard her say:

"Oh!... Oh!"

For her pace was increasing. And she dared not strike her pole into the ground. She had, in fact, no control whatever over those two planks to which her feet were strapped. She might have been Mazeppa and they mustangs. She could not even fall. So she fled down the preliminary straight of the track, and ecstatic spectators cried: "Look how *well* Mrs Machin is doing!"

Mrs Machin would have given all her furs to be anywhere off those planks. On the adjacent fields of glittering snow the Captain had been giving his adored Countess a lesson in the use of skis; and they stood together, the Countess somewhat insecure, by the side of the track at its first curve.

Nellie, dumb with excitement and amazement, swept towards them.

"Look out!" cried the Captain.

In vain! He himself might perhaps have escaped, but he could not abandon his Countess in the moment of peril, and the Countess could only move after much thought and many efforts, being scarce more advanced than Nellie. Nellie's wilful planks quite ignored the curve, and, as it were afloat on them, she charged off the track, and into the Captain and the Countess. The impact was tremendous. Six skis waved like semaphores in the air. Then all was still. Then, as the beholders hastened to the scene of the disaster, the Countess laughed and Nellie laughed. The laugh of the Captain was not heard. The sole casualty was a wound about a foot long in the hinterland of the Captain's unique knicker-bockers. And as threads of that beautiful check pattern were afterwards found attached to the wheel of Nellie's pole, the cause of the wound was indisputable. The Captain departed home, chiefly backwards, but with great rapidity.

In the afternoon Denry went down to Montreux and returned with an opal bracelet, which Nellie wore at dinner.

"Oh! What a ripping bracelet!" said a girl.

"Yes," said Nellie. "My husband gave it me only to-day."

"I suppose it's your birthday or something," the inquisitive girl ventured.

"No," said Nellie.

"How nice of him!" said the girl.

The next day Captain Deverax appeared in riding breeches. They were not correct for ski-running, but they were the best he could do. He visited a tailor's in Montreux.

V

The Countess Ruhl had a large sleigh of her own, also a horse; both were hired from Montreux. In this vehicle, sometimes alone, sometimes with a male servant, she would drive at Russian speed over the undulating mountain roads; and for such expeditions she always wore a large red cloak with a hood. Often she was thus seen, in the afternoon; the scarlet made a bright moving patch on the vast expanses of snow. Once, at some distance from the village, two tale-tellers observed a man on skis careering in the neighbourhood of the sleigh. It was Captain Deverax. The flirtation, therefore, was growing warmer and warmer. The hotels hummed with the tidings of it. But the Countess never said anything; nor could anything be extracted from her by even the most experienced gossips. She was an agreeable but a mysterious woman, as befitted a Russian Countess. Again and again were she and the Captain seen together afar off in the landscape. Certainly it was a novelty in flirtations. People wondered what might happen between the two at the fancy-dress ball which the Hôtel Beau-Site was to give in return for the hospitality of the Hôtel Métropole. The ball was offered not in love, but in emulation, almost in hate; for the jealousy displayed by the Beau-Site against the increasing insolence of the Métropole had become acute. The airs of the Captain and his lieges, the Clutterbuck party, had reached the limit of the Beau-Site's endurance. The Métropole seemed to take it for granted that the Captain would lead the cotillon at the Beau-Site's ball as he had led it at the Métropole's.

And then, on the very afternoon of the ball, the Countess received a telegram—it was said from St Petersburg—which necessitated her instant departure. And she went, in an hour, down to Montreux by the funicular railway, and was lost to the Beau-Site. This was a blow to the prestige of the Beau-Site. For the Countess was its chief star, and, moreover, much loved by her fellow-guests, despite her curious weakness for the popinjay, and the mystery of her outings with him.

In the stables Denry saw the Countess's hired sleigh and horse, and in the sleigh her glowing red cloak. And he had one of his ideas, which he executed, although snow was beginning to fall. In ten minutes he and Nellie were driving forth, and Nellie in the red cloak held the reins. Denry, in a coachman's furs, sat behind. They whirled past the Hôtel Métropole. And shortly afterwards, on the wild road towards Attalens, Denry saw a pair of skis scudding as quickly as skis can scud in their rear. It was astonishing how the sleigh, with all the merry jingle of its bells, kept that pair of skis at a distance of about a hundred yards. It seemed to invite the skis to overtake it, and then to regret the invitation and flee further. Up the hills it would crawl, for the skis climbed slowly. Down them it galloped, for the skis slid on the slopes at a dizzy pace. Occasionally a shout came from the skis. And the snow fell thicker and thicker. So for four or five miles. Starlight commenced. Then the road made a huge descending curve round a hollowed meadow, and the horse galloped its best. But the skis, making a straight line down the snow, acquired the speed of an express, and gained on the sleigh one yard in every three. At the bottom, where the curve met the straight line, was a farmhouse and outbuildings and a hedge and a stone wall and other matters. The sleigh arrived at the point first, but only by a trifle. "Mind your toes," Denry muttered to himself, meaning an injunction to the skis, whose toes were three feet long. The skis, through the eddying snow, yelled frantically to the sleigh to give room. The skis shot up into the road, and in swerving aside swerved into a snow-laden hedge, and clean over it into the farmyard, where they stuck themselves up in the air, as skis will when the person to whose feet they are attached is lying prone. The door of the farm opened and a woman appeared.

She saw the skis at her doorstep. She heard the sleigh-bells, but the sleigh had already vanished into the dusk.

"Well, that was a bit of a lark, that was, Countess!" said Denry to Nellie. "That will be something to talk about. We'd better drive home through Corsier, and quick too! It'll be quite dark soon."

"Supposing he's dead!" Nellie breathed, aghast, reining in the horse.

"Not he!" said Denry. "I saw him beginning to sit up."

"But how will he get home?"

"It looks a very nice farmhouse," said Denry. "I should think he'd be sorry to leave it."

VI

When Denry entered the dining-room of the Beau-Site, which had been cleared for the ball, his costume drew attention not so much by its splendour or ingenuity as by its peculiarity. He wore a short Chinese-shaped jacket, which his wife had made out of blue linen, and a flat Chinese hat to match, which they had constructed together on a basis of cardboard. But his thighs were enclosed in a pair of absurdly ample riding-breeches of an impressive check and cut to a comic exaggeration of the English pattern. He had bought the cloth for these at the tailor's in Montreux. Below them were very tight leggings, also English. In reply to a question as to what or whom he supposed himself to represent, he replied:

"A Captain of Chinese cavalry, of course."

And he put an eyeglass into his left eye and stared.

Now it had been understood that Nellie was to appear as Lady Jane Grey. But she appeared as Little Red Riding-Hood, wearing over her frock the forgotten cloak of the Countess Ruhl.

Instantly he saw her, Denry hurried towards her, with a movement of the legs and a flourish of the eyeglass in his left hand which powerfully suggested a figure familiar to every member of the company. There was laughter. People saw that the idea was immensely funny and clever, and the laughter ran about like fire. At the same time some persons were not quite sure whether Denry had not lapsed a little from the finest taste in this caricature. And all of them were secretly afraid that the uncomfortable might happen when Captain Deverax arrived.

However, Captain Deverax did not arrive. The party from the Métropole came with the news that he had not been seen at the hotel for dinner; it was assumed that he had been to Montreux and missed the funicular back.

"Our two stars simultaneously eclipsed!" said Denry, as the Clutterbucks (representing all the history of England) stared at him curiously.

"Why?" exclaimed the Clutterbuck cousin, "who's the other?"

"The Countess," said Denry. "She went this afternoon—three o'clock."

And all the Métropole party fell into grief.

"It's a world of coincidences," said Denry, with emphasis.

"You don't mean to insinuate," said Mrs Clutterbuck, with a nervous laugh, "that Captain Deverax has—er—gone after the Countess?"

"Oh no!" said Denry, with unction. "Such a thought never entered my head."

"I think you're a very strange man, Mr Machin," retorted Mrs Clutterbuck, hostile and not a bit reassured. "May one ask what that costume is supposed to be?"

"A Captain of Chinese cavalry," said Denry, lifting his eyeglass.

Nevertheless, the dance was a remarkable success, and little by little even the sternest adherents of the absent Captain Deverax deigned to be amused by Denry's Chinese gestures. Also, Denry led the cotillon, and was thereafter greatly applauded by the Beau-Site. The visitors agreed among themselves that, considering that his name was not Deverax, Denry acquitted himself honourably. Later he went to the bureau, and, returning, whispered to his wife:

"It's all right. He's come back safe."

"How do you know?"

"I've just telephoned to ask."

Denry's subsequent humour was wildly gay. And for some reason which nobody could comprehend, he put a sling round his left arm. His efforts to insert the eyeglass into his left eye with his right hand were insistently ludicrous and became a sure source of laughter for all beholders. When the Métropole party were getting into their sleighs to go home—it had ceased snowing—Denry was still trying to insert his eyeglass into his left eye with his right hand, to the universal joy.

VII

But the joy of the night was feeble in comparison with the violent joy of the next morning. Denry was wandering, apparently aimless, between the finish of the tobogganing track and the portals of the Métropole. The snowfall had repaired the defects of the worn track, but it needed to be flattened down by use, and a number of conscientious "lugeurs" were flattening it by frequent descents, which grew faster at each repetition. Other holiday-makers were idling about in the sunshine. A page-boy of the Métropole departed in the direction of the Beau-Site with a note.

At length—the hour was nearing eleven—Captain Deverax, languid, put his head out of the Métropole and sniffed the air. Finding the air sufferable, he came forth on to the steps. His left arm was in a sling. He was wearing the new knickerbockers which he had ordered at Montreux, and which were of precisely the same vast check as had ornamented Denry's legs on the previous night.

"Hullo!" said Denry, sympathetically. "What's this?"

The Captain needed sympathy.

"Ski-ing yesterday afternoon," said he, with a little laugh. "Hasn't the Countess told any of you?"

"No," said Denry, "not a word."

The Captain seemed to pause a moment.

"Yes," said he. "A trifling accident. I was ski-ing with the Countess. That is, I was ski-ing and she was in her sleigh."

"Then this is why you didn't turn up at the dance?"

"Yes," said the Captain.

"Well," said Denry, "I hope it's not serious. I can tell you one thing, the cotillon was a most fearful frost without you." The Captain seemed grateful.

They strolled together toward the track.

The first group of people that caught sight of the Captain with his checked legs and his arm in a sling began to smile. Observing this smile, and fancying himself deceived, the Captain attempted to put his eyeglass into his left eye with his right hand, and regularly failed. His efforts towards this feat changed the smiles to enormous laughter.

"I daresay it's awfully funny," said he. "But what can a fellow do with one arm in a sling?"

The laughter was merely intensified. And the group, growing as luge after luge arrived at the end of the track, seemed to give itself up to mirth, to the exclusion of even a proper curiosity about the nature of the Captain's damage. Each fresh attempt to put the eyeglass to his eye was coal on the crackling fire. The Clutterbucks alone seemed glum.

"What on earth is the joke?" Denry asked primly. "Captain Deverax came to grief late yesterday afternoon, ski-ing with the Countess Ruhl. That's why he didn't turn up last night. By the way, where was it, Captain?"

"On the mountain, near Attalens," Deverax answered gloomily. "Happily there was a farmhouse near—it was almost dark."

"With the Countess?" demanded a young impulsive schoolgirl.

"You did say the Countess, didn't you?" Denry asked.

"Why, certainly," said the Captain, testily.

"Well," said the schoolgirl with the nonchalant thoughtless cruelty of youth, "considering that we all saw the Countess off in the funicular at three o'clock, I don't see how you could have been ski-ing with her when it was nearly dark." And the child turned up the hill with her luge, leaving her elders to unknot the situation.

"Oh, yes!" said Denry. "I forgot to tell you that the Countess left yesterday after lunch."

At the same moment the page-boy, reappearing, touched his cap and placed a note in the Captain's only free hand.

"Couldn't deliver it, sir. The Comtesse left early yesterday afternoon."

Convicted of imaginary adventure with noble ladies, the Captain made his retreat, muttering, back to the hotel. At lunch Denry related the exact circumstances to a delighted table, and the exact circumstances soon reached the Clutterbuck faction at the Métropole. On the following day the Clutterbuck faction and Captain Deverax (now fully enlightened) left Mont Pridoux for some paradise unknown. If murderous thoughts could kill, Denry would have lain dead. But he survived to go with about half the Beau-Site guests to the funicular station to wish the Clutterbucks a pleasant journey. The Captain might have challenged him to a duel but a haughty and icy ceremoniousness was deemed the best treatment for Denry. "Never show a wound" must have been the Captain's motto.

The Beau-Site had scored effectively. And, now that its rival had lost eleven clients by one single train, it beat the Métropole even in vulgar numbers.

Denry had an embryo of a conscience somewhere, and Nellie's was fully developed.

"Well," said Denry, in reply to Nellie's conscience, "it serves him right for making me look a fool over that Geneva business. And besides, I can't stand uppishness, and I won't. I'm from the Five Towns, I am."

Upon which singular utterance the incident closed.

CHAPTER XII

THE SUPREME HONOUR

I

Denry was not as regular in his goings and comings as the generality of business men in the Five Towns; no doubt because he was not by nature a business man at all, but an adventurous spirit who happened to be in a business which was much too good to leave. He was continually, as they say there, "up to something" that caused changes in daily habits. Moreover, the Universal Thrift Club (Limited) was so automatic and self-winding that Denry ran no risks in leaving it often to the care of his highly drilled staff. Still, he did usually come home to his tea about six o'clock of an evening, like the rest, and like the rest, he brought with him a copy of the *Signal* to glance at during tea.

One afternoon in July he arrived thus upon his waiting wife at Machin House, Bleakridge. And she could see that an idea was fermenting in his head. Nellie understood him. One of the most delightful and reassuring things about his married life was Nellie's instinctive comprehension of him. His mother understood him profoundly. But she understood him in a manner sardonic, slightly malicious and even hostile, whereas Nellie understood him with her absurd love. According to his mother's attitude, Denry was guilty till he had proved himself innocent. According to Nellie's, he was always right and always clever in what he did, until he himself said that he had been wrong and stupid— and not always then. Nevertheless, his mother was just as ridiculously proud of him as Nellie was; but she would have perished on the scaffold rather than admit that Denry differed in any detail from the common run of sons. Mrs Machin had departed from Machin House without waiting to be asked. It was characteristic of her that she had returned to Brougham Street and rented there an out-of-date cottage without a single one of the labour-saving contrivances that distinguished the residence which her son had originally built for her.

It was still delicious for Denry to sit down to tea in the dining-room, that miracle of conveniences, opposite the smile of his wife, which told him (*a*) that he was wonderful, (*b*) that she was enchanted to be alive, and (*c*) that he had deserved her particular caressing attentions and would receive them. On the afternoon in July the smile told him (*d*) that he was possessed by one of his ideas.

"Extraordinary how she tumbles to things!" he reflected.

Nellie's new fox-terrier had come in from the garden through the French window, and eaten part of a muffin, and Denry had eaten a muffin and a half, before Nellie, straightening herself proudly and putting her shoulders back (a gesture of hers) thought fit to murmur:

"Well, anything thrilling happened to-day?"

Denry opened the green sheet and read:

"'Sudden death of Alderman Bloor in London.' What price that?"

"Oh!" exclaimed Nellie. "How shocked father will be! They were always rather friendly. By the way, I had a letter from mother this morning. It appears as if Toronto was a sort of paradise. But you can see the old thing prefers Bursley. Father's had a boil on his neck, just at the edge of his collar. He says it's because he's too well. What did Mr Bloor die off?"

"He was in the fashion," said Denry.

"How?"

"Appendicitis, of course. Operation—domino! All over in three days."

"Poor man!" Nellie murmured, trying to feel sad for a change and not succeeding. "And he was to have been mayor in November, wasn't he? How disappointing for him."

"I expect he's got something else to think about," said Denry.

After a pause Nellie asked suddenly:

"Who'll be mayor—now?"

"Well," said Denry, "his Worship Councillor Barlow, J.P., will be extremely cross if *he* isn't."

"How horrid!" said Nellie, frankly. "And he's got nobody at all to be mayoress."

"Mrs Prettyman would be mayoress," said Denry. "When there's no wife or daughter, it's always a sister if there is one."

"But can you *imagine* Mrs Prettyman as mayoress? Why, they say she scrubs her own doorstep—after dark. They ought to make you mayor."

"Do you fancy yourself as mayoress?" he inquired.

"I should be better than Mrs Prettyman, anyhow."

"I believe you'd make an A1 mayoress," said Denry.

"I should be frightfully nervous," she confidentially admitted.

"I doubt it," said he.

The fact was, that since her return to Bursley from the honeymoon, Nellie was an altered woman. She had acquired, as it were in a day, to an astonishing extent, what in the Five Towns is called "a nerve."

"I should like to try it," said she.

"One day you'll have to try it, whether you want to or not."

"When will that be?"

"Don't know. Might be next year but one. Old Barlow's pretty certain to be chosen for next November. It's looked on as his turn next. I know there's been a good bit of talk about me for the year after Barlow. Of course, Bloor's death will advance everything by a year. But even if I come next after Barlow it'll be too late."

"Too late? Too late for what?"

"I'll tell you," said Denry. "I wanted to be the youngest mayor that Bursley's ever had. It was only a kind of notion I had a long time ago. I'd given it up, because I knew there was no chance unless I came before Bloor, which of course I couldn't do. Now he's dead. If I could upset old Barlow's apple-cart I should just be the youngest mayor by the skin of my teeth. Huskinson, the mayor in 1884, was aged thirty-four and six months. I've looked it all up this afternoon."

"How lovely if you *could* be the youngest mayor!"

"Yes. I'll tell you how I feel. I feel as though I didn't want to be mayor at all if I can't be the youngest mayor... you know."

She knew.

"Oh!" she cried, "do upset Mr Barlow's apple-cart. He's a horrid old thing. Should I be the youngest mayoress?"

"Not by chalks," said he. "Huskinson's sister was only sixteen."

"But that's only playing at being mayoress!" Nellie protested. "Anyhow, I do think you might be youngest mayor. Who settles it?"

"The Council, of course."

"Nobody likes Councillor Barlow."

"He'll be still less liked when he's wound up the Bursley Football Club."

"Well, urge him on to wind it up, then. But I don't see what football has got to do with being mayor."

She endeavoured to look like a serious politician.

"You are nothing but a cuckoo," Denry pleasantly informed her. "Football has got to do with everything. And it's been a disastrous mistake in my career that I've never taken any interest in football. Old Barlow wants no urging on to wind up the Football Club. He's absolutely set on it. He's lost too much over it. If I could stop him from winding it up, I might...."

"What?"

"I dunno."

She perceived that his idea was yet vague.

II

Not very many days afterwards the walls of Bursley called attention, by small blue and red posters (blue and red being the historic colours of the Bursley Football Club), to a public meeting, which was to be held in the Town Hall, under the presidency of the Mayor, to consider what steps could be taken to secure the future of the Bursley Football Club.

There were two "great" football clubs in the Five Towns—Knype, one of the oldest clubs in England, and Bursley. Both were in the League, though Knype was in the first division while Bursley was only in the second. Both were, in fact, limited companies, engaged as much in the pursuit of dividends as in the practice of the one ancient and glorious sport which appeals to the reason and the heart of England. (Neither ever paid a dividend.) Both employed professionals, who, by a strange chance, were nearly all born in Scotland; and both also employed trainers who, before an important match, took the teams off to a hydropathic establishment far, far distant from any public-house. (This was called "training.") Now, whereas the Knype Club was struggling along fairly well, the Bursley Club had come to the end of its resources. The great football public had practically deserted it. The explanation, of course, was that Bursley had been losing too many matches. The great football public had no use for anything but victories. It would treat its players like gods—so long as they won. But when they happened to lose, the great football public simply sulked. It did not kick a man that was down; it merely ignored him, well knowing that the man could not get up without help. It cared nothing whatever for fidelity, municipal patriotism, fair play, the chances of war, or dividends on capital. If it could see victories it would pay sixpence, but it would not pay sixpence to assist at defeats.

Still, when at a special general meeting of the Bursley Football Club, Limited, held at the registered office, the Coffee House, Bursley, Councillor Barlow, J.P., Chairman of the Company since the creation of the League, announced that the Directors had reluctantly come to the conclusion that they could not conscientiously embark on the dangerous risks of the approaching season, and that it was the intention of the Directors to wind up the club, in default of adequate public interest— when Bursley read this in the *Signal,* the town was certainly shocked. Was the famous club, then, to disappear for ever, and the football ground to be sold in plots, and the grand stand for firewood? The shock was so severe that the death of Alderman Bloor (none the less a mighty figure in Bursley) had passed as a minor event.

Hence the advertisement of the meeting in the Town Hall caused joy and hope, and people said to themselves: "Something's bound to be done; the old club can't go out like that." And everybody grew quite sentimental. And although nothing is supposed to be capable of filling Bursley Town Hall except a political meeting and an old folk's treat, Bursley Town Hall was as near full as made no matter for the football question. Many men had cheerfully sacrificed a game of billiards and a glass of beer in order to attend it.

The Mayor, in the chair, was a mild old gentleman who knew nothing whatever about football and had probably never seen a football match; but it was essential that the meeting should have august patronage and so the Mayor had been trapped and tamed. On the mere fact that he paid an annual subscription to the golf club, certain parties built up the legend that he was a true sportsman, with the true interests of sport in his soul.

He uttered a few phrases, such as "the manly game," "old associations," "bound up with the history of England," "splendid fellows," "indomitable pluck," "dogged by misfortune" (indeed, he produced quite an impression on the rude and grim audience), and then he called upon Councillor Barlow to make a statement.

Councillor Barlow, on the Mayor's right, was a different kind of man from the Mayor. He was fifty and iron-grey, with whiskers, but no moustache; short, stoutish, raspish.

He said nothing about manliness, pluck, history, or Auld Lang Syne.

He said he had given his services as Chairman to the football club for thirteen years; that he had taken up £2000 worth of shares in the Company; and that as at that moment the Company's liabilities would exactly absorb its assets, his £2000 was worth exactly nothing. "You may say," he said, "I've lost that £2000 in thirteen years. That is, it's the same as if I'd been steadily paying three pun' a week out of my own pocket to provide football matches that you chaps wouldn't take the trouble to go and see. That's the straight of it! What have I got for my pains?

Nothing but worries and these!" (He pointed to his grey hairs.) "And I'm not alone; there's others; and now I have to come and defend myself at a public meeting. I'm supposed not to have the best interests of football at heart. Me and my co-Directors," he proceeded, with even a rougher raspishness, "have warned the town again and again what would happen if the matches weren't better patronised. And now it's happened, and now it's too late, you want to *do* something! You can't! It's too late. There's only one thing the matter with first-class football in Bursley," he concluded, "and it isn't the players. It's the public— it's yourselves. You're the most craven lot of tom-fools that ever a big football club had to do with. When we lose a match, what do you do? Do you come and encourage us next time? No, you stop away, and leave us fifty or sixty pound out of pocket on a match, just to teach us better! Do you expect us to win every match? Why, Preston North End itself"— here he spoke solemnly, of heroes— "Preston North End itself in its great days didn't win every match—it lost to Accrington. But did the Preston public desert it? No! *You*—you haven't got the pluck of a louse, nor the faithfulness of a cat. You've starved your football club to death, and now you call a meeting to weep and grumble. And you have the insolence to write letters to the *Signal* about bad management, forsooth! If anybody in the hall thinks he can manage this club better than me and my co-Directors have done, I may say that we hold a majority of the shares, and we'll part with the whole show to any clever person or persons who care to take it off our hands at a bargain price. That's talking."

He sat down.

Silence fell. Even in the Five Towns a public meeting is seldom bullied as Councillor Barlow had bullied that meeting. It was aghast. Councillor Barlow had never been popular: he had merely been respected; but thenceforward he became even less popular than before.

"I'm sure we shall all find Councillor Barlow's heat quite excusable—" the Mayor diplomatically began.

"No heat at all," the Councillor interrupted. "Simply cold truth!"

A number of speakers followed, and nearly all of them were against the Directors. Some, with prodigious memories for every combination of players in every match that had ever been played, sought to prove by detailed instances that Councillor Barlow and his co-Directors had persistently and regularly muddled their work during thirteen industrious years. And they defended the insulted public by asserting that no public that respected itself would pay sixpence to watch the wretched football provided by Councillor Barlow. They shouted that the team wanted reconstituting, wanted new blood.

"Yes," shouted Councillor Barlow in reply; "And how are you going to get new blood, with transfer fees as high as they are now? You can't get even an average good player for less than £200. Where's the money to come from? Anybody want to lend a thousand or so on second debentures?"

He laughed sneeringly.

No one showed a desire to invest in second debentures of the Bursley F.C. Ltd.

Still, speakers kept harping on the necessity of new blood in the team, and then others, bolder, harped on the necessity of new blood on the board.

"Shares on sale!" cried the Councillor. "Any buyers? Or," he added, "do you want something for nothing—as usual?"

At length a gentleman rose at the back of the hall.

"I don't pretend to be an expert on football," said he, "though I think it's a great game, but I should like to say a few words as to this question of new blood."

The audience craned its neck.

"Will Mr Councillor Machin kindly step up to the platform?" the Mayor suggested.

And up Denry stepped.

The thought in every mind was: "What's he going to do? What's he got up his sleeve—this time?"

"Three cheers for Machin!" people chanted gaily.

"Order!" said the Mayor.

Denry faced the audience. He was now accustomed to audiences. He said:

"If I'm not mistaken, one of the greatest modern footballers is a native of this town."

And scores of voices yelled: "Ay! Callear! Callear! Greatest centre forward in England!"

"Yes," said Denry. "Callear is the man I mean. Callear left the district, unfortunately for the district, at the age of nineteen for Liverpool. And it was not till after he left that his astounding abilities were perceived. It isn't too much to say that he made the fortune of Liverpool City. And I believe it is the fact that he scored more goals in three seasons than any other player has ever done in the League. Then, York County, which was in a tight place last year, bought him from Liverpool for a high price, and, as all the world knows, Callear had his leg broken in the first match he played for his new club. That just happened to be the ruin of the York Club, which is now quite suddenly in bankruptcy (which happily we are not), and which is disposing of its players. Gentlemen, I say that Callear ought to come back to his native town. He is fitter than ever he was, and his proper place is in his native town."

Loud cheers.

"As captain and centre forward of the club of the Mother of the Five Towns, he would be an immense acquisition and attraction, and he would lead us to victory."

Renewed cheers.

"And how," demanded Councillor Barlow, jumping up angrily, "are we to get him back to his precious native town? Councillor Machin admits that he is not an expert on football. It will probably be news to him that Aston Villa have offered £700 to York for the transfer of Callear, and Blackburn Rovers have offered £750, and they're fighting it out between 'em. Any gentleman willing to put down £800 to buy Callear for Bursley?" he sneered. "I don't mind telling you that steam-engines and the King himself couldn't get Callear into our club."

"Quite finished?" Denry inquired, still standing.

Laughter, overtopped by Councillor Barlow's snort as he sat down.

Denry lifted his voice.

"Mr Callear, will you be good enough to step forward and let us all have a look at you?"

The effect of these apparently simple words surpassed any effect previously obtained by the most complex flights of oratory in that hall. A young, blushing, clumsy, long-limbed, small-bodied giant stumbled along the central aisle and climbed the steps to the platform, where Denry pointed him to a seat. He was recognised by all the true votaries of the game. And everybody said to everybody: "By Gosh! It's him, right enough. It's Callear!" And a vast astonishment and expectation of good fortune filled the hall. Applause burst forth, and though no one knew what the appearance of Callear signified, the applause continued and waxed.

"Good old Callear!" The hoarse shouts succeeded each other. "Good old Machin!"

"Anyhow," said Denry, when the storm was stilled, "we've got him here, without either steam-engines or His Majesty. Will the Directors of the club accept him?"

"And what about the transfer?" Councillor Barlow demanded.

"Would you accept him and try another season if you could get him free?" Denry retorted.

Councillor Barlow always knew his mind, and was never afraid to let other people share that knowledge.

"Yes," he said.

"Then I will see that you have the transfer free."

"But what about York?"

"I have settled with York provisionally," said Denry. "That is my affair. I have returned from York to-day. Leave all that to me. This town has had many benefactors far more important than myself. But I shall be able to claim this originality: I'm the first to make a present of a live man to the town. Gentlemen— Mr Mayor—I venture to call for three cheers for the greatest centre forward in England, our fellow-townsman."

The scene, as the *Signal* said, was unique.

And at the Sports Club and the other clubs afterwards, men said to each other: "No one but him would have thought of bringing Callear over specially and showing him on the platform.... That's cost him above twopence, that has!"

Two days later a letter appeared in the *Signal* (signed "Fiat Justitia"), suggesting that Denry, as some reward for his public spirit, ought to be the next mayor of Bursley, in place of Alderman Bloor deceased. The letter urged that he would make an admirable mayor, the sort of mayor the old town wanted in order to wake it up. And also it pointed out that Denry would be the youngest mayor that Bursley had ever had, and probably the youngest mayor in England that year. The sentiment in the last idea appealed to the town. The town decided that it would positively *like* to have the youngest mayor it had ever had, and probably the youngest mayor in England that year. The *Signal* printed dozens of letters on the subject. When the Council met, more informally than formally, to choose a chief magistrate in place of the dead alderman, several councillors urged that what Bursley wanted was a young and *popular* mayor. And, in fine, Councillor Barlow was shelved for a year. On the choice being published the entire town said: "Now we *shall* have a mayoralty—and don't you forget it!"

And Denry said to Nellie: "You'll be mayoress to the youngest mayor, etc., my child. And it's cost me, including hotel and travelling expenses, eight hundred and eleven pounds six and seven-pence."

III

The rightness of the Council in selecting Denry as mayor was confirmed in a singular manner by the behaviour of the football and of Callear at the opening match of the season.

It was a philanthropic match, between Bursley and Axe, for the benefit of a county orphanage, and, according to the custom of such matches, the ball was formally kicked off by a celebrity, a pillar of society. The ceremony of kicking off has no sporting significance; the celebrity merely with gentleness propels the ball out of the white circle and then flies for his life from the *mêlée*; but it is supposed to add to the moral splendour of the game. In the present instance the posters said: "Kick-off at 3.45 by Councillor E.H. Machin, Mayor-designate." And, indeed, no other celebrity could have been decently selected. On the fine afternoon of the match Denry therefore discovered himself with a new football at his toes, a silk hat on his head, and twenty-two Herculean players menacing him in attitudes expressive of an intention to murder him. Bursley had lost the toss, and hence Denry had to kick towards the Bursley goal. As the *Signal* said, he "despatched the sphere" straight into the keeping of Callear, who as centre forward was facing him, and Callear was dodging down the field with it before the Axe players had finished admiring Denry's effrontery. Every reader will remember with a thrill the historic match in which the immortal Jimmy Brown, on the last occasion when he captained Blackburn Rovers, dribbled the ball himself down the length of the field, scored a goal, and went home with the English Cup under his arm. Callear evidently intended to imitate the feat. He was entirely wrong. Dribbling tactics had been killed for ever, years before, by Preston North End, who invented the "passing" game. Yet Callear went on, and good luck seemed to float over him like a cherub. Finally he shot; a wild, high shot; but there was an adverse wind which dragged the ball down, swept it round, and blew it into the net. The first goal had been scored in twenty seconds! (It was also the last in the match.) Callear's reputation was established. Useless for solemn experts to point out that he had simply been larking for the gallery, and that the result was a shocking fluke—Callear's reputation was established. He became at once the idol of the populace. As Denry walked gingerly off the field to the grand stand he, too, was loudly cheered, and he could not help feeling that, somehow, it was he who had scored that goal. And although nobody uttered the precise thought, most people did secretly think, as they gazed at the triumphant Denry, that a man who triumphed like that, because he triumphed like that, was the right sort of man to be mayor, the kind of man they needed.

Denry became identified with the highest class of local football. This fact led to a curious crisis in the history of municipal manners. On Corporation Sunday the mayor walks to church, preceded by the mace, and followed by the aldermen and councillors, the borough officials, the Volunteers and the Fire Brigade; after all these, in the procession, come individuals known as prominent citizens. Now the first and second elevens of the Bursley Football Club, headed by Callear, expressed their desire to occupy a place in Denry's mayoral procession; they felt that some public acknowledgment was due to the Mayor for his services to the national sport. Denry instantly agreed, with thanks: the notion seemed to him entirely admirable. Then some unfortunately-inspired parson wrote to the *Signal* to protest against professional footballers following the chief magistrate of the borough to church. His arguments were that such a thing was unheard-of, and that football was the cause of a great deal of evil gambling. Some people were inclined to agree with the protest, until Denry wrote to the *Signal* and put a few questions: Was Bursley proud of its football team? Or was Bursley ashamed of its football team? Was the practice of football incompatible with good citizenship? Was there anything dishonourable in playing football? Ought professional footballers to be considered as social pariahs? Was there any class of beings to whom the churches ought to be closed?

The parson foundered in a storm of opprobrium, scorn, and ironic laughter. Though the town laughed, it only laughed to hide its disgust of the parson.

People began to wonder whether the teams would attend in costume, carrying the football between them on a charger as a symbol. No such multitudes ever greeted a mayoral procession in Bursley before. The footballers, however, appeared in ordinary costume (many of them in frock-coats); but they wore neckties of the club colours, a device which was agreed to be in the nicest taste. St Luke's Church was crowded; and, what is stranger, the churchyard was also crowded. The church barely held the procession itself and the ladies who, by influence, had been accommodated with seats in advance. Thousands of persons filled the churchyard, and to prevent them from crushing into the packed fane and bursting it at its weakest point, the apse, the doors had to be locked and guarded. Four women swooned during the service: neither Mrs Machin, senior, nor Nellie, was among the four. It was the first time that any one had been known to swoon at a religious service held in November. This fact alone gave a tremendous prestige to Denry's mayoralty. When, with Nellie on his arm, he emerged from the church to the thunders of the organ, the greeting which he received in the churchyard, though the solemnity of the occasion forbade clapping, lacked naught in brilliance and efficacy.

The real point and delight of that Corporation Sunday was not fully appreciated till later. It had been expected that the collection after the sermon would be much larger than usual, because the congregation was much larger than usual. But the church-wardens were startled to find it four times as large as usual. They were further startled to find only three threepenny-bits among all the coins.

This singularity led to comment and to note-comparing. Everybody had noticed for weeks past a growing dearth of threepenny-bits. Indeed, threepenny-bits had practically vanished from circulation in the Five Towns. On the Monday it became known that the clerks of the various branches of the Universal Thrift Club, Limited, had paid into the banks enormous and unparalleled quantities of threepenny-bits, and for at least a week afterwards everybody paid for everything in threepenny-bits. And the piquant news passed from mouth to mouth that Denry, to the simple end of ensuring a thumping collection for charities on Corporation Sunday, had used the vast organisation of the Thrift Club to bring about a famine of threepenny-bits. In the annals of the town that Sunday is referred to as "Threepenny-bit Sunday," because it was so happily devoid of threepenny-bits.

A little group of councillors were discussing Denry.

"What a card!" said one, laughing joyously. "He's a rare 'un, no mistake."

"Of course, this'll make him more popular than ever," said another. "We've never had a man to touch him for that."

"And yet," demanded Councillor Barlow, "what's he done? Has he ever done a day's work in his life? What great cause is he identified with?"

"He's identified," said the speaker, "with the great cause of cheering us all up."

Printed by Jarrold & Sons Ltd. Norwich

Also Published by the Echo Library By Arnold Bennett

NOVELS
Leonora
Sacred and Profane Love
Buried Alive
The Old Wives' Tale
Helen with the High Hand
Hilda Lessways
The Card
The Regent
The Price of Love
The Lion's Share
The Pretty Lady

FANTASIAS

The Grand Babylon Hotel

SHORT STORIES

Tales of the Five Towns
The Grim Smile of the Five Towns
The Matador of the Five Towns

BELLES-LETTRES

Over There
The Author's Craft (In Large Print)